MARTA PERRY

DANGER *in* PLAIN SIGHT

If you purchased this book without a cover you should be aware that this book is stolen property. It was reported as "unsold and destroyed" to the publisher, and neither the author nor the publisher has received any payment for this "stripped book."

Recycling programs for this product may not exist in your area.

ISBN-13: 978-0-373-77668-9

DANGER IN PLAIN SIGHT

Copyright © 2012 by Martha Johnson

All rights reserved. Except for use in any review, the reproduction or utilization of this work in whole or in part in any form by any electronic, mechanical or other means, now known or hereafter invented, including xerography, photocopying and recording, or in any information storage or retrieval system, is forbidden without the written permission of the publisher, Harlequin Enterprises Limited, 225 Duncan Mill Road, Don Mills, Ontario M3B 3K9, Canada.

This is a work of fiction. Names, characters, places and incidents are either the product of the author's imagination or are used fictitiously, and any resemblance to actual persons, living or dead, business establishments, events or locales is entirely coincidental.

This edition published by arrangement with Harlequin Books S.A.

For questions and comments about the quality of this book please contact us at Customer_eCare@Harlequin.ca.

® and TM are trademarks of the publisher. Trademarks indicated with ® are registered in the United States Patent and Trademark Office, the Canadian Trade Marks Office and in other countries.

www.Harlequin.com

Printed in U.S.A.

Dear Reader,

Thank you for deciding to read this third book in my Amish suspense series. As a lifelong resident of rural Pennsylvania, I have always lived near the Plain People. My own family heritage is Pennsylvania Dutch, so it has been a pleasure and a challenge to draw on those experiences in my books.

It can be difficult for outsiders to understand the constraints in the Amish community that prevent them from calling on the police or seeking legal help in any but extraordinary situations. Some outsiders think this attitude is foolish, while others seek to take advantage of it, knowing that it is rare for the Amish to involve the police in their troubles. In truth, most Amish are among the most law-abiding people one could meet, and their belief in nonviolence is a significant part of the core of their faith.

In this story, Libby Morgan returns home to Lancaster County to help her dearest friend, an Amish teacher, but she arrives too late. Esther has been critically injured in a hit-and-run accident, and convincing both the Amish community and the police that Esther is still in danger has life-threatening consequences. I've tried to present Amish belief and practices as honestly and respectfully as I can, and any errors are my own.

I hope you'll let me know how you like my book, and I'd love to send you a signed bookmark and my free brochure of Pennsylvania Dutch recipes. You can email me at marta@martaperry.com, visit me on the web at www.martaperry.com or on Facebook at Marta Perry books, or write to me at HQN Books, 233 Broadway, Suite 1001, New York, NY 10279.

Blessings,

Marta Perry

This story is dedicated to those of my friends who like mysteries best. And, as always, to Brian.

Acknowledgments

I'd like to express my thanks to all those whose expertise helped me in writing this book: to Erik Wesner, whose Amish America blog is enormously helpful; to Donald Kraybill and John Hostetler, whose books are the definitive resources on Amish life and beliefs; to the Plain People I have known and respected; and to my family, for giving me such a rich heritage on which to draw.

The righteousness of the blameless
makes a straight way for them, but the wicked
are brought down by their own wickedness.

—*Proverbs* 11: 5

PROLOGUE

AMISH BUGGIES WEREN'T built for speed. If the men were following her, she couldn't outrun them.

Esther Zook shivered in the December cold, turning her head to peer behind her, her view narrowed by the brim of her bonnet.

Nothing. The township road lay dark and empty behind the buggy...as dark as every farmhouse she'd passed, surrounded by their blankets of snow. Country people went to bed early in the winter, especially the Amish, without electric lights and televisions to keep them awake.

Libby Morgan would be awake, though. If she could get to Libby, everything would be all right. Libby would know what to do.

If only she'd told Libby more in her letters...but Esther hadn't known, then, just how frightening this was.

The Amish didn't go to the law. They settled matters among themselves. But the Amish of Spring Township had never dealt with a problem like this before.

Esther had shrunk from putting her suspicions down in black and white, thinking that when Libby returned it would be time enough to seek her advice. But now suspicion had turned to certainty, and she feared she had delayed too long. If they were following her—

Even as she thought it, she heard the roar of an engine behind her. Panic sent her heart racing; she tried to think, tried to pray, but it was too late. The roar turned to a scream, to a crash which deafened her, to total blackness.

CHAPTER ONE

IT WAS NICE to see someone else's love life turning out well, especially when her own was such a train wreck, Libby Morgan decided. Now that her big brother Trey was married, Mom could turn her obvious desire for grandchildren to Trey and Jessica and stop asking her only daughter if she'd met anyone special yet.

Libby put down the bridesmaid's bouquet she'd been clutching for what seemed like hours and picked up her camera instead. She'd discovered long ago that the camera could be useful camouflage. It would help her get through the rest of the wedding reception without, she hoped, too much conversation with people who'd known her from childhood and seemed compelled to try and find out how her life was going.

Then, once the flurry of wedding-related activities were over, she'd be free to dig into the other reason she'd come home to Spring Township, deep in Pennsylvania's Amish country.

"You know the Amish don't go to the law." Esther's last letter had sounded almost frightened, and Esther Zook, teacher at the local Amish one-room school, didn't frighten easily.

But I fear this is one time when we should. I must talk to you as soon as you get home. You know the Englisch world. You'll be able to tell me if I'm right about this.

Libby snapped off a few shots, more to keep the camera in front of her face than anything else. She hadn't reached Pennsylvania from San Francisco as early as she'd intended, partly because of the weather, but mainly because of the upset at the newspaper that had led to a final showdown with her boss…final in more ways than one.

Well, maybe she could set up in business as a wedding photographer. She framed Trey and Jessica in the pine-wreathed archway of the Springville Inn's ballroom, seeming oblivious of everything but each other, and snapped several quick shots.

"No doubt about how those two feel."

That particular deep male voice, coming from close behind her, made her hands jerk so that she undoubtedly got a great picture of the parquet floor. She turned, arranging a smile on her face. She'd had plenty of practice since fate, in the form of the bride, had paired her with Police Chief Adam Byler for the wedding.

"There isn't, is there? This is one relationship that's destined to last."

As opposed to ours, which lasted for about a minute and a half. That being the case, why did she persist in comparing every man she met to Adam Byler?

Adam's slate-blue eyes didn't show any sign he caught

an undercurrent in her words. But then, he wouldn't. Strong features, brown hair in a military cut, equally military posture—stoic didn't begin to describe Adam. Whatever he felt wouldn't be easily read on his face.

"I was beginning to think Trey would never take the plunge, especially after your dad's death, when he had to take over the company." Adam flicked an assessing glance at her face, as if wondering whether she could take a casual reference to the loss of her father, over a year and a half ago now.

She tried for a stoic expression of her own. "Trey's had his hands full, I know." She raised an eyebrow, casually, she hoped. "Or were you implying that I should have come home to take on some of the burden?"

Adam lifted his hands in quick denial. "Never thought of it. Trey probably wouldn't have let you, anyway. He was born for the job."

Trey, the oldest, had been groomed from birth to take over the extensive holdings that made up the Morgan family company. Link, her twin brother, the best man today, hadn't had that pressure on him, but since an injury cut short his military career, he'd come home to recuperate, fallen in love and stayed to take over the construction arm of the family business.

And then there was Libby, always considered the baby, even though Link had been born only twenty minutes before her. She'd been Daddy's princess. Too bad that role hadn't prepared her very well for the outside world. For an instant a fierce longing for her father's warm, reassuring presence swept through her.

Adam shifted his weight slightly, looking as if he'd rather be wearing his gray uniform on his six feet of solid muscle than the rented tuxedo. Or maybe she had actually succeeded in making him uncomfortable.

"I guess I'd better get back to my groomsman duties." A smile disturbed the gravity of his face. "Your mother gave strict orders. I even have a detailed list."

"That's Mom, all right. She might play the featherbrain at times, but she's the most organized person I know."

Funny, that only her mother could bring that softness to Adam's expression. Or maybe not so funny. Geneva Morgan had looked at a ragged eight-year-old Adam and seen a person worth cultivating instead of the son of the town drunk. Adam wasn't the sort to forget that.

Libby watched Adam walk across the room through the shielding lens of the camera, lingering a bit on those broad shoulders. He was as solid now as he'd been back in high school.

The family had gone to every Spring Township High football game to cheer on Trey, the quarterback. Nobody had known that Libby's eyes were on his best friend, the lineman who'd been that same six feet of solid muscle even then. A crush, she told herself now. It had been nothing but a crush, turned humiliating when she'd thrown herself at him.

In an odd way, when the rumors started going around that he'd gotten Sally Dailey pregnant, she'd felt better about his rejection of her. If that was the kind of girl he wanted, she was done with him.

Only she hadn't been, not really.

Enough, she chided herself. Being home again was having a ridiculous effect on her…her emotions had been riding a roller coaster all day. At least, after another hour or two of the reception, the bride and groom would slip away.

Lucky them. Libby had no doubt that Mom had another of her famous lists ready for the rest of the family. Still, there should be time tomorrow to talk with Esther.

It was impossible to do it before then. Even if she could have left the reception, it grew dark early in December. Amish families, like the Zooks, would be in bed by this time.

"Well, now, if it isn't Libby Morgan, all grown-up."

She wasn't quite fast enough to escape the arm that snaked around her waist…probably because she'd been watching Adam.

"Mr. Barclay." She grabbed his cold hand and shook it, using the move to get him at arm's length.

Owen Barclay, manager of the Springville Inn, did a marvelous job of running the Revolutionary-era showplace for its distant owners, so everyone in town said. Everyone also said he'd chase after any attractive female who crossed his path.

"Owen, please. After all, we've known each other a long time, haven't we?" He made the words sound ridiculously intimate.

"The family is so pleased with the reception." She turned the conversation to the only business they had between them. "The setting is perfect." Her gesture took in the spacious, Christmas-decorated room that could and did host everything from the local high school prom to political rallies.

Owen nodded, flashing a white smile. Everything about Owen was polished, from his sleek dark hair to the tan—that had to come from a tanning booth—to the expensive cut of his suit. He might have been made for the position he held as manager of the historic inn.

"My staff is well trained to handle an event like this. Naturally we want to provide the perfect setting for any wedding, but your brother's is very special. It isn't every day a member of the Morgan family gets married."

"It's so nice that the bride decided to have the wedding here in Springville." Sandra Smalley paused next to them, patting her silver-blond hair. "One does wonder why she didn't have it at her home, of course."

Libby's smile tightened. Sandra had always had aspirations to be the social leader of Springville, and she probably still did. More to the point, she was a notorious gossip. Libby certainly wasn't going to mention Jessica's strained relationship with her father, who was her only relative.

"Well, I can answer that." Libby leaned close to Sandra, as if about to impart a secret. "She actually thinks people here are nice."

"Oh. Well, of course." Sandra blinked, perhaps wondering if she'd just been insulted. "That's good, isn't it?" She backed up, nearly stepping on her husband, waiting behind her. "Come along, Leonard. I'm sure Libby has a great deal to do."

They moved away between the tables, and Owen shook

his head at her in mock disapproval. "Shame on you. What would your mother say about your baiting Sandra that way?"

"She'd say I should know better, which I should." She raised her camera. "So I'd better get back to taking photographs. Good seeing you, Owen."

While she was at it, she really needed to readjust her thinking to the small-town mindset. Libby moved among the tables, snapping photos, agreeing that the bride was beautiful, the ceremony had been perfect, and yes, it was sad that her father wasn't here to see this day. This last one required gritting her teeth a few times, but she managed. Mom would be proud of her.

Her gaze sought out her mother in the crowded room. Geneva Morgan was doing her duty, of course, speaking to every single person here. She probably hadn't had a bite of her dinner, but her smile was radiant as she greeted guests.

Would Mom be proud when she learned that her only daughter was now unemployed? Possibly, when she knew the circumstances. Mom was a great one for standing up for what was right. As for Libby's own sense of that... maybe living in the competitive world of news photography had blurred her vision. If so, it was past time to regain her moral compass.

She stopped at the Smalleys' table, taking several photos of them out of a delayed sense of social guilt. Sandra beamed, adjusting the collar of her pink sequined top. Leonard, whose habitual expression was one of faintly worried absentmindedness, looked like a white rabbit that had strayed into the party by mistake.

"Smile, Leonard. You're happy for the bride and groom, aren't you?"

He produced something that was more of a grimace, and she snapped the photo.

"That's great," she said. At least when she photographed car smashups, she didn't have to coax a smile from people. A faint memory teased at her mind. "By the way, didn't I see—"

She stopped, glancing across the room, her gaze caught by Adam Byler. He stood a little apart from the crowd, cell phone pressed to his ear.

A small, icy thread traced its way down her spine. Adam looked solemn—there was nothing in that. He always did. But something about the call had frozen him into immobility for just a moment. Then his gaze swung around the room. It reached her. It stopped.

Something was wrong. The thread became a torrent of cold. Something was very wrong, because Adam was moving through the crowd toward her, his eyes never leaving hers.

She clutched the back of the nearest chair as he reached her. "What is it? What's happened?"

He took her arm, leading her a few steps away from the interested glances of the people at the table.

"I'm sorry." His voice was low, for her ears only. "I don't want to disrupt the reception, but I know how close you two are." He paused for the space of a heartbeat, his hand firm and strong on her arm. "There's been an accident. Esther Zook's buggy has been hit."

"How bad?" Her frozen lips could barely form the words.

"Bad," he said, clenching his jaw. "She's on her way to the hospital, but...it's bad."

It hadn't been any part of Adam's plan to bring Libby with him. But when she'd learned he was headed for the hospital after a brief stop at the accident scene, she'd been adamant.

He might have overruled her, but when Geneva found out what was happening she'd been equally insistent. He hadn't been able to hold out against both of them.

Ripping off the tie that went with the tux, he tossed it into the backseat, glancing at Libby. She huddled into a thick winter coat—apparently not thick enough, because she was shivering. He flicked the heat up to full blast.

"It'll warm up soon."

She didn't seem to hear him. The brief light provided by a passing car showed him the pale oval of her face, stiff and frozen. Only her lips moved silently, as if in prayer.

Would Carmody have done everything he'd told him? The kid was fairly new, but he seemed intelligent enough. Which probably meant he wouldn't hang around long. The smart kids he got in the township police generally used it as a stepping stone to something else.

Well, he'd see for himself soon enough. The accident site wasn't far from Springville.

What had Esther been doing out in her buggy at this hour, anyway? That was unusual, to put it mildly.

He turned onto the township road, slowing, wary of patches of black ice. Not far now. His mind ticked over all the things that had to be set in motion with a hit-and-run, but that wasn't enough to distract him from the silent figure at his side.

"I'm sorry we have to stop at the scene. Maybe you should have had someone else take you."

She shook her head, roused for the moment, at least. "We came from the house in the limo, remember? None of the family had a car at the inn. Anyway, I shouldn't take them away from the reception. Esther is..." Her voice choked on the words.

He felt as if he'd been hit in the heart. "I know. You've been friends since you were kids."

He had a quick mental picture of Libby as a child, hair so light a blond it looked like dandelion fluff dancing in the breeze when she and Esther darted among the apple trees behind the Morgan house, playing some fanciful game. Tonight her slightly darker blond hair was swept up into a complicated twist adorned with a wisp of lace that matched her bridesmaid's dress.

"We couldn't have been much more than four or five when her mother started helping at the house and brought her along." Once she got started, Libby's voice seemed to ease. "Mom was glad I had a girl to play with, instead of just my brothers."

"Your friendship lasted even after you went away to

school?" If he kept her talking, maybe she wouldn't get that frozen look again.

"Nobody writes letters anymore, except the Amish." She almost smiled. "Esther's letters...I don't know, I think they grounded me, in a way. Reminded me of home. They still do." She sucked in a breath. "If the paramedics took her to the hospital, there must be hope. There must be," she repeated, as if he'd argued the point.

He didn't want to tell her what he'd heard. "The paramedics got to her quickly. I'm sure they would have a surgeon waiting when she reached the hospital."

"Her injuries...what were they?" Her voice quavered, then steadied. She wanted the truth, he knew.

"Trust me, my guys aren't experts on trauma. When you get to the hospital—"

"What did they say?" Her tone was uncompromising.

"She has what looks like a bad head injury."

I figured she was a goner. That was what the patrolman on duty actually said. *All that blood.* He'd sounded a little sick. Adam could only hope Carmody hadn't disgraced himself at the scene. This was the kid's first bad crash...not that anyone ever got used to seeing mangled bodies at an accident scene.

Not just an accident, he reminded himself. A hit-and-run. That made the site a crime scene. He'd called for a crime scene investigation team from the state police. His tiny department didn't have the resources for anything like that. The driver was bound to have left some traces behind.

Libby stirred. "Esther's mother…has someone told her?"

He nodded. "I sent someone to pick up Bishop Amos to help break the news. They should be at the hospital by the time we are."

The strip of black macadam went over another rise and he spotted the flares and reflective tape. Good. He didn't want anything messed with before the crime scene team got here. He pulled to a stop and turned on his flashers.

Joe Carmody was at his door the moment he opened it, a little green around the gills over being first on the scene.

"Everything's cordoned off, just like you wanted it, Chief. I had the volunteer firefighters bring along their battery lamps so we could see better."

"Good thinking, Carmody." He hadn't expected that display of initiative from the kid.

The lights flashed on as soon as the words were out of his mouth, and the scene sprang to life—tangled wreckage of a gray buggy, its battery lantern still flickering, one twisted wheel sunk at an angle in the ditch a few yards down the road, the horse lying dead in a tangle of lines.

"The horse was still alive when I got here." The kid's voice shook despite his best efforts to steady it. "Pretty bad. I had to—" He stopped, leaving the rest unsaid.

Adam gave a short nod. "You did the right thing. Nothing else has been touched?"

"Just what the paramedics had to do to get in," Carmody said quickly, obviously glad to get away from the subject of the horse. "I put the tape up right away after

I made the calls. Hasn't been any other traffic along the road, though."

"Nobody else through at all?" That would be a break for the crime scene guys. Maybe they'd actually pick up something to identify the vehicle.

Carmody jerked his head toward the nearest lane, where a pony cart was pulled up, an Amishman leaning against it, staring morosely at the scene. "Just Paul Miller. He's the one made the call. Seems like his teenage boy has a cell phone."

Amish didn't have phones in the homes, generally, but cell phones were becoming more and more common with the teens, and the parents usually turned a blind eye to that until the kids were old enough to join the church. A good thing, in this case.

"Did Miller see anything?"

Carmody shook his head. "Vehicle was long gone by the time he got out here. His wife sent out a thermos of coffee, if you want any."

"Not now." He walked along the edge of the tape, looking, not touching, just assessing. Esther had been headed toward Springville, and she'd been hit from behind. Those battery lights on the buggy—they could be plainly seen by anyone coming up from the other direction. Why didn't the driver stop, or at least swerve? Looked like he'd hit square on.

Anger burned along Adam's veins. "No excuse for this."

"Drunk maybe. Or high." Carmody seemed to know what he meant. He gestured down the road, the way the vehicle must have come. "There's no curves or hills for a good hundred yards. He had to have seen the lights."

A sound behind him like a choked-off cry, and Adam swung around. Libby stood there, staring at the horse, lips clamped together.

He grabbed her arm and turned her away. "Stay in the car, Libby. Please," he added, softening his tone. "We need to keep the area clean for the crime scene people."

"Crime?" She repeated the word, eyes searching his face.

"Hit-and-run is a crime," he said. And if Esther didn't make it, that would be vehicular homicide at the very least. Still, they had to find the driver first. "Libby..."

She took a step, wobbling a little on the macadam in those ridiculously high heels she wore. He held her arm securely. There was nothing much he could do here at the moment. He needed to get to the hospital, to see if Esther had said anything.

"Extend that tape along the road on either side for another fifty feet or so." He spoke over his shoulder to Carmody. "Maybe we'll get lucky and he swerved off onto the verge after the collision. I'm going to the hospital. I'll be back."

"Yessir." Carmody looked as if he'd like to salute, but didn't. The boy was recovering from his initial shock, and it would help him recover his dignity to be left in charge.

Adam propelled Libby to the car, not letting go until she was safely inside. If he hadn't brought her—but that wouldn't really change anything. He'd still have to run by the hospital, talk to the mother, find out if Esther had said anything and when she could be questioned. Or if.

Once they'd driven past the scene, he glanced at Libby. "I'm sorry you had to see that."

She let out a shaky breath. "Esther…she'd have heard the car, wouldn't she? Known it was going to hit her?"

He couldn't lie to her. "Probably. But it would have been very fast." His fingers tightened on the wheel, and he felt a totally unprofessional surge of fury. "He must have been blind drunk not to see her lights."

"Or he intended to hit her. That would explain it, wouldn't it?"

He hung on to his exasperation. This was bad enough without making it worse. "Libby, no one would deliberately hit a buggy straight on like that. No one would want to harm Esther."

"You don't know that." She snapped the words. "You can't."

"Look, I know you're upset about your friend—"

She was shaking her head. "You don't understand. Esther wasn't just my childhood friend. She's always been like a sister to me. We exchanged letters every week without fail, and we confided in each other. I told her things in my letters I didn't tell anyone, and she did the same. And the last couple of times Esther wrote to me she was worried, upset. Afraid."

"Afraid?" He seized on the word. "Of what?"

"She didn't say." Libby pressed her fingers against her forehead. "She wanted me to get in touch with her as soon as I got home, but I didn't get here until nearly time for the rehearsal, and—"

"But what did she say? Had someone threatened her?" It happened, even to someone as blameless as an Amish schoolteacher. Some nut job, fixating on her?

Libby sucked in an audible breath. "Sorry. I'm not making sense." She closed her eyes for a second, and then opened them. "Like I said, Libby wrote to me every week. The past few times, she'd sounded as if she were worried about something. I tried to find out what it was, but she didn't say. Then this last letter came."

She paused, and he thought she was visualizing it in her mind's eye. "She said that something was very wrong in the Amish community. She talked about how they won't go to the law, but said maybe in this case they should have. She said she was counting the days until I got home, because I'd understand the situation better than she could." Her voice shook. "But I didn't get here in time, did I?"

"Libby, you don't know that." He reached across to touch her sleeve. "Chances are her accident is nothing more or less than it seems. Car and buggy collisions do happen, especially at night."

She jerked away from his touch, turning to stare at him. "Didn't you understand what I said? She was afraid. Esther, afraid. Esther Zook was never afraid of anything."

"If it was a situation she didn't understand—" he began, but she didn't let him finish.

"She said something was wrong in the community.

And it must have involved outsiders, because she implied my experience in the English world would help."

He weighed the words, weighed too his impression of Libby. She was strung up, distraught about her friend, but she wouldn't make up the contents of Esther's letters. Still, she might be exaggerating, making connections that weren't justified.

"Do you think I could see the letters?"

"Don't you believe me?"

He didn't need to look at her to know that those dark blue eyes were snapping.

"I believe you, but I'd like to read her exact words for myself." They were entering Lancaster now, and he could see Libby's face a little better in the glow of the streetlights. In her fear for her friend, she would lash out at anyone who got in her way. Especially him.

Finally she nodded. "I brought the letters home with me, thinking I might show them to Mom to see if she knew anything helpful. She's usually pretty up-to-date about what goes on in the Amish community. They're at the house. I'll show them to you. You'll see I'm right."

He didn't suppose a word of caution would be welcome, but he had to try. "Look, even if Esther was concerned about some problem in the community, it doesn't necessarily follow that her accident was deliberate. I'd need to know a lot more before I could assume that." To his relief, the lights of the hospital gleamed ahead.

She bit her lip, probably to keep from telling him what she thought of him and his assumptions.

"Fine." She snapped off the word. "Look at it from all

angles. Investigate. Deliberate. And in the end you'll find I'm right. Esther knew about something wrong going on, and someone made sure she couldn't tell."

CHAPTER TWO

THE LIGHTS OF the hospital glowed icily in the cold night. Adam pulled up to the emergency room door and stopped. Libby fumbled with the door handle, her fingers cold and stiff despite the heat that had poured from the car heater.

"Wait," Adam said. "I'll take you in."

He was out his door and around the car before she could bolt for the emergency room entrance. He took her arm in a firm clasp.

"You don't need to go in with me." It was all she could do to prevent her teeth from chattering, whether from cold or fear she wasn't sure.

He swept her inside, not bothering to answer, and strode toward the desk. She had to hurry, but she managed to reach the receptionist first.

"Esther Zook…how is she?" She gripped the edge of the counter.

"I'm sorry, but I can't give out…" The woman's denial faded away when Adam flashed his badge.

"Where is she?" he asked, his voice crisp with authority.

The woman consulted her computer. "She's already in surgery. The family is in the third-floor waiting room."

Ignoring the interested glances from the few waiting

patients, Adam took Libby's arm again, steering her down the corridor toward the elevator. The swags of plastic greenery that draped each door along the hallway were a dismal counterpoint to her feelings.

"You don't need to hold on to me." She tried to tug free of his hand. "I can walk."

"In those shoes?" He sent a dismissive glance toward the heels that had been dyed deep green to match her dress, discolored now with slush from the road.

The elevator doors swished open and as promptly closed behind them. Not long now, and she'd know for herself how serious Esther's condition was.

"That's good, isn't it? That she's in surgery, I mean." She wanted to, needed to, find a shred of hope.

Adam turned a grave face toward her. "I hope so."

That was all. For a second she wanted to storm at him, demand that he say something encouraging, but false hope wouldn't help. Adam would tell her the truth, or he wouldn't speak at all. Anyone who knew him must certainly know that.

Would he tell her the truth about his feelings over what had happened between them? The thought popped into her head, and she chased it away. Adam had clearly managed to forget it. To him, she would always be his best friend's kid sister, nothing more. And maybe that was for the best. She'd embarrassed herself too many times where Adam was concerned.

The doors slid open, and Libby's stomach tightened.

"The waiting room is to the right." Adam put a hand on the door.

"I know." She'd waited there a time or two with Mom and Dad, once when Link smashed up his motorcycle and again when Trey had appendicitis. She hurried her steps, but Adam's long stride kept pace with her.

Libby pushed open the door, and the two figures in the room swung toward her, wearing identical expressions of fear. She blinked, identifying the faces above the dark Amish dresses. Esther's mother, Rebecca, and Esther's sister-in-law, Mary Ann Zook.

"Rebecca, I'm so sorry…" Libby took a step forward and was enveloped in Rebecca's motherly embrace.

"Ach, Libby, I am ser glad you are here. Esther—" She stopped, seeming to choke on her daughter's name.

"It will be all right," Libby said, with no assurance that her words were true. Still, Rebecca had to have hope, didn't she?

She took a step back, trying not to let tears flow. "I'd expected to see you on this trip, but not here."

"Ja." Rebecca closed her eyes for a moment, probably in prayer.

She had aged in the past few years. Her hair was almost entirely gray now, the center part widening as it so often did with Amish women after years of pulling their hair back tightly under their kapp, the small white covering over their hair. Rebecca's faded hazel eyes were red-rimmed from crying.

The younger woman put her arm around Rebecca's waist. "We must have hope, Mamm Rebecca." She reached out to clasp Libby's hand. "It's wonderful gut that you are here. I know that Esther was counting the days."

"Ach, what am I thinking?" Rebecca straightened, as if calling on some reserve of strength. "Libby, you remember Mary Ann, Isaac's wife."

"Of course I do." Libby managed a smile. Mary Ann was the wife of Esther's older brother, Isaac, who ran the farm now. Esther and her mother shared the grandparents' house, the daadi haus, next to the farmhouse. "How are the children?"

"All well." Mary Ann, plump and rosy with a face made for smiling, looked distracted for a moment, as if her mind scampered off after her seven children. "Isaac stayed with them until a neighbor could komm. He and Bishop Amos are on their way here."

"I'm glad you'll have them with you." Adam spoke for the first time, his voice gentle. "I'm afraid I have to ask you a few questions."

The two women exchanged glances. "Isaac could answer better than we can," Mary Ann said.

"I'm sure you can help. It's nothing very hard. Why don't you sit down?" He led Rebecca to a chair. Once she was seated, he knelt beside her. "Mrs. Zook, do you have any idea where Esther was going tonight?"

She shook her head. "She left right after supper. She said she had an errand to run, but that she wouldn't be late. I thought it was something to do with school—maybe working on the Christmas program, or a parent she had to speak to."

"Did she tell you which parent?" Adam asked, obviously hoping for someone who could tell him more about what Esther had been doing on that road at night.

Rebecca shook her head. "She would never talk about it if a child was having trouble in school. Chust to the parents." Rebecca's voice seemed to gain a bit of strength as she talked. "I waited and waited, there in the daadi haus, and she didn't komm. Finally I went over to speak to Mary Ann, but she didn't know where Esther had gone, either." She clasped her hands together so tightly that the knuckles were white. "We didn't know what to do." Her voice seemed to run down.

Mary Ann sat down next to her, clasping her mother-in-law's hands. "I didn't know where Esther had gone, either."

Adam surveyed her as if weighing her words. "Even if she didn't say, you might have had an idea."

"But I didn't. I didn't even know she was going out on such a cold night, or I'd have tried to get her to stay home, or have Isaac go with her."

Libby could imagine what Esther would have said to that. She'd always resisted her brother's efforts to take care of her, saying she could take care of herself. But this time, she couldn't.

"Has anything been bothering Esther lately?" Adam's tone was patient.

Both women shook their heads, but Libby thought she saw some faint reservation in the younger woman's eyes.

Adam seemed to notice it, as well. He looked at Mary Ann for a long moment, but she didn't speak.

Rebecca turned away from him, her hands twisting in Mary Ann's grasp. "Why have we not heard anything?"

"What did the doctor say?" Libby brushed past Adam

to sit down on Rebecca's other side, the silky folds of her green dress touching his shoulder.

"Chust that she had to go into surgery right away if… if they were going to save her." Tears filled Mary Ann's eyes at the words.

Libby reached out to her, and the three women sat, hands linked. *Please. Please, don't take Esther away from us.*

The door burst open. Isaac, Esther's brother, surged through, followed at a more moderate pace by the bishop of the local Amish church district.

"Was ist…?" Isaac went straight to his mother, breaking off the question in Pennsylvania Dutch when he saw there were others in the room. "What is happening with Esther?" His face was white above the straw-colored beard.

Libby's throat tightened. She and Esther had joked, sometimes, about their brothers, pretending total exasperation with them, but knowing all the while that the bond ran deep. Isaac might have disagreed with Esther on almost every subject, but there was no doubt about his love for his sister.

Adam rose, stepping away to give the others space, and she slipped from her chair, letting Isaac sit next to his mother. He barely glanced at Libby, all his focus on Rebecca, and they spoke to each other in broken murmurs of Pennsylvania Dutch.

She took a step back and found Bishop Amos at her elbow. The elderly man shook his head gravely, his face lined with a thousand wrinkles that bore testimony to his years of service to his people.

"This is a bad business," he said softly, almost to himself.

"Esther is still in surgery," she said, answering the question he didn't ask. "We won't know anything until she comes out." If she comes out. Libby tried to dismiss the thought, but it clung, tenacious.

Bishop Amos nodded, his wise eyes curious when they rested on her. "This has been a strange homecoming for you, Libby Morgan. Happiness and sorrow all mixed together."

He spoke to her with the same easy familiarity he'd have used years ago, when she'd hung over his shoulder while he put new shoes on her pony. In addition to being a spiritual leader, Bishop Amos was also a farrier, something the Amish didn't find remotely strange. Even a minister worked to earn his daily bread.

She nodded, tears coming to her eyes when she tried to speak. "I wish I had gotten here sooner."

"It is as God wills," he said softly.

As if to punctuate his words, the door swung open again. The doctor who stood there still wore surgical scrubs, and his gray hair stood up as if he'd just run his hands through it. His face was lined with fatigue. "Mrs. Zook?"

Rebecca rose, Mary Ann and Isaac supporting her on either side. "Ja," she murmured, eyes dark with dread.

"Your daughter has come through the surgery."

"Thank God," Rebecca murmured. "Denke, Doctor."

"The head injury was severe." The doctor seemed to be picking his words carefully, watching her face to be sure she understood. "She is unconscious now."

"But she will wake up," Isaac said. "She will, won't she?"

The doctor looked from him to his mother, and Libby's heart turned to lead. She knew what he was going to say before the words were out of his mouth.

"I can't tell you that. Right now, the best thing I can say is that she is alive." He hesitated, face filled with sympathy. "The chances are not very good, I'm afraid. She may not last the night."

There was a muffled cry from Mary Ann. Rebecca's face seemed to freeze, as if refusing the words.

Libby didn't realize she'd sagged until she felt Adam's strong hand on her arm, supporting her. He held her, his face like a mask, while he addressed the doctor.

"There's no chance that she could answer a question?"

The doctor seemed to take in the uniform as if he registered for the first time that this might be a police matter. "I'm afraid not now." His voice had lowered, and he took a few steps toward them, away from Rebecca and her family. "She is in a coma, and we have to keep her that way for her brain to have any chance to heal."

Libby sucked in a breath, absorbing the blow. Adam's fingers tightened on her arm.

"So." His voice was soft in her ear, maybe not even intended for her. "We may never know the truth."

LIBBY HUNG THE green bridesmaid's dress at the back of the closet. Not that she'd expected to have an occasion to wear the dress again anyway. That never seemed to happen, no matter how well a bridesmaid's dress was chosen.

But this one—she ought to put it right in the trash. She'd never be able to look at it without reliving the fear she'd felt during those long hours at the hospital.

She hadn't reached home until nearly dawn, after spending several hours sitting next to Esther's bed. Isaac had hinted more than once that she ought to leave, but Rebecca clung to her, so she'd stayed. Besides, she couldn't bear to go, thinking her last sight of Esther would be that still, waxworklike figure lying connected to so many tubes and machines.

Not having the patience to style her hair, Libby pulled it back into a ponytail. Mom had wanted her to go back to bed once she'd had some breakfast, but she couldn't. She'd come upstairs to dress instead.

She itched with a restlessness so intense it was surprising she didn't burst out of her skin. She had to do something for Esther, even if it was just sitting in the quiet room listening to the sound of the machines.

Crossing the bedroom, Libby pulled open a dresser drawer for a sweater. When she'd left for her first real job, she'd cleared her personal stuff from this room, insisting Mom use it for guests. Looking back on it, maybe that hadn't been very tactful…like announcing she was never coming home again.

But if she hadn't, Mom would have kept it as it was then, the walls covered with photos of people she barely remembered and events she'd be just as glad to forget. Like Link's room. That had practically become a shrine when he'd joined the military.

But even though her high school mementos were gone, the bedroom still felt, in some way, hers. The quilt her grandmother had made still covered the sleigh bed in which Libby had slept from the time she'd graduated from her crib, and the bow-front dresser had a nick from the time she'd knocked out a baby tooth on it.

And it still bore a childhood photo. She picked up the silver frame. She clowned in front of a campfire with Trey and Link, while Dad looked on indulgently. She and Link must have been about ten, with Trey already turning into a gangling adolescent.

She traced Dad's face with her finger, sorrow building in her. The photo had been taken at the cabin, the site of so many family outings. The place where her father had died.

She set the picture back in place. Mom would have taken it. She'd been the family photographer until Libby reached her teens and realized she could take pictures in which most of the subjects didn't have their heads cut off by the camera, unlike Mom's efforts.

That was the problem with coming home—you spent too much time thinking of what had been. She needed to concentrate on the here and now.

And thinking of photographs, where was her camera? She'd had it at the inn. It had been in her hands when she'd seen Adam walking toward her and known something was wrong. She certainly hadn't taken it into the hospital with her.

A quick search of the room didn't turn it up. She trotted down the stairs. "Mom? Are you here?"

Her mother appeared from the direction of the kitchen, a dish towel in one hand. Today she looked herself again, wearing jeans and an oversize Penn State sweatshirt, her gray curls tousled. "Libby, I thought you had gone back to bed." Her voice was gently chiding.

"I couldn't." She took the last few steps in a hurry. "Have you seen my camera? Did you bring it home from the inn last night?"

Please say yes, she pleaded silently, thinking of all the irreplaceable photos she'd taken yesterday.

But her mother was already shaking her head. "I didn't see it, darling, or I would have. Are you sure it's not in your coat or your bag?"

"It wouldn't fit." She went quickly to the bentwood coatrack where she'd hung her coat when she'd come in, searching the pockets even though she knew it was futile.

No camera, of course, but her groping fingers found a memory card. She'd switched to a second one sometime during the reception. Relief swept through her. At least she hadn't lost the entire day's worth of once-in-a-lifetime shots.

"No camera, but here's the memory card." She dropped it in the basket on the hall table. "I'll upload what I have on it when I get back."

"Back?" Mom's face crinkled with concern. "You're

surely not going out already. You need to get some rest, have some lunch…"

"Mom, you just gave me breakfast an hour ago." The way her mother kept urging food on her children, it was a wonder the three of them hadn't been little butterballs. "I'm going back to the hospital."

Mom grasped her hand, as if to hold her. "Just let me change, and I'll go with you."

She shook her head, impatient to be off. "I'll have to stop at the inn on my way, to see if they have my camera. Maybe you can stop by the hospital later."

She freed her hand, shrugging into her bright red anorak instead of the dressier coat she'd worn last night.

"Can I take a car?" She'd have to do something about a car, if she were going to stay here long, since hers was in San Francisco.

"Use Jessica's." Mom took a set of keys from the basket and handed them to her. "She won't mind at all."

Safely off on her honeymoon, it seemed unlikely that Jessica would even think of her car. Libby grabbed her bag and headed for the door. "Thanks, Mom."

"Be careful, dear." Mom said the familiar words automatically. "Maybe tonight we'll have time to sit down and have a nice chat, now that the wedding's over."

"We'll see." With the classic evasive words, Libby stepped out into the cold sunshine and pulled the door closed.

Now why, exactly, was she so reluctant to have that nice heart-to-heart chat with her mother? Because it wasn't going to be nice?

Mom wouldn't blame her for her actions. Geneva Morgan would never put a job before doing what was right.

But her mother would worry, and that was the last thing Libby wanted. Admitting that she hadn't been able to cut it out there in the big wide world...

She decided not to pursue that path, concentrating instead on pulling out of the gravel driveway onto the two-lane blacktop that led to Springville and beyond it to Lancaster and the hospital. She shouldn't be thinking about her own failings. They were unimportant compared to Esther's situation.

Her fingers tightened on the steering wheel, cold even through her gloves. Nothing could have happened to Esther since she'd left. She'd given the nurse on duty her cell number and firm instructions to call if there was any change.

When the woman had looked mulish and muttered something about regulations, Adam had pulled out that magical badge of his, and the nurse had fallen in line. A badge worked even better than her press credentials.

She passed one of the Amish farms that dotted the roads of Spring Township and realized what day it was. Rows of buggies lined the lane that led to the barn. It was Sunday, and the Amish were obviously worshipping today in the King family's barn. They'd be praying for Esther, of that she had no doubt.

The thought comforted her as she drove the rest of the way to the Springville Inn. Maybe, when she reached the hospital, there'd be good news waiting. Maybe Esther would be awake…weak, hurting, but herself, with characteristic courage in her blue eyes.

The inn's parking lot was crowded, and Libby finally parked illegally, rationalizing that she'd only be inside long enough to see if her camera had turned up.

She hurried through the lobby to the restaurant, nodding absently to the hostess while her gaze scanned the crowded dining room. The inn was a popular place for brunch on Sundays, and today was no exception.

Not seeing her quarry, she turned to the hostess. "Is Mr. Barclay here? I need to speak with him."

The young woman nodded. "He's in his office. Go past the reception desk, and it's the first door on the left."

Libby moved back into the hotel lobby, relieved to leave the noise of the dining room behind. It had been noisy last night, too, when they'd celebrated Trey and Jessica's wedding. The gaiety had died for her when she saw Adam's expression.

She walked quickly back to the office, tapped lightly and opened the door. "Owen?"

"Libby, what a delightful surprise." Owen Barclay circled his desk toward her, looking as fresh and smiling as he had the previous night. "I thought the Morgan family would be exhausted after all of yesterday's festivities."

She took a step back as he approached, holding the office door open. "I just stopped by to see if your staff found my camera. I must have put it down when I rushed out to go to the hospital last night."

No need to say any more. She was certain everyone in

the room had known why she and Adam left within ten minutes of their going.

Owen's face assumed a gravity suitable for a funeral director. "Of course, your friend's accident. I'm so terribly sorry about that. It was pretty bad, or so I've heard."

She nodded, knowing that was an invitation to share details that she had no intention of repeating. "It was a hit-and-run. The police are looking for the driver."

"I certainly hope they find him. It's tragic, the way some people speed along our back roads with no thought for others." He leaned toward her, his face sympathetic. "How is Ms. Zook?"

An image of Esther, white and still, flashed in her mind. But she was going to think positively, wasn't she?

"It was a serious injury, but I'm sure I'll find her improved when I get to the hospital. Now, about my camera..."

He was already shaking his head. "The staff has standing instructions to bring anything of value directly to my office, and nothing has turned up. The room was thoroughly cleared, of course, to get ready for brunch this morning."

Too easy, to think the camera would turn up that fast. "You'll let me know if anyone finds it?"

"I'll check the room thoroughly myself as soon as we've finished serving." Owen clasped her hand before she could escape. "And I'll ask the staff that was on duty if anyone saw a camera."

"Thank you." She detached her hand. "I'd appreciate it."

"And you let me know if there's anything I can do for the Zook family." He followed her, but stopped in the doorway. "We'd be happy to send some meals over, either to the hospital or the house. No charge, of course."

"That's kind of you, Owen. I'll let you know." Would Esther be eating again anytime soon? *Hold the good thought,* she reminded herself, and walked toward the door.

But as she passed the archway that led into the dining room, she realized someone was waving at her. It was Sandra Smalley, sitting across from Leonard at nearly the same spot where they'd been last night.

There was no choice but to stop, trying to manage a polite smile while her nerves screamed at her to move.

"Here we are again," Sandra said. "We just can't stay away from the inn. We come every Sunday for brunch, don't we, Leonard?"

Leonard nodded, his gaze shifting from his wife to Libby. "Our favorite place," he said.

"The holiday decorations are so lovely this year." Sandra swept on, gesturing at the swags of greens and holly and relieving Libby of the duty of answering. "We heard about what happened with your friend. Such a pity. It just shows how dangerous it is, driving a horse and buggy on public roads after dark."

If she throttled Sandra, Libby probably wouldn't be able to ask them whether they remembered what had happened to her camera. She'd taken a photo of them just seconds before she saw Adam, after all.

"Hit-and-run drivers are the worst kind of creatures,"

Leonard said, with surprising heat. "I trust the police will catch up with the person who did this. How is your friend?"

"It's early yet," she said cautiously. "But we're hoping for a good recovery."

"That's wonderful." Sandra seemed to feel she'd been out of the conversation long enough. "I do hope you're right, although you never can tell with head injuries. I heard of someone who—"

"I really must be on my way," Libby said, desperation triumphing over good manners. "But I wanted to ask if you remembered what I did with my camera when I left last night."

"Camera?" Leonard blinked at her.

"You were taking photos of us," Sandra said promptly. "Then the chief came over and whispered something to you, and you went out together without a word to anyone." The mention of Adam was accompanied by an arch smile that annoyed Libby.

Not quite true, but let it pass. "Do you remember if I took my camera?"

"I'm certain you did," Leonard said. "I noticed that you had it in your hand."

That seemed to settle it. "Thank you. That's a relief."

She hurried off before Sandra could decide to finish her story of someone who'd had a head injury. No doubt it would end in disaster.

Pushing open the front door, Libby zipped her jacket against the wind that teased at the door's wreath. She'd said it was a relief to know she'd had her camera when she left, but that wasn't quite true.

If she'd had her camera then, it must be in Adam's car. And that meant she'd have to stop at the police station and see Adam again.

CHAPTER THREE

ADAM SHUFFLED THROUGH the reports on his desk, trying to focus. He was used to nights without sleep…it was the thought of Esther Zook lying in that hospital bed, maybe dying, of Libby's pain and grief, that had his eyes stinging and gritty.

Don't get emotionally involved. He knew that as well as the next cop. All very well if you worked a city district where the victims were totally unknown to you. Here…

He'd known Esther Zook since she was six or seven, probably, chasing around the Morgan place with Libby. Impossible to stay detached when she was the victim.

As for Libby…well, she just made it more difficult. Maybe someday he'd be able to look at her without feeling that complicated mix of longing, guilt and sorrow, but he didn't figure it was happening anytime soon. He'd messed up with Libby twice in his life, letting his emotions overcome his better judgment. The first time she'd been a teenager, and he'd had no earthly excuse for responding to that impetuous kiss she'd given him. If her brothers had known, they'd have rearranged his face for him.

He'd handled it badly, hurt and embarrassed Libby by letting her think he didn't care about her. He should have gone to her afterward, found some better way of explaining that he was too old for her and he wasn't in her league anyway. But then that mess with Sally had exploded in his face, with half the town believing he'd fathered Sally's baby. Libby had clearly been in that half, even though Geneva had come firmly to his defense.

Geneva's reaction had been simple. She knew that if he had been responsible, he'd have taken responsibility. Her confidence in him had gotten him through. Eventually the rumors had died down, Sally had married and moved away, and the incident was over, but it was a reminder, if he'd needed one, that in a small town people were always ready to believe the worst of someone like him.

Old news, Adam reminded himself. Past history. They'd both been over it a long time ago.

He turned to the computer, focusing on whether or not an answer had come through on the paint fragments the CSI guys had scraped off the buggy. Nothing yet, but they'd agreed to rush it.

Running a hand through his hair and rubbing the back of his neck, he looked at the large-scale township map on the wall behind his desk.

What were you doing, Esther? Where were you going that time of night?

The phone buzzed. Ginger, the dispatcher, must be trying to impress someone. Usually she just shouted for him. Ginger had come in unasked this morning to see what she could do to help.

"Libby Morgan here to see you, Chief."

He'd think of an excuse if he could, but it was too late. Ginger must have waved Libby on back, because the office door was already opening. He rose, shoving his chair back, and it hit the wall in protest.

"Libby. I didn't expect to see you this early." His gaze sharpened on her face, drawn and exhausted-looking. "You look beat," he said abruptly. "Didn't you get any rest?"

She shook her head, the blond ponytail and red ski jacket making her look about fifteen if you didn't look at the lines of tension and pain around her eyes.

"I stayed at the hospital until morning. It seemed to comfort Esther's mother to have me there, and I was able to run interference with the medical people."

He nodded, knowing the truth of that. As far as Rebecca Zook was concerned, Libby was like another daughter. Their relationship had deep roots, and even though Libby lived far away, it was still solid. "Is there any change?"

He gestured to his visitor's chair. Libby sat down but perched on the edge of the seat, as if she'd fly off again any minute.

"No change as far as we could tell." Her voice thickened on the words. "The doctor on duty seemed to be surprised that she had survived the night."

He tried to think of something comforting to say and couldn't. "I'm sorry."

Libby's dark blue eyes looked even darker with emotion. "She did get through the night, so I'm taking that as a good sign. Maybe when I get there—"

"You ought to be home, getting some sleep." His voice was gruff as he tried to conceal an uprush of concern.

"You sound like my mother." There was a snap in her voice.

He tried to smile, wanting to ease the tension between them. "Speaking of your mother, I'm surprised Geneva let you go."

"She knows I'm only doing what she would do in this situation." She glanced down, seeming to focus on her hands, clutching together in her lap. "She'll be at the hospital herself later—you can count on that."

His heart twisted. "I wanted to talk to you, but it can wait, if you need to get back."

"Talk about what?" She focused on his face, her gaze so intent it was like being touched.

"Those letters you received from Esther." He frowned. "I don't suppose you brought them?"

"I'm sorry. I forgot you wanted to see them. I can drop them off later, but I've already told you what they said." Her chin lifted. "Are you actually taking me seriously now?"

I always take you seriously, Libby.

"I'm not convinced the letters had anything to do with her accident, but I'm not dismissing the idea." He frowned, glancing toward the map again. "Nobody seems to know what Esther was doing on that road last night. Or if they do, they're not telling me."

She considered that, following his gaze to the map. Then she rose, coming around the desk to stand next to him, staring at it.

"Esther was where? About here?" She put her finger

on the narrow line that represented the road, her sleeve brushing his.

There wasn't enough air in the office. It was always small, but now the walls closed in around him. No, around *them*.

"A little farther along." His touched the map, unable to avoid touching her hand, as well. "You see the problem. The Zook farm is clear up here, and the school is in the opposite direction. I don't see any reason at all that she'd be on Dahl Road. It's not on the way to any of the places she might normally go."

Libby studied the map and then traced her finger along the road to where it intersected with the main road, three miles from Springville. Her breath caught in a strangled gasp.

"Esther knew I was at the reception. She was coming to see me. If I had gotten to her sooner, this never would have happened."

"You don't know that." He made his voice deliberately flat, trying to dampen her emotion. "And even if she was heading for Springville, it doesn't explain anything. Where was she coming from? She wouldn't be on Dahl Road if she were driving from home to Springville."

"N-no, I guess not." She looked up at him. "But it doesn't change the fact that I should have come home sooner."

She was so close. Too close. He couldn't help but remember what had happened the last time he'd made the mistake of getting this near her.

He took a step back, bumping into the desk, his foot

entangling with the wheels of his chair. Like a stupid adolescent, tripping in the presence of the girl he was crazy about.

"It doesn't do Esther or her family any good to have you feeling sorry for yourself," he said, purposely cool.

Her face flamed with anger, as he'd known it would. "I'm not feeling sorry for myself. And I see you haven't learned any tact," she snapped.

"I'm a cop, not a diplomat." He moved away from her, around the desk. "My job is to find out who smashed into Esther's buggy and left her lying there on the road."

Maybe it was the effect of his words or maybe it was her natural courage, but Libby straightened, her chin lifting.

"I'll let you get on with that, then. If you need me, I'll be at the hospital." She walked quickly to the door, and then turned. "And while you're investigating, you might see if you can find my camera. I must have left it in your car last night."

Before he could respond she was gone, the door not quite slamming behind her.

He'd wanted to snap her out of thinking she was responsible for Esther's injury. Looked like he'd succeeded, but at the cost of making her mad at him.

Still, that might be better for both of them.

LIBBY'S HEART TWISTED when she approached the door of Esther's room, an unreasoning panic welling up. If something had happened...

That was stupid. If anything had changed, she'd

have heard. Still, her hand was cold as she pushed the door open.

Esther lay as she had the night before, her face nearly as white as the sheets except for the spreading bruises. Motionless, silent. The only sound in the room came from the machines, throbbing and pumping.

Esther's mother, sitting on the edge of a vinyl chair, was touching her daughter's hand. Another Amish woman sat next to Rebecca, her black dress and apron an echo of Rebecca's.

Rebecca looked up as the door swung shut, and her face creased in a welcoming smile that wiped away a little of the stress and pain. "Ach, Libby. I knew you would be back soon, for sure."

Libby crossed to her and bent to press her cheek against Rebecca's.

"How is she?"

Rebecca took her hand. "No change. That's what the nurse said, ja, Anna?" She glanced at the woman next to her.

The name triggered Libby's memory. Anna King, Esther's Aunt Anna. A former teacher herself, she had encouraged Esther to teach.

"Ja, that's right." Anna managed a smile, even though it was strained. "Libby, it is gut you are here. You have always been one of the family. Komm, sit here." She rose, motioning to her chair.

"I won't take your seat—"

But Anna shoved her gently to the seat. "You will keep

Rebecca and Esther company, and I will go for some coffee. The walk will do me gut."

Libby let herself be persuaded. Alone with her, maybe Rebecca might talk a little more freely. Surely she knew something about what had worried Esther in recent weeks.

"This is gut," Rebecca said. Clasping Libby's hand, she placed it over Esther's. "Maybe she will know that it is you, ain't so?"

She nodded. Esther's hand was slack under hers, limp and almost lifeless.

When they were children, they'd run everywhere holding hands. Laughing. After all these years, they were still so close. Each time she came home, she and Esther picked up again exactly where they'd left off, as if they hadn't been apart.

"She will open her eyes and look at us," Rebecca said. "Maybe not today, but soon."

Did Rebecca realize how serious Esther's condition was? Probably. She was a realist who took things as they came, like most Amish.

"Has the doctor been in again since I left?"

Rebecca shook her head. "But the nurse is very kind."

"That's fine." But she couldn't help wanting to hear an analysis from the doctor. "Before I forget, my mother said to tell you she'll be here a bit later today."

Rebecca's eyes filled with tears. "Geneva is a gut friend. Everyone has been ser kind, offering rides, saying they'll watch the kinder so Mary Ann can be here, bringing food."

"Everyone loves Esther. And you. They want to help."

Rebecca nodded. She looked at her daughter, and her lips pressed together.

Libby knew what she was thinking. She was wondering if Esther would ever know how much people cared about her.

She clasped Rebecca's hand. "She'll get well. She will." Was she assuring Rebecca or herself?

"It will be as God wills," Rebecca said softly. "But it can't be wrong to hope God wills her to stay with us awhile longer, ain't so?"

The door swung open. The doctor who entered was the same one who'd stopped by earlier—not the surgeon, the one who'd shown his surprise that Esther was still alive. Dr. C. Bardo, according to his name badge.

Libby found herself stiffening. If he didn't manage to be a bit more tactful this time…

"Well, let's see how we're doing." He consulted the chart, checked the machines, looking everywhere, it seemed, but at the patient. Rebecca followed his every movement, her gaze painful in its intensity.

He made a notation on the chart and then turned as if to leave.

Libby stood. "How is Esther doing, Dr. Bardo?"

Her crisp voice halted him. He looked from her to Rebecca, as if measuring what to say to them. Or maybe how much they could handle.

"The patient is fairly stable at the moment." He frowned, seeming to search for the right words. "Does she…" He nodded toward Rebecca. "Does she understand what I'm saying?"

Libby took a strong hold on her temper. "Of course Mrs. Zook understands. Please tell us how her daughter is."

"Sorry." He had the grace to look embarrassed. "I wasn't sure. The injuries are serious. Very serious. Frankly, we weren't sure the patient would survive the night."

"Esther," she said clearly. "Her name is Esther."

"Yes, right." He spoke quickly. "Head injuries are tricky things. I'm sure her…Esther's…surgeon will stop by later today, and he'll be able to explain it more thoroughly. Simply put, we're doing everything we can. She's in a medically induced coma to give her brain time to heal. Beyond that—well, no one can say how much she might recover."

"I see. Thank you for telling us." Should she have pressed him? But Rebecca wanted the truth.

"I wish we had better news for you." He was already halfway out the door. This time, Libby let him go.

She sank down in the chair next to Rebecca. "Doctors don't know everything," she said. "And he certainly doesn't know what a strong person Esther is."

"Ja, that is true." Rebecca looked at her daughter, love in her eyes. "Denke, Libby. For making him tell us. It is better to know what they are thinking. And you are right. Esther is a strong person, and she is in God's hands."

Strong. Even motionless, unconscious, with tubes running into her, there was strength in the very bone structure of Esther's face. Esther was a person who would do what she thought was right, no matter the consequences. Was that what had landed her here?

"Rebecca, you know that Esther wrote to me, didn't you?"

"Ja, for sure. Every week. Sometimes she would read me parts of your letters, too." Rebecca smiled gently. "She loved hearing from you."

Libby's throat tightened. "I felt the same. She'd tell me all the little things of her days…funny things the children said, what canning you were doing. It made me feel connected."

"Reminded you of home, is all," Rebecca said. "She wished you would komm back to stay."

She nodded. That wasn't a safe subject. She'd never told anyone, even Esther, about Adam's connection to why she stayed away, but she'd had a feeling Esther guessed even the things she didn't say.

"In the last month, Esther's letters were different," she said, feeling her way cautiously. "She seemed to be worried about something. She said she wanted to talk to me about it when I got here."

"Ja," Rebecca said softly. "I knew she was wanting to see you. But she didn't say anything was worrying her."

Libby looked at her searchingly. "Are you sure she didn't give you any idea that she was troubled in the past few weeks?"

"Nothing." She shook her head. "Now, if you'd said Isaac was troubled…"

A step sounded in the doorway. Libby swung around

to see Esther's brother, Isaac, standing there, watching them, and it was obvious he'd heard what his mother said.

There was an awkward silence, and then Mary Ann slipped around her husband to hurry over to her mother-in-law.

"Mamm Rebecca, you must be so tired. We are here now, so why don't you lie down and rest a bit? That nice nurse said she has a room you can use."

"Ja." Isaac came closer, trying to walk softly, as if afraid of disturbing his sister. "You need some rest. And Libby, also. She can go home now."

Libby managed a smile, trying to see the boy she'd known behind the bearded man in front of her. "I just got back. I'll stay."

"You should go—"

"Of course Libby will stay." Rebecca's voice was firm. "She is Esther's oldest friend. What are you thinking, Isaac?"

Grown man or not, Isaac looked abashed at his mother's words. He stared at his shoes. "I just thought…"

His words trailed off as Anna bustled back into the room, carrying a tray with the promised coffee. Bishop Amos was right behind her, and in a moment the room was filled with low voices, murmuring in a combination of English and Pennsylvania Dutch.

Libby stepped out of the way as the others joined in urging Rebecca to rest for a while. She watched Isaac bend over his sister, reaching out to her tentatively.

What had Rebecca meant? She'd implied that it was Isaac who was worried about something in recent weeks, not Esther. She studied the stiff set of his shoulders. If Isaac had been worried in the past weeks, she had a feeling he'd never admit that.

THE FENCE AT the edge of the road was coming toward her. Libby jerked the wheel, her breath catching, and straightened the car. Obviously she was way too tired to be driving her brand-new sister-in-law's car.

The driveway to the Morgan farm appeared ahead of her, guarded by enormous hemlocks on either side. With a rush of relief, she turned into the narrow lane.

Thursday's snowfall still lay in drifts in the patch of woods that screened the house, but it had melted where the sunlight hit the lawn. It had been thanks to that snowfall that she'd arrived in Lancaster County so late. Too late.

She parked on the gravel drive in front of the white frame house, pulling her key from her bag as she scurried to the front porch. Mom should have locked the door when she left for the hospital, but it was anyone's guess whether she had or not. Mom still seemed to think she lived in the safe, placid, rural community she'd moved to as a bride nearly forty years ago.

Sure enough, the door was unlocked. Libby slung her bag and jacket on the coatrack and walked back through to the family room. "Hello? Anyone home?"

No answer, not even from Sam, the golden retriever. But then, she hadn't expected one. She and Mom had crossed paths when she was coming out of the hospital while her mother went in, and Link was undoubtedly spending the afternoon with Marisa, probably taking the dog with him. Those two were newly engaged, and eager enough that Mom might well have another wedding on her hands soon.

Fatigue dragged at Libby as she went up the stairs, hand running along the smooth, warm wood of the banister. She was happy for Link. Of course she was. He deserved all the happiness in the world.

So why did the thought of Link married leave her so bereft? It wasn't as though they'd seen a lot of each other in the past few years.

But twins were twins, wherever life took them. Link had been the companion of her childhood, even more than Esther. He'd been her partner in countless acts of mischief, her confidant when things had gone wrong.

Stop feeling sorry for yourself, her conscience snapped in a voice that sounded rather like Adam's. That's what he'd said to her, wasn't it?

He didn't know the half of it. There was also the little matter of her job, and the fact that she still hadn't told the family she had joined the ranks of the unemployed. To say nothing of the nagging sense that she didn't know what she was going to do with her life.

Grow up, maybe. That sounded like a good move. She looked longingly at her bed, but another hot shower might do more to take out the kinks induced by hours in a plastic hospital chair.

A few minutes later she was stepping out of the shower, steam fogging the bathroom mirror and window. She wrapped one of Mom's enormous bath sheets around her. This had definitely been the right choice. The shower seemed to have washed away the doubts she'd let debilitate her.

One thing at a time. The important factor now was to keep Esther safe, in case the accident had been deliberate. Since it was unlikely that Adam would agree to put a guard on her door, she'd just have to make sure there was always someone in Esther's room with her.

Libby opened the bathroom door, letting the steam escape into the bedroom. She'd snatch a few hours of sleep and go back to the hospital. At some point she'd have to stop at a store and pick up a few more incidental Christmas gifts, with the holiday headed for them so quickly. At least nobody was questioning her staying for so long a visit, since the wedding had fallen less than a week before Christmas.

A door closed downstairs. Mom? A glance at the clock on the nightstand told her it was impossible for her mother to be back already. Maybe Link and Marisa, in which case it would be only tactful to let them know someone was here.

She traded the bath sheet for the fluffy pink robe she'd worn in high school and opened the bedroom door. "Link, is that you? I'm upstairs."

No one answered. But from downstairs came the creak of a floorboard. She froze, clutching the door. She knew exactly which board made that sound...the one in the hallway near the family room door. They'd joked, as kids, about having their own private alarm system to let them know when Mom was about to appear in the door to the family room.

She listened, holding her breath. The faintest of sounds, like a hand brushing the wall. Her imagination? Or someone being careful, trying to avoid hitting any more creaky boards?

She gripped the door, undecided. She wouldn't let herself panic. Maybe—

A footstep, definitely.

She moved backward, bare feet making no sound on the wide floorboards. Ease the door shut, carefully, carefully. She held her breath, releasing the knob ever so slowly. The snick of the lock sounded ridiculously loud.

In two steps she was at the phone, and in less than a minute she'd dialed 911. Adam's voice, crisp and professional, took her aback for an instant, but of course it was Sunday. Probably the only reason the dispatcher had been there earlier was because of the current investigation.

"Adam, it's Libby." She kept her voice barely above the whisper. Whoever was in the house knew now that she was there, but maybe not exactly where. "Someone's in the house."

He didn't waste time questioning how she knew. "Where are you?"

The wail of a siren punctuated his words. He was in the police car, then. With luck, not clear at the other end of the township.

"Locked in my bedroom. He's downstairs."

"Shove something in front of the door, and don't come out until I tell you to. Understand?"

She'd resent his tone, but at the moment she was too eager to see him. "Yes. I understand."

"Keep the phone line open."

He didn't need to tell her that twice. She set it down long enough to shove the dresser across the door. Then she leaned over the dresser, trying to listen over the thudding of her heart.

Nothing. Or at least, nothing she could hear. A smart burglar would get out quickly once he realized someone was in the house. Maybe he was gone already.

Or maybe not. She had no desire to find out. She sat on the edge of the bed, the phone cradled in her hands, and waited.

The sound of the siren was suddenly coming both from the phone and from outside. She reached the window in time to see the police car skid to a stop, gravel spraying. Adam got out, and just the sight of his tall figure was enough to make her stomach do a flip.

Going to the dresser, she put her hands on it to push it back into place, then thought the better of it. She'd wait until she heard Adam's voice first.

She heard the front door open, then the sound of footsteps moving through the downstairs. She waited, and it felt like forever.

Finally the footsteps came up the stairs. "Nobody here now. You can come out."

She slid the dresser back, unlocked the door and opened it.

Adam lifted an eyebrow, and she realized how she

must look—wet hair, damp robe, bare feet, her face bare of makeup.

"Are you okay?"

She nodded, trying to hang on to whatever shreds of dignity she had left. "Did he take anything?" She had a sudden vision of her mother's sterling silver gone while she was cowering in her room. "Maybe I should have—"

"You did exactly the right thing," he said, his tone repressive. "I suppose you think it would have been better to go after him armed with a tennis racket."

"My mother would have." She could picture it perfectly.

"I love your mother dearly, but common sense is not her strong suit." A smile tugged at the corner of his mouth. "Come on. Let's see if anything's missing before I launch a full investigation."

She slanted a sideways glance at him as they went down the stairs side by side. "Thanks for getting here so fast."

"I wasn't far away." His gaze was fixed on the front door, not on her. "That door was unlocked. Did you leave it that way?"

"Mom had left it unlocked when she went to the hospital."

"So you decided to do the same? I thought you big-city types were safety conscious."

She clenched her teeth for an instant. "I intended to talk to her about it when she came in, but I didn't want to lock her out, in case she hadn't taken her keys."

"There's one under the third flowerpot on the left."

At her surprised glance, he shrugged.

"She told me, in case I ever needed to get in. She's probably told about half the township for one reason or another."

That was her mother, all right. "If I knew, I'd forgotten. And since I was going in the shower, I might not have heard her when she came back."

"So I see." He glanced at her robe, and she had a feeling she was blushing.

Hurrying down the last few steps, she headed for the dining room. "I'll check the silver. Isn't that the first thing a burglar would take?"

"Only the sophisticated types. Around here, they're more likely to grab the electronics." He followed her to the sideboard, which was adorned with greens and holly in Mom's silver punch bowl.

She bent to open the door and grabbed the chest, opening the lid. "It's here." The tightness in her throat eased as she slid the silver chest back in place. "Maybe he didn't come in this room. The board I heard creak is at the entrance to the family room."

The family room, where most of the electronic equipment would be. If Adam was right…

He was ahead of her, and she heard the board creak under his foot.

"That's what I heard. Dad tried I don't know how many times to fix that, but it always creaked."

Adam moved into the family room and stopped, blocking her view.

"How bad is it?" She squeezed past him, expecting a

mess. The family room was never all that neat, since that was where most of the family living was done, but Mom and her helpers had no doubt tidied up before the wedding. The mantelpiece was filled with greens and candles, and the family Christmas tree in the corner carried its usual array of ornaments made by her and her brothers. More to the point, her laptop still sat on the desk, in obvious view.

Adam didn't speak, but it seemed to her that his very silence was skeptical. She glared at him.

"I did not imagine it. Someone was in the house. I heard him."

He shrugged, his face impassive. "Could have been a neighbor, dropping something off. Or one of the Amish girls who helps your mother." He held up his hand, stopping her protest. "Or it could have been a sneak thief, thinking no one was here and scared off when he realized he was wrong. I'll check the rest of the downstairs more carefully, but it doesn't look as if anything is missing."

She should be pleased. She was pleased, except for the fact that Adam probably thought she was letting her nerves get away from her. Or, worse, that she wanted his attention.

She turned toward the desk, not eager to see his face right now. And found she was staring at a blank blue screen.

For a moment all she could do was stare. The computer should have been in sleep mode. It wasn't. It took only a few keystrokes to show her the truth.

"Something is missing." She felt numb. All her work, her business files, her personal data. "Someone has wiped my hard drive clean."

CHAPTER FOUR

ADAM STUDIED LIBBY'S face. She obviously believed that. But was it really likely that someone had broken into the Morgan house just to damage Libby's computer?

At his silence, Libby's cheeks flushed. "I suppose you think I'm making that up."

"Don't put words in my mouth, Libby. I don't think that at all. I can see for myself that the computer has crashed."

"Everything's gone." She raked her fingers through her damp hair. "What a mess. All my photo files—"

"Don't you have backup?" He took a step closer, impelled by the distress in her face. He didn't quite get it himself, since he used the computer only when his job required, but he knew people who insisted their whole lives were on their computers.

"Yes, of course." She managed a feeble smile. "I'm overreacting, I guess. I use an online backup system, so it's not really lost. Sorry. I didn't mean to sound as if it was the end of civilization as we know it."

"That's okay. You're entitled, after the time you've had lately."

That flash of the old, spunky kid sister encouraged him, but he was going to have to be careful what he said to her. Libby was fragile, more so than he'd ever seen her.

"Okay, let's assume someone came in the house while you were upstairs. You didn't see a vehicle?"

She shook her head. "But someone planning a break-in wouldn't leave a vehicle in plain sight."

"True, but it'd also be pretty obvious if he walked in, with the snow cover." He prolonged the conversation, since Libby looked better for concentrating on possibilities. "I'll take a look around outside while you get dressed, and then we can do a more careful check of the house."

She nodded, wrapping the fuzzy robe more tightly around her, as if just becoming aware that she stood there in robe and bare feet, looking as if she'd just stepped from the shower.

Whoa. Better not let his mind go there. Maybe getting dressed would help restore Libby's balance. And the cold air would certainly do him some good right now.

Libby hurried up the stairs without another word, and he went back out the front door. He hadn't taken the time for a good look around when he'd arrived, too intent on getting to Libby.

The massive wreath on the front door rustled as he closed the door. Adam stood on the front porch, surveying the area. The Morgan place stood in its own acreage some seven miles from Springville, a large, gracious house, set well back from the road. Everything about it screamed out the difference between Libby's life and his own.

Not that something like that would necessarily stand between them if… Well, that was a stupid train of thought. He'd made too many mistakes with Libby to start over now, and for that matter, she'd never exactly shown a lot of confidence in him, either, jumping to conclusions about his guilt where Sally was concerned.

Focus, he ordered himself. The stand of evergreens that screened the house from view might provide cover for an intruder. The lawns were snow-covered in patches, but maybe there was enough bare ground that a man could approach without leaving prints in the snow.

Adam stepped down from the porch to the gravel-covered parking area. Nothing to be seen here, but it would take nerve to drive straight in from the road if you were intent on burglary. Still, there were no neighbors near enough to see, assuming you were sure no one was home.

He started around the house. The Morgan place had begun life as a classic Pennsylvania double-plank farmhouse, but succeeding generations had added on as the family became larger. And more prominent.

He could spot no signs of anyone coming near the house this way, but when he reached the rear, there were too many. Obviously plenty of vehicles had been in and out in the past few days because of the wedding. It was impossible to separate out any tracks that had been made today.

Trying the kitchen door, he discovered without surprise that it was unlocked. Geneva drove Trey crazy with her carelessness about safety. He'd installed a security system at one point, but after several dozen false alarms caused by Geneva's habit of forgetting to shut the thing off, he'd given up on that.

The kitchen seemed bright and welcoming on even a gray day, with its pale yellow walls and warm wood cabinets. Adam rested a hand on the pine table where he'd had more meals than he could count. Geneva had always acted as if he were half-starved when he was a kid, which had more truth in it than she'd probably known.

The old man hadn't wanted to waste money on food when it could be better spent, according to him, on drink. Adam's jaw tightened, and he yanked his attention back to the present.

A basket sat on the counter, the casserole dish it contained covered with a napkin. So maybe a neighbor had been in, and that had been the sound Libby heard.

Libby appeared in the kitchen door. "Did you find anything?" She looked more like herself now, in blue jeans and with her damp hair fastened at the nape of her neck, but she still had a brittle edge that concerned him.

"Too much traffic in and out with the wedding," he said. He nodded toward the basket. "It looks as if a neighbor might have been here. Maybe that was what you heard." He suspected that wouldn't satisfy her.

It didn't…he could see that from her expression even before she spoke.

"Then what happened to my computer? A neighbor delivering a casserole wouldn't be likely to touch that."

"Computers do crash," he said mildly.

"Yes." Doubt flickered in her eyes. "But that would be awfully coincidental."

"Why?" Frustration was getting the better of him.

"How could your computer possibly link up with Esther's letters?"

Her jaw set with typical Morgan stubbornness. "I don't know. But I still say it's odd."

She wouldn't admit it, he knew, but at least he'd succeeded in planting some doubt in her mind. "You just want to find a mystery in everything. Natural enough. You're a reporter."

"Not anymore." She clamped her lips together, looking as if she regretted saying the words.

"Oh?" He stood. Waited. He could see she wanted to say more, but if he urged her, she'd back off. Libby hadn't changed all that much, and he knew her too well.

She smoothed still-damp hair back from the perfect oval of her face. "Yes, well, I lost my job. Quit, actually, but it came to the same thing." Concern drew her brows together. "I haven't told my mother yet, so don't say anything."

"I won't." He waited, knowing there was more.

"It had been coming on for a long time, actually." She shrugged, moving restlessly around the kitchen table to the counter. "Too many crime scenes, too many photos of mangled cars and mangled bodies and burned-out buildings and…

"The last straw was the scene of a gang shooting. The mother, crying over her son's body. I was snapping shots, trying not to register what I was seeing, and all of a sudden the woman raised her head and looked right at me."

Her lips trembled, making him want to put his arms

around her. She pressed her lips together, hands gripping the edge of the counter.

"I told her I wouldn't run the photo. I told my editor that. But he did it anyway. Said that was what a news reporter did, and if I couldn't hack it, I should quit. I just stood there looking at him, and it all gelled in my mind. I didn't belong there, taking pictures of one disaster after another. So I'm officially unemployed."

He couldn't stay away from her any longer, but he contented himself with going to lean against the counter next to her, looking down at her averted face. "Why haven't you told your mother yet? If I know Geneva, she's likely to want to give you a medal for that."

Libby shook her head, still not looking at him. "I…I didn't want to distract from the wedding. I'll tell her. Then I'll figure out what I'm going to do with my life."

His heart lurched at the bereft sound in her words. He leaned closer, needing to comfort her, wanting to tell her everything would work out—

"Hello?" The front door banged. "What's going on? Is something wrong?" Geneva's light voice echoed in the hallway, and then she erupted into the kitchen. "What's happening?"

"It's nothing, Mom." Libby spoke quickly, before he could explain. "I thought I heard someone in the house earlier, so Adam came to check it out for me, but it was nothing."

Geneva eyed her searchingly, and then she turned the same gaze on him. "Is that all? Are you sure?"

"I checked the whole house," he said. Obviously Libby

wanted to protect her mother from knowing anything about this. Admirable, but not very realistic. Geneva always found out about things, and she could never be persuaded to stay out of anything.

"Nothing was missing?" Geneva glanced around, running a hand through her short gray curls. "How could someone get in?"

"Through the doors you so obligingly left unlocked." He gave her a stern frown. "What do you suppose Trey would say about that?"

"Well, Trey's off on his honeymoon, so he won't know." She gave him the winsome smile that had half the township ready to do whatever Geneva asked. "And you won't tell him, will you?"

"Not if you promise to be more careful in the future." He glanced at his watch. "I've got to get back to the office. If anything turns up missing..."

"We'll call you," Geneva said promptly. "But why don't you come for supper? We can talk it over then. Along with whatever you two are trying to keep from me."

"We're not—" Libby began, but let it drop at her mother's look.

"It's nice of you to invite me, but I'm in the middle of an investigation," he said quickly, moving toward the door.

"You still have to eat," Geneva said. "Come back around six. Link and Marisa will be here by then, and we can talk it over while we eat." She smiled, seeming confident that he'd obey.

Which he would. He couldn't refuse Geneva anything. He owed her too much for that. She'd looked at the ragged, angry son of the town drunk and seen a person worth cultivating where the rest of the township had seen trash.

He'd never forget what he owed her, as well as the rest of the Morgan family. Which was why any feelings he had for Libby were best buried…too deep to be found.

CHAPTER FIVE

LIBBY GLANCED LONGINGLY at her bed, something she seemed to be doing a lot lately. She'd spent what was left of the day trying to get her operating system reloaded so that she could start downloading the files from her off-site storage. It had, of course, been a frustrating experience, but once she started, she hadn't been willing to stop.

Adam would probably say she was being obsessive about it, just as he so clearly thought she was obsessive about the attack on Esther.

Why was she thinking about Adam again? She attacked her hair with the hairbrush. Being home, seeing him again, had brought up feelings she was sure she'd banished ages ago. Well, she'd just have to chase them back out. Anything else just led to problems—witness the fact that she'd opened up to him about her job, when she hadn't told anyone else yet.

She stared blindly into the mirror, seeing, instead of her own face, an image of that grieving mother. When their eyes met, it was as if she'd seen herself as she must appear to that poor woman.

She'd seen a Libby she didn't know. A Libby she didn't like much. It wouldn't have taken the final indignity of that fight with her editor. That moment had been the end of her career.

Voices sounded from downstairs, and the clatter of china and silverware. She tossed the brush on the dresser. Time to stop going over these fruitless thoughts and get on with things.

She hurried down the stairs, consciously trying for the usual spring to her step. The voices came from the dining room. She went in to find that Adam, Link and Marisa were all helping her mother get supper on the table.

Of course. It was Sunday, and Mom's usual Amish helpers didn't work on the Sabbath.

"You all look busy." She forced the lilt into her voice. "What can I do?"

"Put water in the glasses," Link said promptly, glancing at her and then taking another, longer look and frowning. "What's wrong?"

So, maybe the twin connection between them hadn't been entirely vanquished by his love for Marisa. "Nothing. I'll get the water." She escaped into the kitchen.

Not that she wasn't relieved to know the bond with Link still existed, but she hadn't decided yet how much she wanted to tell her family. Always assuming that Adam didn't take it out of her hands and tell them everything.

With everyone helping, they had the simple meal on the table in no time.

"Chicken potpie," her mother said, taking her seat at the foot of the table nearest the kitchen. "Thomas Esch dropped it off from his mother right after church. She knew we'd be tired from the wedding, not that we did all the cooking, the way the Amish do for their weddings."

Libby frowned, trying to pick out the important fact from her mother's tale. "Were you here when Thomas brought it, Mom?"

Her mother gave her a wide-eyed look. "Of course, how else would I know what his mother said? Why? What difference does it make?"

"None," she said quickly, fearing she hadn't been quick enough. She glanced at Adam, to make sure he hadn't missed the implication. Whoever her mystery guest had been, it hadn't been the neighbor bringing the casserole. "How is Thomas?"

The teenage son of their Amish neighbors had gone through a terrible ordeal during the summer, when he'd been accused of killing a woman. That was the case which had brought Jessica to Springville to defend him, and incidentally to fall in love with Trey.

"He seems to be doing all right," her mother said, frowning a little. "He's very quiet, but at least he's stopped refusing to leave the farm."

"Poor kid," Link said. "If it hadn't been for Trey and Jessica, I hate to think what would have happened to him."

"And your mother," Adam added. "She's the one who was determined to defend Thomas."

That action had had unintended consequences, as the investigation had eventually led to the man who'd killed Dad. Tough for all of them, but at least they no longer had to face the thought that he'd committed suicide.

"Another case of the Morgan family butting into other people's business," Link said lightly. He put down his fork to cover Marisa's hand with his. Marisa returned his look with one so tender that it nearly brought tears to Libby's eyes.

She didn't envy them their happiness. Marisa was perfect for Link—gentle, kind, artistic, with a shy warmth that seemed to bring out Link's gentleness. They'd met through a twist of fate just a few months ago, when Link had found a clue to the long-ago disappearance of Marisa's Amish mother in the house their uncle left him.

Link glanced at Adam. "I understand you made a house call this afternoon?" His tone made it a question.

"Your sister heard someone in the house when she came back this afternoon," Adam said, before anyone else could begin explanations. "She called me, so I came over and checked it out. Nothing seems to be missing."

She managed not to remind him of her computer. Pointless to keep going over it.

Link's expression darkened. "Are you sure? How did they get in?"

Libby wasn't going to give her mother away, but it seemed likely that Geneva's guilty look had done that already.

"Mom." Link's tone was close to a howl of frustration. "You left the house open again, didn't you?"

"It's not going to happen again," Adam said. "By the way, I thought you invited me here to pump me about the investigation." He put a large forkful of chicken potpie in his mouth.

"Not exactly that," her mother said, clearly ready to change the subject. "But we do want to know what's happening."

"We got a preliminary report back on the vehicle," Adam said. "Based on the paint scrapings and the height at which the buggy was hit, we're looking for a black pickup truck or van." He shrugged. "Doesn't exactly narrow it down a lot. I'd hate to guess how many there are in the county, and it doesn't have to be someone local."

Link shook his head. "I'd think only a local was likely to be on Dahl Road at that hour. It's not as if it's midsummer, when you stumble over tourists everywhere you turn."

"I just don't understand what Esther was doing there, for that matter." Mom's face crinkled in distress. "Where on earth was she going?"

"Good question," Link said. "It's not on her way home from anywhere she'd be likely to go." Everyone who knew the area and the Zook family would be bound to see that.

"Your sister thinks Esther was coming to see her." Adam's tone expressed his doubt. "Based on Esther's letters—"

"Letters?" Mom was on that in an instant, as Libby had known she would be. "What letters?"

Libby glared at Adam, but he spread his hands, as if to say that it had to come out. And he was probably right.

"You know that Esther and I write to each other," she said. "In the last few letters I received, Esther was worried about something. She was eager for me to get here, so that she could ask my advice about it. But by that time..." She let that trail off. It was obvious.

"Elizabeth Amanda Morgan." Mom was truly upset when she used all three names. "Why on earth didn't you tell me about this?"

"Come on, Mom. When did I have a chance to? When we were rushing off to the rehearsal, or scurrying around hosting the rehearsal dinner? You've been so preoccupied with Trey's wedding that there was no time for anything else. As you should be," she added hastily. "I brought the letters with me because I wanted to hear what you thought of them, but..." She shrugged.

"You think the hit-and-run was connected to this whatever-it-was that had Esther worried." Link could connect the dots quickly when it came to how his twin thought.

"I think so." She darted a glance at Adam. "Adam doesn't agree."

"You don't have any idea what she meant?" Marisa's brown eyes were warm with concern.

Libby shook her head. "I asked Rebecca, Esther's mother, if she'd noticed that Esther was upset lately, but she said no. She said..." She stopped, frowning.

"She said what?" Adam's tone demanded an answer.

"She said Esther seemed fine, but that Isaac had been upset about something. But that can't have been what Esther wrote to me about. She wouldn't want my advice on handling her brother."

"No." Link said the word slowly. "You're right. If she

wanted your help, it would have to be something that involved the English."

"The English and the Amish," Mom amended. "If it was strictly an English concern, Esther wouldn't be involved."

"True." Adam looked as if he'd prefer not to be discussing this at the Morgan dinner table. "I've been thinking about it since Libby mentioned the letters, but I'm drawing a blank."

"Could we see the letters?" Marisa asked. "Maybe we'd pick up on…well, not anything you missed. But sometimes a different viewpoint helps in seeing something more clearly."

Libby made an effort not to resent that. Marisa meant well. "I'll get them." She slid from her chair.

But getting the letters proved more difficult than she anticipated. She'd put them in the case she always carried on a plane, one that contained her laptop and any work she had with her.

It wasn't in her room. She came back down the stairs, not looking toward the dining room to encounter any skeptical stares, and hurried into the family room, hearing the familiar squeak of the board.

It wasn't there. Surely she'd left it next to the desk, hadn't she, when she took the computer out?

She went back to the archway into the dining room. "It looks as if something was taken after all this afternoon. My computer case is missing."

"Are you sure you looked everywhere?" Her mother

sprang up, always ready to jump into the finding of lost objects. "Where did you last have it?"

That was the same thing she'd always asked when homework was missing.

"It had to be either in my bedroom or by the desk in the family room. It's not at either place." She couldn't help giving Adam a challenging look. Maybe now he'd admit that she was right.

"Oh, dear." Her mother sounded guilty. "You know, when I was rushing around trying to make sure the house was picked up in case anyone came back here after the wedding, it's possible that I moved it. I don't remember doing that, but you know what I'm like when I clean up."

She did indeed. Mom's clean sweeps were legendary. Things that were put away at Christmas sometimes didn't turn up until Easter.

"I'll have a good look around for it later," her mother said. "If it's here, I'll find it. And anyway, when Esther wakes up, she'll be able to tell us all about whatever it was."

If, Libby thought, unable to help herself. If Esther woke up. If she remembered.

A chill went down her spine. And if the person who'd hit her buggy heard that Esther was waking up, what might he do to keep her from talking?

LIBBY SLEPT LATER than she'd intended the next morning, and she hurried down the stairs, intent on grabbing something to eat before she went to the hospital. The house was quiet. She could only hope Mom was sleeping in this morning. She'd been looking tired after all the festivities, though of course she'd never admit it.

There was no sign of her mother, but when Libby reached the kitchen, Link was there, nursing a mug of coffee with the morning paper spread out on the table in front of him.

"Hey, little sister." He looked up, his lean face, tanned even in winter, relaxing in a grin. "I thought you'd sleep till noon today."

She gave him the light slap on the back of the head that had passed for a hug when they were teenagers. "We're twins. I am not your little sister." The familiar banter was comforting.

Link caught her hand and gave it a squeeze. "I'm twenty minutes older. That makes you my little sister. Coffee?" He stood, lifting the coffeepot.

"Sounds great." She found a half grapefruit in the fridge, already cut the way she liked it, and set it on the table.

Link put the coffee mug next to the grapefruit and shoved the sugar bowl in her direction. "How about a sticky bun? Or walnut streusel coffee cake?"

"Coffee cake." She sat down, eyeing her twin with suspicion. "Okay, out with it. What do you want?"

He put a slab of coffee cake in front of her, his grin sheepish. "How about an idea of what to get Marisa for Christmas?"

"You haven't done your shopping yet?" She stared at him with horror that wasn't entirely teasing. "It's only two days until Christmas. What on earth have you been doing?"

He shrugged. "Getting my brother married off, same as you. Anyway, I can't decide. It has to be just right. This is our first Christmas together."

Libby repressed a pang of envy. "Christmas did kind of get lost in the shuffle, with Trey and Jessica getting married the week before. But you know Marisa better than I do. What do you think she'd like?"

Manlike, he shrugged helplessly. "I don't know. Maybe a flat screen television?"

"So she could watch sports?" She let sarcasm creep into her voice. "That's what *you* want. What about jewelry?"

"I just gave her an engagement ring," he protested. "She wouldn't want more jewelry, would she?"

"You really are hopeless, you know that?" She considered smacking him again, but that might lead to all-out war, and as tempting as it was, she didn't have time for it now. Still, she had to grin, remembering the series of practical jokes they'd played on each other the last time she was home.

"Listen carefully," she said. "No woman, especially one newly engaged, wants an appliance for Christmas. She wants something that reminds her you love her. What about a watch? Marisa always wears one, and you could have it engraved with something romantic."

"Good idea." His face brightened. "You want to go shopping and help me pick it out?"

"Can't. I've got to go to the hospital to see Esther. But

do it today, or you'll never get it engraved by Christmas. And make it something small and delicate and feminine."

"Right, I will." His face sobered. "Listen, it's not going to bother you that Adam Byler is joining us for Christmas, is it?"

It took an effort to keep her face from changing. "I didn't know he was."

Link nodded. "Him and Leo Frost."

Leo Frost was the family's attorney and an old friend. His inclusion didn't surprise her.

"Why did Mom decide to invite Adam?"

"You know Mom." He shrugged his shoulders. "She can't stand the thought of anyone being alone on Christmas. She invites him every year, and this time he said yes."

Okay, she could handle this. "Why would you think it might bother me?"

He avoided her eyes. "Look, I know how you felt about him when we were in high school, remember? And it seems to me sparks have been flying since you've been back this time."

"That's your imagination." She caught his look and knew he didn't believe her. "Whatever sparks you see are the result of our disagreeing over what happened to Esther."

He held up his hands, evidently wishing he hadn't asked. "Okay, if you say so. But just remember, sparks can sometimes cause a fire. Give my best to Esther's family, will you? Is there anything I can do?"

"Not unless you can figure out who did this to her."

"Afraid not," he said, his voice slowing. "But something did occur to me after we talked last night—something that's happening in the township that affects both English and Amish. Still, I don't see how Esther could be involved."

"Tell me," she demanded, mind racing. Was she actually going to learn something helpful?

Link frowned. "Like I say, I don't see how it could affect Esther. But there's been a lot of talk going around about a new motel being built on a piece of prime Amish farmland. Nobody can understand how the builder got permission to build there. Not a word of it leaked out until it was a done deal and he broke ground. Word has it several Amish farmers had an eye on that piece of land, just waiting for it to come on the market."

She didn't see how Esther could be concerned in that, either, but it *was* the sort of thing she might ask Libby's advice on.

"Who's the builder?" She set her mug down. The coffee had cooled while they'd been talking.

"That's just it. It's Tom Sylvester. I can't imagine him doing anything sleazy to get a project through."

"I thought he retired and went to Florida. Isn't that why you're running Morgan Construction now?" She remembered Tom, of course. He'd run the family's construction business for what seemed most of her life.

"Retiring was all he talked about." Link's frown deepened. "It was kind of odd, now that I think about it. He came back after just a few weeks, saying he couldn't stand doing nothing. He didn't want his job back—just said he'd be taking on a few small jobs on his own. Next thing we knew, he was digging the foundation for a new motel just this side of Springville."

She nodded. "I saw that something was going up there. I can't imagine any reason Esther would be interested, but it's worth looking into."

"But Tom—" Link's face showed his doubt.

She had never been as impressed with Tom Sylvester as the boys had been. His bluff, hearty manner didn't seem quite real, and his habit of calling her "little princess" annoyed her. That was for Daddy to say, no one else.

"It might be worth taking a look at this new project of his. I'll stop at the site on my way to the hospital and see if Tom is there." She stood, abandoning her half-eaten breakfast. "See you later. Do that shopping today."

He grinned. "I will. And you be careful."

"I will," she echoed. But what could happen to her?

ADAM SHOVED HIS chair back from his desk with an impatient movement. Reports, reports and more reports…all negative. The canvass of local garages for repairs hadn't produced a thing so far, but he didn't have the manpower to do it any faster. His two part-timers had been let go at the end of the tourist season, leaving him with only three officers.

The state police were circulating a request to all garages in the tricounty area, but they knew, as he did, that there were places that would do repairs and conveniently forget if questioned.

The lab tests on the paint had narrowed the possibilities down slightly. They were looking for a late-model black van or pickup truck, American made. Unfortunately that wasn't enough to point in any particular direction.

He moved toward the door. He may as well join in the check on garages as sit here. There weren't any other investigations pressing—winter was the quiet season in their little corner of the county.

He reached the dispatcher's desk in time to see the outer door open. Jason Smalley, one of the three township supervisors, came in, wiping his shoes carefully on the mat.

Jason was always what the old-timers called "finicky" in his actions…maybe the result of growing up with a mother like Sandra. Too bad his flawless exterior didn't match up with his inside. Adam looked at him and saw, not the successful real estate developer, but the bully who'd made an elementary school career out of taking lunch money from younger kids.

Once his shoes were clean enough to suit him, Jason brushed a melting snowflake from the sleeve of his navy wool coat and strode toward Adam, smile wide and hand extended.

"Adam. Just the person I wanted to see."

He nodded, unable to feel any matching enthusiasm. "What can I do for you, Jason?"

Jason shot a glance at Ginger, the dispatcher, who promptly turned back to her keyboard.

"Let's go into your office."

Since Jason, as a township supervisor, was in a sense Adam's boss, he could hardly refuse. He stepped back, gesturing Jason in, and thinking fleetingly of the day he'd put an end to Jason's bullying by giving him a bloody nose. He'd been the one to get into trouble for it, of course, but it had been worth the detention.

He closed the door and returned to his desk, nodding at the visitor's chair. "What is it, Jason? I was just heading out to join the search for the hit-and-run car."

"The accident, of course." Jason sat. "I came by to see how the investigation is coming along. On behalf of the supervisors, of course."

Adam sat motionless, studying Jason's face for a clue to his thoughts. The township supervisors, three elected officials, generally concerned themselves with keeping the township roads clear and following up on decisions of the township planning commission. He couldn't remember a time when they'd asked for more than the latest department statistics.

That stare must be making Jason nervous. He crossed his legs, swinging one foot in quick, jerky motions.

"The department is following all the leads to the driver," he said.

Jason frowned. "We'd like a few more details than that. The supervisors are responsible for the police department."

He'd guess the bully was still there, hidden behind that glossy facade. Still, he didn't really have a reason to refuse.

"We know that the vehicle was a late-model van or truck, black, American made. There must have been considerable damage to the front end of the vehicle, so we're checking all the garages in the township. The state police have circulated a request for information to all repair facilities in the tricounty. There's really not a lot more we can do from that angle."

"Of course, of course." Jason's lips twitched in a smile. "You're doing all you can. No one can fault us if you're not able to arrest the driver. Probably someone from out of the area, driving too fast on an unfamiliar road. Likely you'll never know."

That smug assumption of failure got under Adam's skin. "It may not be as simple as that." He hesitated. Better not to mention Libby. "We've learned that Esther wrote several letters which hinted that she was worried about a problem that apparently involved the English community. There's a suggestion the crime was connected with that."

"Crime?" Smalley looked startled. "You mean the accident."

"Hit-and-run driving is a crime," Adam said. He didn't believe in sugarcoating wrongdoing. "The driver faces a stiff penalty, even if Esther recovers."

"Yes, well, I suppose you're right. But these letters..." He paused, eyes narrowing. "They were to Libby Morgan, I suppose. I should have known the Morgan family would be involved somehow."

His fingers tightened around his pen. "What do you mean by that?"

Jason seemed to sense he'd gone too far. "Nothing, nothing. I suppose the Morgans have gotten used to being the big fish in the pond, but times are changing.

People like the Morgans aren't so important these days. You don't have to pursue a pointless investigation just to please them."

Resisting the urge to throw his pen, Adam put it down carefully. "I follow where the evidence leads. That's my job. I won't ignore any leads, no matter how slight."

Jason stood, shoving the chair back, his face stiff. "We know where you stand, don't we?"

Adam rose and planted his fists on the desk very deliberately. "You keep saying 'we,' Jason. Somehow I wonder if you really represent the other supervisors. Or if they even know about your attempt to influence the investigation."

Anger flared in Jason's face. "I see it's useless to talk to you." He walked to the door and paused for a parting shot. "You always were the Morgan family's little pet, weren't you? The trash they picked up from the gutter to do their dirty work for them."

He was gone before Adam could react.

That was a good thing. Adam unclenched his fists, a finger at a time. He might have bloodied Jason's nose for him again, and if he had, the consequences this time would be considerably more serious.

Stupid to let anger steer him away from the central point. He didn't believe the other supervisors knew anything about Jason's visit, or if they did, they hadn't instigated it. So what was Jason up to?

CHAPTER SIX

LIBBY SLOWED THE car as she neared the outskirts of Springville, watching for the building site Link had mentioned. She didn't share Link's high opinion of Tom Sylvester, and it had been obvious to her that her brother had some doubts, even if he didn't want to admit that.

Just what strings had Tom pulled to get permission to build on what was apparently prime farmland? The township planning commission would be the body that ruled on such a question. Her reporter's instincts kicked into gear. Too bad she no longer had press credentials to back them up.

She stepped on the brake pedal. The raw, unfinished construction site, barely yards from the road, stood in stark contrast to the simple Amish farms tucked back on their narrow lanes.

Spotting a gravel access road into the site, Libby turned in, parked and stared at the building, speculating. Based on what Link had told her, the first anyone knew about the project work had already started and was moving fast, odd enough at this time of year.

Speed was smart on Tom's part, though, if he feared a challenge. The zoning commission would be less likely to reverse its decision if the building was already up.

Funny, how all the things she'd heard her father say about the importance of the land came back to her now. Dad had considered it a family responsibility to protect the township from the kind of haphazard development that had occurred elsewhere in the county.

She slid out of the car, zipping her anorak against the cold wind. She'd borrowed a small digital camera from her mother, mainly because she didn't feel right without one, though she could snap photos on her cell phone if need be. She dropped the camera into her pocket and picked her way through patches of snow and half-frozen mud toward the building.

It was going to be two stories, and much bigger than she'd imagined. She'd pictured Tom Sylvester putting up a little mom-and-pop operation to amuse himself in his retirement, but this place was big enough to rival the more upscale chains.

Pulling the camera out, Libby snapped a few photos. No point to it, maybe, but still…the situation was odd, to put it mildly.

She'd convinced herself that whatever had upset Esther, it had to be something that involved both English and Amish in some way. This project apparently qualified, even though she couldn't see what Esther's connection to it might be. Her family didn't live near enough that Isaac would have been trying to add acreage.

Look for the connection. She'd heard that often enough in the newsroom. So, she'd look.

A couple of wooden planks laid together over a trench seemed the only access to the building itself. No one was here. She wouldn't get a better chance to have a look inside.

She started up the slanted planks. Hiking boots would have been a better choice than the leather ones she had on. She took another step, her foot sliding, and flung her arms out for balance, breath coming quickly.

Okay. Worst-case scenario was that she'd fall into the trench and end up wet and muddy. No need to panic. Inching her way, she reached the top and stepped inside.

The first floor was already partially partitioned off. If she was interpreting it correctly, there was going to be a restaurant as well as the hotel lobby in this area. Frowning, she snapped off a few more pictures. Where did Tom Sylvester get the funds to put up something this extensive?

She walked around another partition, trying to visualize the layout. Her boots echoed on the wooden subfloor, the only sound. Eerie, how quiet it was. The snow that still blanketed the earth seemed to muffle ordinary noises.

A chill slid down her back. She ought to be at the hospital, seeing how Esther was, instead of playing girl detective. Even if this building was what had Esther upset, she wouldn't learn anything by looking at it. She'd have to dig deeper than that.

She turned back the way she'd come, camera still in her hand, and froze. Footsteps. She wasn't the only one here.

For a moment Libby couldn't move. Then she shook her head. Stupid. It would be one of the workmen, or maybe a watchman who'd seen her car and come to investigate. Well, there was nothing to be done but to brazen it out.

"Hello?" She strode toward the exit with more assurance than she felt. "Is someone there?"

No answer for a few seconds. And then a burly figure stepped from behind a partition into her path, filling it entirely, a dark silhouette against the rectangle of the entrance beyond him.

"What are you doing here?" He growled the words, taking a step toward her. "This is private property."

"Just having a look around. There's no harm in that, is there?" She forced herself to move toward him.

Big, though not as big as she'd thought in that first instant. He was hefty rather than tall, wearing faded jeans that sagged below his belly and a camouflage jacket. The stains on the jacket and the stubble on his face suggested that he didn't care much about his appearance.

"Private property," he growled again.

"Yes, I get that. I understand Tom Sylvester is putting up this building. When is it scheduled to be finished?"

He blinked. "If you know Mr. Sylvester, you better ask him yourself."

"I'll do that." She started past him, moving briskly.

"Hey, what are you doing with that camera? You can't go around taking pictures in here." He reached for the camera.

She skittered past, headed for the ramp. If he chased her—

He took a few menacing steps, raising his hand, and she realized that he held a hammer.

"Stay away, 'less you want to get hurt. You hear?" He took another step.

Libby went down the planks considerably faster than she'd gone up them. *Don't give him the satisfaction of running, but don't dawdle, either.* She went quickly toward the car and opened the door. Then she looked back.

He was turning, apparently satisfied that he'd chased her off.

"Hey!" she shouted.

He spun. Raising the camera, she snapped off a picture of him and slid into the car.

Smart. Too smart, maybe, because the wheels spun uselessly in the slush, and he was coming toward her, the hammer raised—

The wheels caught, and she spun out the gravel lane and lurched onto the road.

She took a deep breath, then another. She'd been too cocky for her own good, probably, but she didn't like being scared.

And whatever the man had intended, he'd just succeeded in rousing her curiosity. Tom Sylvester didn't know it, but he was about to have a visitor.

A FEW MINUTES later, Libby was trying the doorknob at the small storefront office that was apparently the headquarters of Sylvester Construction. It was locked, and no one seemed to be stirring inside. Shielding her eyes with her hand against the glare, she peered in.

Sylvester's new business didn't look particularly prosperous. A battered aluminum desk, a chair, a filing cabinet. No phones, no computers, nothing much to suggest that business was conducted here.

She eyed the filing cabinet. Lacking a computer, Sylvester's secrets might be found there, but she could hardly break in.

A tall figure loomed next to hers in the glass. "Planning a break-in?" Adam asked.

"Of course not." She jerked back from the window, hoping her face didn't give her away at his echoing her thoughts. Adam had a remarkably piercing gaze when he wanted to.

He raised an eyebrow. "So what are you doing? This doesn't look like your kind of place."

She responded in kind. "My kind of place? What is my kind of place?"

She'd actually succeeded in disturbing that stoic facade. His eyes flickered.

"Anything other than an empty construction company office," he said.

She shrugged. "I'm just a hardworking photojournalist. I've been in a lot worse places, believe me."

"That doesn't exactly answer the question of what you're doing here." He folded his arms across the front of his heavy uniform jacket and leaned against the doorjamb, apparently ready to stay there as long as it took.

"Link remembered something this morning," she said abruptly, then realized Adam still might not know what she was talking about. "You remember what we discussed last night…trying to think what Esther could have wanted to see me about."

He nodded. "You said it had to be something that would affect both Amish and English."

So he did remember. "I still think that. And this morning Link told me about that new motel Tom Sylvester is building, and how he'd snatched the land away from some Amish farmers who wanted it. And that no one could understand why the planning commission had given him permission to build there—"

"What would be Esther's involvement with that?" His cool tone dumped water on her enthusiasm.

"I don't know," she admitted. "But I thought it was worth looking into. Do you know how he got that project okayed?"

He shrugged. "Not my business. That's why we have a planning commission."

"I would have found out. I'd want to know." She preferred to believe it was reporter's instinct rather than rampant curiosity.

"So you planned to tackle Tom at his office and demand answers?"

Again with the raised eyebrow. That was beginning to seriously annoy her.

"Actually, I stopped at the site and had a look around first. And I had a rather unpleasant encounter with a workman."

"You were snooping around a construction site? Libby, don't you have any sense? You could have been hurt."

"I was perfectly safe, except maybe from the worker or watchman or whatever he was. He told me to stay away or I'd get hurt, and from him, that sounded like a threat."

Adam blew out a breath of what was probably exasperation. "I might do the same, if I caught a stray female snooping around a construction area."

Her temper rose. "That's a sexist remark, Chief Byler. Better watch it."

She watched in fascination as he obviously tried to control himself. Was she actually about to see stoic Adam lose his temper?

"That's not what I meant, and you know it. Just leave the investigating to me, will you?"

"How can I?" All of her frustration and worry seemed to boil over. "How can I, when you're not willing to take my suspicions seriously? Maybe you're too afraid to make waves—"

She didn't finish that sentence, not that she even wanted to, because Adam grabbed her arm and hustled her into the police car that sat at the curb. He got in after her.

She managed to catch her breath once he'd let her go. She turned, so that she could see his face. "Are you going to arrest me for being annoying?"

The corner of his mouth twitched before he got it under control. "If I were arresting you, you'd be in the backseat. That was not a conversation I wanted to have on a public street. Do you want your suspicions all over the township by nightfall?"

"No." She took a breath. "Sorry."

Adam turned sideways in the seat so that he was facing her. Facing her and way too close to her in the confines of the police car. Her pulse skittered, and her breath seemed to get caught in her throat. He wasn't touching her, but he might as well have been, given the way she was reacting.

Get a grip, she ordered herself, but the words didn't seem to help much. Even Link had noticed the sparks between her and Adam, and Link wasn't the most observant person in the world when it came to emotions.

She'd basically thrown herself at Adam, back when they were in high school, acting on the crush she'd had on him. And he'd responded, just for an instant, before he made her feel like a fool.

Then all the talk had started about him and Sally, and she'd been only too eager to believe it, because it meant she could tell herself she hated him with a clear conscience. And when she had found out the truth, her apologies had led to a moment so real, so true, that she'd been sure they loved each other, right up until the moment he'd walked out. Or run out, more likely.

She still didn't understand what happened that night. They'd both been old enough to know what they were doing by then. He'd stopped to see her when he was in the city for some police seminar; she'd invited him to dinner and they'd spent hours talking and reminiscing. When they'd kissed, it had seemed something that was always meant to happen. But apparently she was the only one who thought that.

Did Adam sense her emotions? For a moment he seemed almost confused. Unsure of himself, and Adam was never unsure. He knew his duty and he did it.

He shook his head slightly. "Libby, this is an ongoing police investigation. I can't discuss the particulars with you, but I promise I'm not ignoring any possibilities. If there is something else behind Esther's hit-and-run, I'll find it."

His sincerity grabbed her by the heart.

"Please, Libby." His fingers closed over hers, and she couldn't breathe. "Trust me to deal with this. Will you?"

She couldn't speak. She nodded.

Apparently satisfied, Adam let go of her. She shot out of the car, knowing it looked as if she was running and not caring.

"Libby." He lowered the window to speak. "About your camera—it wasn't in my car. Do you want to file a stolen item report?"

"No, that's okay." She didn't want to do anything that would keep her in his company a minute longer.

She raised her hand in a wave, trying to manage a smile, and walked quickly to her own car. She trusted Adam. She'd trust him with her life.

But that wasn't what was at stake. She couldn't leave this alone. Esther was counting on her.

THE QUIET HOSPITAL floor seemed safe and insulated when Libby reached it. Insulated—that was a nice feeling. Now if only she could be insulated from her own feelings, she might find the balance she needed to deal with this situation. Esther was important now, not the fruitless emotion she thought she'd buried years ago.

That was the trouble with coming home, maybe. It showed you too clearly all the things you'd been able to ignore out in the world.

She pushed open the door to Esther's room. She had time for no more than a quick glance at Esther, still motionless, before Rebecca rushed to her. Grasped her, poured out a flood of words in a mix of English and Pennsylvania Dutch so scrambled that Libby couldn't make out a thing.

Libby caught Rebecca's hands in hers, heart thudding with fear. "Rebecca, what is it? Calm down and talk to me. Is it bad news about Esther?"

"Ach, no." Rebecca seemed to make a major effort to control herself. "I am so sorry. I didn't mean to frighten you. I am chust so glad to see someone I can tell."

"Tell what?" Libby's fear ebbed slowly. "If it's not Esther…"

"No, no. She is better today, I think. Her color is better, ain't so? And she hears me when I talk to her, I am sure. Don't you see it?"

Rebecca was looking at her so anxiously that Libby couldn't bring herself to say that Esther seemed much the same as yesterday to her. "I'm sure you're right," she said. She clasped Rebecca's hand and led her to a chair, sitting down next to her.

"Now, tell me what has you so upset."

Rebecca put her fingers to her lips. "Maybe…I didn't know if I should say anything. But I knew when you came, I could tell you, for sure."

Another little nail of guilt. She'd been playing detective when Rebecca was longing for her to be here.

"You can tell me anything."

Rebecca nodded. "Ja. I know." She patted Libby's

hand. "It was in the night. Right around four in the morning." She pointed to the clock on the wall above the television set. "I looked after he was gone."

Rebecca's method of telling the story would try the patience of a saint. "After who was gone? Tell me from the beginning."

Rebecca took a deep breath, seeming to organize her thoughts. "I had been talking to Esther. The nurse said she might be able to hear my voice and be comforted, even if she could not respond. But I was so tired. I fell asleep."

The guilt in Rebecca's face touched her heart. Libby knew that feeling. "That's only natural. You can't stay awake all the time. You must get some rest."

Rebecca nodded, but she seemed to be looking inward, as if reliving something in her mind. "I woke. Opened my eyes. Someone was standing over our Esther. He had a pillow in his hands. I was afraid."

At the bald words, Libby was suddenly afraid, too. "Who was it?"

Rebecca shook her head, paling. "I could not say. He wore those clothes the hospital people wear."

"His face? His hair?"

"He had a kind of cap over his hair, and a mask, like the surgeon had. But I know he was English, not Amish."

"How can you be sure?" She tried to visualize it. Someone in hospital garb—a nurse or orderly on some legitimate errand? But the pillow frightened her. She was imagining the pillow pressed against Esther's face….

"No beard," Rebecca said simply.

Of course. The beard would show, even in such a disguise.

"Maybe it was a hospital worker, trying to make her more comfortable." Somehow she found that hard to believe.

"I made some sound. Asked what he was doing. He threw the pillow down and went out."

Surely anyone on legitimate business wouldn't do that. Still, sometimes people didn't know how to act around the Amish. They thought, as that doctor had, that an Amish person might not understand English, or sometimes even that the Amish were stupid because of their way of life.

"Did you call the nurse? Tell anyone what happened?"

Rebecca put her fingers to her lips again. "I rang for the nurse. I told her, but she said no one had been in. That I must have been dreaming." She raised a troubled gaze to Libby's face. "I wasn't. Someone was here."

"I believe you." She patted Rebecca's hand. "I'm going to call Adam Byler."

"The police?" Concern filled her face. "We do not go to the police."

Libby had to suppress her frustration at this typically Amish response. The Amish didn't count on civil authorities to settle their problems. But this wasn't a situation that could be resolved by the church family or the bishop.

"The police are already involved, Rebecca." She kept her tone calm and firm. "There's no way to keep them out. It's Adam Byler's job to find the person who did this to Esther and to protect her from harm."

"I don't know what the bishop would say..."

"I'm sure Bishop Amos would agree with me on this." She wasn't, really, but she had a high regard for Bishop Amos's common sense. "Besides, you're not calling the police. I am."

That seemed to satisfy Rebecca. She nodded, looking relieved at having someone else take the responsibility, and sank back in the chair.

Libby started to pull her cell phone out of her bag, remembered the ban on cell phones in this area, and went to the room phone instead. Her fingers hesitated for a moment. After those moments in the car with him, Adam was the last person she wanted to see right now. But she didn't have a choice. She dialed the number of Adam's cell.

Adam answered on the first ring, and she toyed briefly with the notion that he'd been expecting her call.

"Adam? It's Libby." She made an effort to keep the words steady.

"What's wrong?" He must know her voice too well to be fooled.

"I'm at the hospital." She glanced at Rebecca, who was watching her anxiously. Best to keep this brief. "Something happened last night that could have been serious. Can you come?"

"I'll be there in twenty minutes." Never one to waste time on useless words, he disconnected.

Twenty minutes could seem like a very long time when you spent it trying to convince an Amish person that it really was all right to talk to the police. Libby reminded herself of all the reasons why Rebecca's attitude was understandable. The Amish had endured terrible persecution from the authorities in the old country, and they had long memories. They trusted in God, not in other people, especially not Englischers wearing uniforms and carrying guns.

Finally the door swung open, and Adam was there.

Libby's breath caught. She had fallen in love with Adam Byler when she was fifteen. Despite everything that had happened since, no matter how they'd grown or changed, it seemed she'd never managed to fall back out again.

CHAPTER SEVEN

LIBBY WAS LOOKING at him with an expression Adam couldn't interpret. He froze for an instant. He'd have said he knew every mood that flickered across her face, but maybe he was wrong.

He stood for a moment as straight as if he were on the parade ground and then moved toward the women, assessing the emotional temperature of the room.

Esther looked much the same as she had the previous day—immobile, pale save for the bruises that marred her face. Rebecca touched her daughter's hand, her gaze sliding away from his. Whatever had brought him here, he suspected he'd hear most of it from Libby, not from Rebecca.

A folding chair leaned against the wall. He took it, opened it and sat down, giving Rebecca a moment to become used to his presence.

"Not an emergency, I guess." He glanced again toward Esther, silent on the white bed.

Libby stiffened as if he'd criticized her for calling him, and he wanted to bite his tongue. Why did he always get off on the wrong foot with her?

"Not an emergency," she repeated. "But serious. During the night, something happened that frightened Rebecca."

When he shifted his focus to Rebecca, Libby spoke quickly.

"She'd like me to tell you, and then she'll answer any questions you have."

Annoying as it was to have Libby acting as intermediary, he appreciated the delicate balance that was contained in her suggestion. Rebecca wouldn't have called him. No Amish woman in her position would have—that was a foregone conclusion. It was only with Libby to smooth the way that he'd hear this story at all.

"Good idea," he said, trying to sound as nonthreatening as possible. "I have no problem handling it that way."

He did, of course. He wanted Libby out of this situation—far, far out of it. Hadn't she just agreed to leave the investigation to him not an hour ago? He should have known better than to think that would happen.

Libby seemed to take a moment to organize her thoughts. "Rebecca was sitting with Esther last night. She dropped off to sleep, and when she woke, a man in hospital scrubs, his face and hair covered, was leaning over Esther with a pillow in his hands."

Libby was obviously trying to keep her voice calm, but he could read the tension in it easily enough.

"Rebecca spoke, and the man tossed the pillow aside and rushed out of the room." She stopped, maybe waiting for his response.

"It could have been someone on a legitimate errand."

But he didn't like that image of the man hurrying away when Rebecca spoke.

"Rebecca called the nurse and asked. The nurse claimed no one was in here. Rebecca couldn't identify him…his clothes, face and hair were covered. But he was English."

Rebecca nodded at that, and then lowered her gaze to her hands, clasping them in her lap.

He had to force himself to lean back, giving Rebecca plenty of space before he addressed her directly. "Mrs. Zook, did you notice anything else about the man? Hair color, eye color?"

She shook her head. A brief glimpse in the night, the lights dimmed—he could fill in the reasons for himself.

"What about his shoes? Could you see them?"

Rebecca frowned, as if trying to see the image in her mind. "He had something over them…" Her hands moved, as if trying to trace an amorphous shape. "Soft, like baby booties, it was."

This character hadn't missed a trick. Those elaborate precautions convinced him more than anything that this was serious.

He studied Rebecca's face for a long moment. She was exhausted, and he had enough sense to know that he'd get nothing more from her. The whole episode probably hadn't taken more than a minute or two.

He slid back his chair, rising. "Thank you, Mrs. Zook. Denke." She had a faint smile for his use of the Pennsylvania Dutch word. "I'll go and have a word with the nursing staff."

Libby followed him to the door, as he'd known she would.

"You can't tell me this wasn't serious." Her expression dared him to argue the point.

"Take it easy, Libby. I agree with you."

That seemed to disarm her, at least for the moment. "I just don't understand." Her voice held anguish. "What could make someone take such desperate measures against Esther, of all people?"

He didn't have an answer to that. "Let's do this a step at a time. We can't get at why before we know who."

Libby nodded, some of the pain ebbing away from her face.

He'd guess, by the determined set to her chin, that Libby intended to follow him right out to the nurses' station to make sure he investigated properly. He could be just as determined, but guile might serve him better at the moment.

"Rebecca's exhausted," he said softly, glancing at the woman. "Can't you persuade her to sleep, or at least lie down, now that you can stay with Esther until some other family member arrives?"

That distracted her, as he'd been sure it would. For a moment she looked stricken.

"I should have done that the minute I arrived. But after I heard what she had to say, I knew I had to reach you before she changed her mind about talking to you."

"I know. I appreciate what you did." For a perilous moment they were too close, too much in sympathy, and he had to step back. "I doubt she'd have said anything to me about it if it hadn't been for you. But right now…"

"Right now you want me to leave you alone to deal with your investigation." Amusement sparked briefly in her blue eyes. "All right. I'll work on Rebecca. But don't you dare leave without touching base with me."

"You've got it." With a sketchy salute, he made his escape.

The staff on duty wasn't able to add much to what he already knew. The night nurse Rebecca had spoken to had apparently not taken the incident seriously enough to do anything, certainly not calling security.

He considered, his jaw tight. Little though he liked to admit it, the staff hadn't done anything wrong. They had no reason to think that Esther Zook was anything other than an accident victim. Maybe it was time to change that.

He leaned on the counter, trusting his size and his uniform to make an impression on the nurse who'd been answering his questions. "Call the security office and ask the officer in charge to come up here right now. We need to talk."

Her eyes widened slightly, and she grabbed for the phone.

Ten minutes later Adam was closeted in a miniscule waiting room with Lew Thomas, the hospital's security chief. His first sight of the man had reassured him. Thomas was obviously retired military…he'd seen the type too often to mistake it. Stocky and muscled, even his gray hair didn't detract from the sense that here was someone to be relied upon in a tight spot.

"Trouble is, the hospital's security cameras don't cover this hallway," Thomas was saying. "I recommended total coverage, but…" He shrugged. "You know the answer to that."

"Budget won't allow it. Right." That was an issue everyone in public service faced.

"You think someone actually penetrated the hospital with the intent of silencing the victim?" Thomas's tone made it a question.

"I think what happened last night is potentially too serious not to take precautions."

"Right." Thomas seemed to be collecting his thoughts, or maybe marshaling his resources. "I can have a camera moved up here from one of the less sensitive areas, and I'll take a look at the footage we do have from last night to see if any anomalies show up."

"Good. They might have caught someone leaving the building that shouldn't have been here." Although he doubted the man would allow a camera to film him.

"Trouble is, I only have two men on at night, and they have to cover the whole place. I'll rearrange their routes to bring them through here more often, but otherwise…" Thomas shrugged.

"I'd appreciate it."

But it wasn't enough. Adam knew that, even as he thanked the man and headed back toward Esther's room. He needed more, and his manpower shortage was as bad as the hospital's was.

He eased the door open to find that only Libby sat next to the hospital bed.

Libby was talking to her friend, he realized, and he stood where he was, not sure whether he wanted to advance or retreat.

"…the time we pretended we were spies and followed the boys all the way to the quarry? Trey and Link and Adam. They thought they were so clever, and they never knew we were there."

Actually they had. He remembered that day—a fall Saturday, the leaves turning red and yellow and orange, drifting down to crunch underfoot as they made their way toward the forbidden quarry. They'd spotted the two little girls following them, creeping from tree to tree under the illusion they hadn't been spotted.

Link had wanted to turn the tables and scare them; Trey had wanted to lecture them and send them home. But he'd persuaded them to play along with the little girls. It had been—

Libby's voice cut off abruptly, and she swung to look at him, as if she'd sensed his presence.

"Adam. What did you find out?" She rose and came quickly toward him.

He let the door swing shut. Hadn't they recently had a discussion about the fact that he couldn't share details of the investigation with her? Unfortunately, none of the rules seemed to apply when it came to Libby.

"Not much more than you already know." He kept his voice low, though it seemed impossible to disturb Esther. "The security chief will increase patrols, but—"

"That's not enough. She needs a guard on the door all night. Don't you see that?"

He held on to his patience with an effort. Give Libby an inch and she'd take a mile, especially where someone she cared about was concerned.

"That would be the best solution, but he doesn't have the manpower, and neither do I."

"We'll hire someone," she said instantly. "Just give me the name of a reputable firm."

That, he thought, summed up one of the differences between him and the Morgan family very neatly. Libby had no idea of the cost of putting on a security guard, but that didn't matter.

"That's not necessary. I've got a friend in the Lancaster city police who owes me some favors. I'll bring them in on this, since the hospital is in their jurisdiction. They ought to be able to spare an officer for nights, and that's the crucial time. Somebody's always with her during the day."

"Good." She hesitated, frowning a little. "I suppose you heard me talking to Libby when you came in."

He nodded.

"Silly, I guess." She folded her arms around herself defensively. "But she might be able to hear. She might be comforted."

That momentary switch to vulnerability touched him. "She might," he agreed, though he doubted it. "You're a good friend, Libby."

She looked up at him, those dark blue eyes shrouded with misery. "Not good enough."

She said the words softly, but they set up a reverberation in his soul. There was no point in expecting Libby to stay out of this. She couldn't.

And as much as he admired that loyalty of hers, it scared him to death.

LIBBY STEPPED OUT of the hospital room the next day, hearing the spate of Pennsylvania Dutch erupt in her wake. It was the day before Christmas, and Esther's family was there in force. She'd begun to feel very much the fifth wheel.

She paused, frowning, her hand still on the door. It had been more than that, though. There'd been an undercurrent in the room...something she didn't understand but that somehow affected her. She'd caught the sideways glances, heard the soft whispers.

Libby gave herself a shake. She should be concentrating on the positive, not the negative. Esther had been better today...it hadn't just been her mother's imagination. Her coma seemed lighter, she stirred more often, one almost had the feeling she'd open her eyes and join the conversation.

That wasn't likely. Libby had sat with Rebecca when the doctor talked with her. Nothing he'd said had been promising as far as getting the Esther they'd known back, but she was breathing without the breathing tube for short periods. They'd cling to every small positive sign.

Christmas was a time for hope, after all. Libby turned and walked quickly toward the elevator. Christmas Eve, and she had a ton of things to do before the festivities began.

The elevator doors swung open before she reached it, and a lone Amish man got off, probably yet another visitor for Esther. She nodded in greeting, and the man stopped, staring at her.

Was he someone she should know? She gave him a tentative smile. She'd been away so long, and naturally she didn't remember everyone from the Amish community. The length of his dark beard put him in middle age, and his narrow face and piercing eyes didn't rouse any hint of recognition.

"You are Elizabeth Morgan." His voice was harsh and guttural, the accent strong.

She nodded, opening her lips to apologize for not recognizing him, but he swept on.

"You are the one who has brought this trouble on us."

She blinked. Had she really heard that? "I don't know what you mean."

"The police," he said, his stare intensifying. "I have heard. You are the one. You brought the police here, at the very sickbed of one of our sisters."

What on earth? "Esther was the victim of a hit-and-run. That's a crime. No one can keep the police from being involved."

He dismissed that with an abrupt, chopping gesture, taking a step closer. "There was a policeman standing at Esther's door last night. All night. I have been told of this."

So that's what his antagonism was about. In a way, she supposed she was responsible for that, but didn't he realize it was for Esther's safety?

"I'm sorry if you disapprove, but the policeman was there to keep her safe." Libby shot a quick glance around. The corridor, usually so busy, was empty right now except for the two of them.

"It is not a question of what I think. It is the Amish way. We do not go to the law with our problems. Esther's life and her safety are in the hands of God."

Anger boiled up in her, washing away the faint traces of anxiety. "That policeman might be God's way of protecting her. Did you ever think of that?"

The moment the words were out, she regretted them. She had no right to criticize Amish beliefs.

The man took a step closer, his face mottling an unpleasant shade of red. "You cannot—"

He cut off abruptly as the elevator doors slid open behind him. Libby's breath went out in a whoosh of relief that startled her. She hadn't realized she was holding her breath.

"Owen." She greeted Owen Barclay with a warmth that was probably a mistake. "How nice to see you."

"Libby, I hoped I'd run into you here." He gestured with the shopping bags he carried, one in each hand, emblazoned with the inn's logo. "I told you I'd drop off a meal, and this seemed like a good day to do so. I'm sure Esther's family is getting tired of the cuisine at the hotel cafeteria."

Almost before he got the words out, the Amish man stalked off, leaving the air frosty with disapproval.

Owen looked after him. "What did you do to get Ezra Burkhalter so upset?"

"Is that who he is?" She knew the name, if not the face. Burkhalter was one of the ministers of the Amish congregation. "I'm afraid he didn't approve of my part in…"

She let that sentence die. In her relief, she was saying too much.

Owen didn't seem to notice. "Some of the Amish don't approve of friendships with the English, I've heard. And he's apparently pretty strict."

That attitude was actually rare among the Amish in Lancaster County, who had lived for generations in such close proximity with their Englisch neighbors. It would be more common in some of the remote settlements out West of very conservative Amish. But she didn't want to get into a discussion with Owen.

"I suppose that's it. I'm sure the family will appreciate the food. There are several people in with Esther right now." She gestured toward the door.

"How is she doing?" Owen's face assumed an expression of appropriate gravity.

"She seems a little better today." Libby tried to force some enthusiasm into her voice. "As if the coma isn't as deep."

"Well, that's very good news. I'm delighted to hear it."

She suspected that if his hands hadn't been full, Owen would have attempted to hug her.

"She has a long way to go, of course. And I'd better get going, or I won't have all my errands accomplished. Merry Christmas, Owen."

He nodded. "Give your family my best. Merry Christmas."

Libby stepped into the elevator, feeling a sense of relief when the doors closed and she could stop trying to smile. *Merry Christmas.*

How merry a Christmas could it be for Esther's family, with doubt about her recovery hanging over their heads? To say nothing of the expense of her treatment—the Amish didn't believe in commercial insurance. The family and the church would take care of their own.

Was there any way her family could help? The Zooks wouldn't accept charity from outsiders, but maybe her mother could think of something.

Still, whatever happened, the faith of Esther's family was strong, and they had a belief in God's will that wouldn't be easily daunted. But an attacker might take advantage of that belief.

CHAPTER EIGHT

CANDLELIGHT FROM THE branched candelabra mounted at the ends of the pews cast a radiant glow on the faces around Libby. The organist launched into "Oh Come All Ye Faithful," and the congregation rose, the movement sending the candle flames flickering.

The candlelight service in the small clapboard church in Springville didn't seem to have changed since she'd been a small child, breathless with excitement. She remembered standing on tiptoe between her brothers to peer between the bodies ahead of her, trying to see the Baby Jesus in the manger.

A lump formed in her throat, making it more difficult to sing the familiar words, and she tried to think of anything other than the fact that it was Christmas Eve, and Dad was not here for the service.

She was squeezed between Link and Mom, with Link's fiancée, Marisa, on his other side and their guests, Leo Frost and Adam, sitting beyond Mom. Libby had done a certain amount of shuffling as they'd filed into the pew, determined to be sure she wouldn't be sitting next to Adam. She didn't want to be that close to him at a time when her emotions were as near the surface as they were tonight.

The carol ended, catching her by surprise since she'd been singing the words somewhat automatically, and she sat down half a beat behind the others.

The small sanctuary was as full for Christmas Eve as it would be for Easter Sunday, maybe more. The candlelight service was a tradition in Springville, and even those who never darkened the door of a church the rest of the year seemed to show up. It was almost like a reunion, with kids and grandkids home to visit. She'd already spied half a dozen people from her graduating class.

The reading of the next lesson began, and she tried to corral her straying thoughts. None of Spring Township's Amish were here, of course. Christmas Eve was a quieter observance in their homes, and Christmas Day was a time of worship and reverent celebration. The next day, Second Christmas, was the time for visiting and gift-giving. The holiday would be even quieter for Esther's family, probably.

Her thoughts formed a silent prayer for Esther…for her safety, for her recovery. And for light to be shed on the darkness that surrounded her injury.

It hadn't done all that much good, maneuvering herself away from Adam. She was still too aware of him, sitting on the other side of her mother. His strong hands, tanned even at this time of year, were within view each time she let her gaze slip that way.

The choir began to sing "The First Noel," and she had to blink back tears. That had been her father's favorite carol, and he'd belt it out in a mellow baritone at odd times during the holiday season.

Was her mother thinking of him, too? Impossible to tell. Geneva Morgan came from a tradition which said that a lady did not show her sorrow in public, no matter how much she might weep in private.

It was stupid, Libby told herself, to resent the changes time had brought here. After all, she was the one who'd moved away. She could hardly expect that everything would stay the same, waiting for her return.

The service moved through the familiar passages…the angels, the shepherds, the kings. Finally the congregation sang one final triumphant verse of "Joy to the World" and, clutching their candles, moved out into the cold night.

Libby was so intent shielding her candle flame from accidental contact with someone's coat in the crowd that she'd reached the sidewalk before she realized it was snowing.

"How beautiful," she breathed, more to herself than anyone else, as she watched the flakes swirl in the lights and coat the branches of the evergreens on either side of the church walk.

"As long as no one decides to ignore a patch of ice and plows into a tree." Adam's deep voice was so close that her hand holding the candle jerked, setting the flame flickering wildly. Fortunately he seemed too intent on checking his cell phone to notice.

"Don't tell me you're on duty Christmas Eve," she said.

Adam shrugged. "I'm always on duty. Have you forgotten how small the township police force is?"

She watched him slide the cell phone into the pocket

of his heavy jacket. Even when Adam wasn't in uniform, he wore that air of being in charge like a second skin.

"But surely someone else could be on call tonight," she protested.

"I gave them the night off. They've got family or girlfriends to spend Christmas with. Since I don't have either—" He cut that short, as if he regretted saying it. "Anyway, it's just a matter of taking any calls that come in."

In all the years she'd known him, she'd never heard Adam speak, even obliquely, about his family. His father was buried in the church cemetery, just as hers was, and the falling snow rendered all the markers anonymous.

"Do you ever hear from your mother?" The question was out quickly and just as quickly regretted when the mask came down over Adam's expression.

"No." The word was so curt that it was almost painful, and Adam's lips twisted. He seemed to make an effort to turn away from whatever bitterness burned toward the mother who'd been more interested in herself than in protecting her son from his drunken father.

"Sorry. I wish…" She let that trail off, because there was really nothing she could say.

"Were you thinking about your dad in there?" Adam jerked his head toward the sanctuary, his voice gentle.

She nodded, tears filling her eyes, and he clasped her cold fingers in his warm hands.

"He was a good man." His voice was deep.

People milled around them, greeting each other, welcoming visitors, reminiscing about past Christmases.

But it was as if she was alone with Adam in their own private circle.

She looked into his face, seeing the sympathy there. "I can't help thinking what a jerk I am to resent the changes that took place while I was away. After all, it was my choice to leave."

"I understand. Leo is good for your mother, but she never forgets your dad. Not for a minute." Adam's hand tightened on hers in silent comfort.

"I know. It's just…hard."

"Yes." His touch was gentle, but there was strength in it, as well. That was who Adam was, all through.

THE CROWD BEGAN to thin out as the snow thickened. "I thought maybe you had been looking around in church, speculating on which of them might be guilty."

His words jolted through her like an electric shock. "I guess I hadn't thought that it could be someone I know."

"Most likely would be." Adam said the words absently, his gaze moving over those who lingered on the church walk. "How would Esther learn anything dangerous about a stranger?"

Libby gave herself a mental shake. "I can't even guess. I've been gone so long—you'd think everyone here would feel like a stranger to me. But some of them haven't changed at all." She nodded toward the Smalley family, just exiting the church. "Sandra Smalley's personality hasn't changed. Just intensified, if anything."

"Did you know their son is a township supervisor now?" Adam's voice grew hard.

"Jason? He never struck me as very civic-minded." Not that she'd thought much of him at all.

"He likes power." Adam's mouth clamped shut, and he shook his head slightly. "I shouldn't have said that."

"Why not? The police chief is allowed to have opinions, isn't he?"

"Not about local politicians." His smile flickered. "Or at least, not to voice them out loud."

The Smalley family passed them then, not stopping, thank goodness, although it seemed to her that Jason took a long look at them. He couldn't have known they were talking about him, could he? She was watching them walk away when a voice sounded.

"Well, look who's here. If it's not the little princess."

She had to compose her face before turning to face Tom Sylvester. "Hello, Tom. Merry Christmas to both of you." She smiled at Tom's wife, trying vainly to remember her name.

"Same to you. And you, Adam." Tom's ruddy face creased in a broad smile. "Libby, I hear you're interested in that project of mine."

Now, how exactly had he known that? She hadn't mentioned her name to the man who'd chased her off the building site, and he hadn't given any sign he recognized her.

"Just naturally curious, I guess." She kept her tone light. "Link mentioned the new motel to me, so I had to stop and see for myself."

"Great, great." There seemed to be an edge behind

the jovial smile. “I’d love to show you around, anytime. Just give me a call.”

“I’ll do that, as soon as the holiday is past,” she said promptly, feeling Adam tense next to her. But he could hardly criticize when Tom himself invited her.

Tom looked taken aback for an instant before he regained his smile. “Sure thing. I just thought maybe you were too busy, with your friend in the hospital and all.”

“I have been.” Now she was the one who had to force her smile. “But I can spare the time.”

“Fine, fine. Stop by my office or give me a call, and I’ll take you out to the job site myself.”

“Great. I’d like that.” And she’d like asking a few hard questions, as well.

“Say, I hear Esther is doing better, breathing on her own and all,” Tom said. “She’ll probably be sitting up and talking before long.”

For a moment she could only gape at him, praying her face didn’t betray her feelings. “Where did you hear that?”

Tom shrugged. “That’s what people are saying.”

“I’m afraid that’s too optimistic,” she said, with no expectation that it would do any good. Nobody ever succeeded in stopping a rumor, even with the truth, and she felt almost superstitious about trying to make Esther’s condition sound worse.

“Well, you give her our best when you see her.” Tom patted his wife’s arm. “Guess we’d better get on home.” They headed down the walk toward the street.

Libby turned to Adam, realizing that she was instinctively looking to him for reassurance. "I had no idea people were saying that."

"Rumors go around. You can't stop them." He didn't seem to grasp the importance.

"No." She shivered, suddenly feeling the cold. "But don't you see? If people think Esther is regaining consciousness, she could be in even more danger."

ADAM STEPPED ONTO the hospital elevator on his way to Esther's room. The day after Christmas meant back to work in the English world.

Not so for the Amish, though. For them, this was Second Christmas, a time for visiting friends and relatives to celebrate the season.

That meant Esther's room would probably be crowded with people—not really the best time for the police to barge in. But he hadn't been able to rid his mind of the fear Libby had voiced on Christmas Eve. If rumors were going around about Esther's recovery, someone might think she could remember…the same someone who'd been behind the wheel of the van or truck that hit her.

He realized he was tensing and deliberately relaxed his muscles. It was useless to get angry over the fact that they'd found no trace of the vehicle. Logic said that indicated the driver wasn't from the area, which swung the odds toward accident.

But that would be ignoring the man who'd entered Esther's room, and he couldn't forget the image Esther's mother had planted in his mind—the masked figure bending over Esther, pillow in his hands.

He also couldn't forget the fear in Libby's eyes at the danger to Esther.

No use kidding himself. What he wanted at this point was to have Libby safely out of this situation. Too bad she'd lost that job on the West Coast and didn't have to rush back. Then he wouldn't have to run into her everywhere he turned.

The elevator stopped, and he stepped off and headed for Esther's room. He'd see for himself whether there was any truth to the rumors about her recovery.

The door stood ajar, and a babble of Pennsylvania Dutch flowed out. He'd been right, it seemed. The room was crowded with people, so many that he'd expect the nurses to be chasing some of them out.

He lingered in the doorway for a moment, suspecting he wouldn't be welcome, and glanced around. In a sea of dark colors and white kapps, Libby's bright coral sweater drew his eyes irresistibly. She stood a few feet from the hospital bed, talking to Bishop Amos.

Rebecca, Esther's mother, emerged from the crowd and rushed up to him, beaming. It was so far from the reception he'd been expecting that he had to blink.

"You have komm to share our gut news, ja?" Rebecca looked as if she'd shed ten years overnight. Her cheeks were flushed, and her eyes had come alive. "God has answered our prayers."

That could mean only one thing. "Esther is better, then?"

"Ja, ja, such a wonderful gut Christmas gift. Esther

has opened her eyes. She squeezed my hand. She is coming back to us."

"That's great news." And dangerous, as well. "Has she spoken yet?"

Rebecca shook her head, still smiling. "No, but that will happen. I know it. Soon our Esther will be home where she belongs."

Before he could respond she'd hurried away to greet an Amish couple who'd squeezed into the room behind him. But he wasn't alone long enough to think this through. Libby grabbed his arm.

"I have to talk to you," she said, her voice low. "Come on." Hand clutching his sleeve, she tugged him toward the door.

"I wanted to see…" He let the protest die in the face of Libby's determination. He may as well let her have her say. Knowing Libby, she wouldn't give up.

She led him down the hall, probably looking for a quiet spot. The door to the chapel appeared on their right, and Libby propelled him through it, letting it close behind them. They were alone in the small, wood-paneled room that was furnished with a few rows of pine pews and some carefully nondenominational inspirational art.

He faced her, registering the concern and alarm in her expressive face. "Okay, calm down. What's so important that you had to drag me out of there?"

"Esther's better, opening her eyes, beginning to regain consciousness." Libby stopped, shaking her head, and tears filled her eyes for a moment until she blinked them back. "That sounds terrible, to be upset because she's doing better. But don't you see? That puts her in more danger, and there's no way to keep people from talking about it."

"I know." He'd like to wipe the worry from her face, but that was impossible. "If the person who hit her was local, he'll find out."

"If?" Scorn filled her voice.

He'd distracted her for a moment, at least. "Take it easy, Libby. I agree there's reason to suspect that someone wants to silence Esther, even if there's precious little proof. You're thinking of Tom Sylvester, I bet, but nothing links them. Esther isn't really in any further danger because she's improving. She still has people with her all day and a guard on her door at night."

"As long as she's here, yes. But what if Rebecca takes her home?"

He forced himself not to react to Libby's emotion. "Is it really likely that the doctors will release Esther anytime soon?"

Libby wrapped her arms around herself. "Not likely, but possible. She's breathing on her own, and they've taken the feeding tube out. Every step forward makes Rebecca more determined to have her home."

"That's only natural," he said, intending to soothe her.

It didn't. Passion flared in her face. "It could be deadly. You know how isolated the Zook farm is. How vulnerable."

"If they'd accept protection..." he began.

"They won't. I've already mentioned it, but you know how strong their pacifist views are. They won't hear of having guards at their place." Libby's expression lost its drive, suddenly afraid. She looked up at him, taking a step closer and touching his arm. "Adam, you have to do something."

That look, her voice, went right under his guard and hit his heart. Catching his breath, he took a step back. Being alone with Libby wasn't a good idea. It never had been.

"I know you're worried, but you're leaping ahead too far. We'll work something out by the time the doctors are willing to send Esther home, and—"

"Will you stop backing away from me?" Libby flared up in an instant. "Am I that scary? Just because I had a stupid crush on you when I was a kid, that doesn't mean I'm going to attack you every time we're alone."

It wasn't her he was worried about, but saying so would just make things worse. And Libby was conveniently leaving out another time when they'd gotten too close, and they'd both been old enough to know better.

But he certainly wasn't going to bring that up.

"It doesn't have anything to do with that." He paused, sure she knew that for the lie it was. "Look, about what happened the night of that high school dance…I didn't handle the situation very well. I was too dumb and inexperienced."

She shook her head, smiling faintly. "No, dumb and inexperienced was me. You did pretty well, considering that someone you considered basically a kid sister threw herself at you."

The words brought the picture back too clearly for his comfort—Libby in her first grown-up party dress, something soft and silky and pink that showed off curves he hadn't known she possessed. The feel of her soft lips on his…

His rebellious memory took him back to the more recent time…to Libby's apartment in San Francisco three years ago, to the moment when she'd been so close he'd taken her in his arms, losing himself in her kisses until reality had crashed in on him. He'd known he had to get out of there before they went too far.

He'd never succeeded in wiping out the results of that episode with Sally. He'd learned then that someone like him was always teetering on the edge of respectability, with plenty of people around to cheer if he fell off. He couldn't take chances with his reputation, just as he couldn't take advantage of whatever Libby might imagine she felt for him. The results could be disastrous.

The very fact that Libby didn't mention that event told him feelings were still raw—for her as well as for him.

"I've known you most of my life, Libby. I don't want to have bad feelings because of anything that happened between us."

Libby pressed her lips together for a moment, as if she held back words she didn't want to say. Finally she managed a smile. "What's past is past. Can we be friends now? That's what Esther needs from us."

"Friends," he said, holding out his hand.

She put hers into it. "Friends," she echoed.

He released her hand as quickly as he decently could. "But that doesn't mean you can interfere with my investigation," he warned.

Libby gave him that look of wide-eyed innocence that couldn't be trusted an inch. "I wouldn't dream of it."

LIBBY FINALLY HAD an opportunity to be alone with Esther after what seemed like weeks. Christmas was past, and life was going back to normal. Or the new normal, in this case.

She'd made it to the hospital in the afternoon after driving cautiously over roads hiding patches of black ice and gritty with salt. Living in San Francisco for five years had eroded her driving skills when it came to Pennsylvania winters.

Libby pulled the green vinyl chair close to Esther's bed and touched the hand that lay lax on the white sheet. "I persuaded your aunt to take your mamm down to the cafeteria for a bite of supper so we could have some time together."

It still seemed strange to talk to an unresponsive Esther, but even someone as medically ignorant as she was could see that Esther was improving. Some of the tubes were gone now, and her color was definitely better. She simply looked as if she were sleeping.

"Your mamm says you've been opening your eyes more. I wish you'd open them for me. Please?"

Fine lines appeared between Esther's brows, and Libby's breath caught.

"That's it, Esther. Open your eyes. It's me, Libby. I want to see you."

Esther's eyelids flickered slightly. Her frown deepened. With what seemed a struggle, she opened her eyes.

"That's it." She wanted to jump up and down with delight, but this didn't seem the place for it. "Esther, I can't tell you how glad I am to see your blue eyes. It's about time you were waking up."

Esther's face turned slightly, her gaze seeking Libby. She seemed to be trying to focus, and her troubled expression intensified, as if she fought to figure out what was happening.

"It's okay, Essie." The childhood nickname came easily to Libby's tongue. "You're in the hospital. In Lancaster. Remember?"

No response.

"The doctors say you're doing much better. Honestly. And everyone is thinking about you and praying for you." Libby's heart hurt. Was it easier to see Esther unconscious or to watch this struggle to understand?

"My mom's been in to see you several times. She's still getting over the wedding, I think. I caught her up in the attic yesterday—supposedly she was putting Christmas decorations away, but she was dusting off the old cradle, anticipating grandchildren before Trey and Jessica are back from their honeymoon." She smiled, remembering Mom's expression at being caught.

Esther's hand moved in hers, and she looked up to see a smile—a genuine smile.

"You heard. You understood. Didn't you?"

"Ja." It was hardly more than a whisper, but it made her want to dance.

The door behind her swung open. Libby turned, eager

to tell Rebecca what had happened. But it wasn't Rebecca. It was a nurse's aide.

"Are you Ms. Morgan?" The young woman looked uncertainly at a slip of paper in her hand.

"That's right." Libby stood.

"I wasn't sure of the name." The aide shoved the paper in the pocket of her scrubs. "Someone called the desk with a message for you. Said your car had been hit in the parking lot. He wants you to come down right away."

Her car…no, her brand-new sister-in-law's car. Her stomach tightened. What a way to start their relationship.

It would be Trey who'd have something to say about it, most likely, not Jessica, but that didn't make her feel any better.

"Thanks. I'll go and take care of it."

The aide nodded, losing interest now that her message was delivered, and went out.

Libby grabbed her jacket off the chair. If she could get the car to a garage right away, maybe there'd be a chance of having it fixed before Jessica returned. She'd have to—

Halfway to the door, she stopped. Wait a minute. She'd been driving Jessica's car. How could anyone know that? There was nothing in the car to identify her as the driver. Even if the police had traced the license plate, it would lead to Jessica, not to her.

Libby frowned, looking at the window that overlooked the parking lot. Darkness drew in early this time of year. A gray day had already turned to a gray dusk. Wisps of fog wreathed the lampposts, and shadows deepened between the vehicles.

If she rushed out, the way she'd intended, Esther would be alone here. Alone and vulnerable. Someone might be trying to get to her.

Libby went quickly to the bedside table and picked up the phone. She hesitated a moment, but how could she weigh her discomfort against a possible threat to Esther? She dialed Adam's number.

"Chief Byler." He answered quickly, always on duty, it seemed.

"Adam, it's Libby." It took less than a minute to explain what happened, and telling it made it seem less and less important. Maybe there really was someone down in the parking lot, growing impatient as he waited for her.

"I'll come over," Adam said crisply. "Don't leave the room until I get there."

"Maybe I'm just making monsters out of thin air. You don't need to come. I'll stay until Esther's mother and aunt—"

"I'm coming. Stay put." He clicked off, leaving her torn between relief and embarrassment.

CHAPTER NINE

BY THE TIME Esther's mother and her aunt came back in the door, Libby was pacing back and forth across the room, casting glances out at the parking lot as if she could pierce the fog and the darkness and see what was going on out there. Which was ridiculous, because the spot where she'd parked wouldn't be visible from this window even in broad daylight.

"Ach, Libby, we have been a long time, ain't so?" Rebecca looked guilty. "I am sorry that we have held you up."

"No, of course you haven't. I was just stretching a little." Now she was the one to feel guilty. "I was happy to spend time with Esther."

As the door swung shut, Libby glimpsed the sleeve of a blue uniform. The policeman wasn't due until six, a half-hour from now. Had Adam made sure he came early?

"She is better, ja? You see it?" Rebecca crossed to Esther, but she looked anxiously at Libby, obviously needing reassurance.

"Definitely better," she said, managing to smile, her need to encourage Rebecca stronger than her caution. "I'd been talking to her, telling her something funny about my mother, and she actually smiled at me. And spoke a word."

"That is wonderful gut." Anna clasped her hand, face wreathed in smiles.

"Wonderful gut," Rebecca echoed. She put her arms around Libby. "I knew you would be gut for Esther."

Libby's tension melted away in the warmth of their rejoicing. She had to concentrate on Esther and stop letting herself get sidetracked by her own muddled feelings.

Libby stayed for a few more minutes, but Esther didn't open her eyes again. Finally she bent over the bed to kiss her cheek.

"Sleep well," she whispered. "I'll see you tomorrow."

Leaving wasn't quite that easy, of course. Rebecca had a string of messages to be delivered to Libby's mother, mostly thanks for various helpful things Libby's mother had set up. Promising she'd remember every one, Libby went out, nodding to the police officer next to the door.

Why did leaving a hospital room always feel like escaping? She'd never been able to figure that one out. Maybe it had something to do with reminders of one's own vulnerability.

She was headed toward the elevator when the doors opened. Adam stepped out, saw her and glowered.

"What part of *stay in the room until I get here* didn't you understand?" He came to a stop a foot away, forcing her to look up to see his face.

"I don't see what difference it makes." She wasn't about to start letting him dictate to her. "Esther's mother and her aunt are in there, and there's a cop on the door. Nobody can get at her."

"And nobody could have known you'd driven that car today, either." His glare didn't soften. "Which one gave you the message?" He nodded toward the nurses' station.

"The blonde heavyset one." She knew she sounded sulky. "But I don't think…" She let that die off, because he was walking away.

He turned before he'd taken a dozen paces. "Stay right where I can see you." His tone made it clear that was an order.

So she stayed, watching him. She wasn't the only one with eyes on that tall, muscular figure. When he leaned on the desk, three or four women hurried to help him. The tall brunette got there first, but she lost points when he asked for the short blonde. He bent over her, obviously flustering her with the display of attention.

It was instructive, seeing how other women responded to Adam. He obviously had an effect on women wherever he went, even though he seemed oblivious to the attention. The blonde's face was animated, and she seemed to be telling him a heck of a lot more than she'd said to Libby.

Libby waited, less than patient. If he didn't finish up soon, she'd see what happened if she punched the elevator button.

But Adam headed back before she could resort to that, detouring to have a word with the officer on duty and then joining her. He was frowning, and he took her arm and piloted her toward the elevator.

She held on to her patience until they were on the elevator. "Well?"

"It was just a male voice on the phone. No indication of who it was. She didn't know whether he was calling from the lobby or the parking lot."

She nodded. "That's basically what she told me. And it might be perfectly legitimate. If Jessica's car—"

"Forget the car. At least, if it's dented, that means this was real and not an attempt to get Esther alone."

That was true. Strange as it seemed, she'd welcome a crumpled fender at this point.

They stepped outside, and Libby zipped her jacket, turning the collar up. Her driving gloves were in her pocket, but Adam had grabbed her hand, and she didn't pull away.

She shot a glance at that tense, strong face. There was nothing remotely romantic about the way he was tugging her along. He might have been taking a reluctant puppy back to its kennel.

"Where's the car?" he asked abruptly.

She pointed. "Down that aisle, almost to the end."

They walked in silence, and she had to hurry to keep up with his long strides. As they passed car after car, she realized he was looking between each of them.

"You picked the darkest section of the parking lot, you realize that?" he growled.

"It wasn't dark when I got here," she snapped. She tugged at his hand. "Do you mind slowing down a little? There's too much slush on the ground to rush."

"Sorry." He slowed, almost imperceptibly.

"There it is." She pressed the remote, and the lights blinked a few yards ahead of them.

"Stay right here, in the middle of the lane where I can see you."

He started to move away. She hung on to his hand, stopping him. "Why?"

He frowned down at her. "That call could have been just what it seemed. Or it could have been designed to get Esther alone. Or someone might have wanted to get you in this dark parking lot alone."

She stared at him, trying to understand. "But I don't get it. Why would anyone want to silence me? Because that's what it would amount to—trying to silence me the way they did Esther."

His frowning dark eyes seemed to nail her to the spot. "Just stay put so I can make sure no one's waiting near the car. Then we'll talk about it."

She started to protest but clamped her lips shut instead. There was no point in arguing when Adam wore that forbidding look. But they weren't done with this.

Apparently assured that she'd do as he told her, at least this once, Adam walked toward the car, and she realized that he carried a heavy flashlight in his left hand.

She shivered a little in the cold wind that blew through the parking lot. Why would anyone be after her? She didn't know anything. Bitter, but true. She knew no more than she had the night Esther was hit.

Suspicions? She had plenty of those, and no way of proving any of them.

Adam closed in on the car. The hand holding the flashlight swung up. Holding it above his head, Adam switched it on, and a bright beam pierced the shadows between the vehicles.

Nothing. She could see from here that no one was there, but that didn't prevent Adam from moving cautiously around the car, even shining the lights under it.

She was rubbing her arms, thoroughly chilled, by the time he returned to her. "You see? No one was there."

"Given the way you kept talking as we approached, he had plenty to time to hear us and slip away."

"Will you stop?" Her exasperation mounted. "No one is stalking me. It's Esther who is in danger."

"Someone broke into your house, remember? And crashed your computer. And maybe lifted your camera. To say nothing of decoying you out here."

"Definitely took my camera." That was still a sore subject. "We don't know that it was a decoy…" She let the words trail off, because he was shaking his head.

"No damage to your car," Adam said briefly. "The call was definitely a phony. Either they wanted Esther or you alone. I admit Esther is the more likely possibility, but I'm not about to ignore the possibility of danger to you."

Libby stiffened, determined not to let him think he'd scared her. "I thought you didn't believe in the break-in."

"Don't quote my words back at me." Adam sounded as if he were gritting his teeth. Probably trying to hang on to his temper. "Any one of those things could mean nothing. Taken together, they start to form a pattern. Did your mother ever locate your case with the letters from Esther?"

"No, but you know my mother. It might not turn up until spring." She stopped and shook her head, knowing she was fighting with him out of a mix of fear and frustration. "All right. I get it, and I agree. But I still think Esther is the target. I'm just in the way."

"Being in the way can be dangerous. It's my responsibility to keep you safe."

The words flicked her on the place in her heart that was still raw. "You're not responsible for me, Adam. You weren't three years ago, and you're not now." She regretted it the instant the words were out. Talking about what had happened between them that night in San Francisco was a mistake.

Adam glared at her, and she could feel the anger radiating like heat from him. His gaze seemed to slip, focusing on her lips. His eyes darkened, but not with anger this time. He pulled her into his arms, and his lips closed on hers.

A tiny voice at the back of her mind insisted that kissing Adam never ended well. She ignored it, sliding her arms around him, giving herself up to his embrace.

Adam let go of her slowly, maybe reluctantly. He shook his head, as if trying to clear it, and took a step back. "Sorry." It was almost a snarl. "Get in the car. Start it and lock the doors. I'll bring the patrol car around and follow you home."

She wanted to protest, to tell him neither of them needed to be sorry for what they felt.

He was attracted to her. He couldn't possibly deny it.

But for some reason he didn't want to recognize that attraction, and there was nothing at all that she could do about it.

"As SOON as I realized that the police might need my information, I called you." The manager of the convenience store near the highway looked at Adam's uniform with dark, worried eyes. "The driver merely stopped for gas as I was walking in. There was nothing I could do."

"We appreciate your call, Mr. Amir." In Adam's opinion, the man already regretted making the call. The fact that he'd delayed calling until today seemed to prove that. "If you'll just tell me everything you can remember about the vehicle and the driver, that's all we need."

"Yes, well, I noticed very little. Very little," he repeated, glancing around as if to be sure he wasn't attracting attention from his customers. "It was a black van, maybe a year or two old. The front end was damaged, but it was still drivable."

That narrowed it down a little. "You didn't happen to notice the license number, I suppose?"

"Not the number, no. But the plate was from Canada," he added, brightening. "We don't see that many of those this time of year, so I took note of it."

"Good." It was good. In fact, it was the first solid lead they'd had to the vehicle. "Could you tell the province?"

"Ontario. In fact, the driver mentioned that he was from Ontario and was on his way back there. I asked him if he wanted me to refer him to a body shop, but he said that he'd wait and have it fixed when he got home."

If he'd hit Esther's buggy, he'd probably thought it safer to get away from the area as quickly as possible. "What did the driver look like? Was he alone in the vehicle?"

"Just an ordinary middle-aged man." The manager spread his hands. "His wife was with him. They looked like any other tourists visiting the county."

That sounded less like a hit-and-run driver…most often the driver who ran was alone in the car. "Did he pay with a credit card?" That, at least, could be traced.

"He paid in cash. I rang him up myself. And then he drove off." He shrugged. "I didn't have reason to notice anything else."

"You didn't ask him about what happened to the vehicle?"

"He said that someone hit his car in a parking lot, that's all." The manager turned away as a customer approached the counter, obviously eager to have this conversation over.

"Did he say what parking lot?"

The manager shook his head, pausing in the act of ringing up a two-liter bottle of soda. "He did mention that they had been staying at the inn. Maybe they'll be able to help."

Adam's energy soared. The inn's management would have to know more about the couple, if not about the damage to the vehicle. Finally the tedious routine had paid off. With a quick expression of thanks, he headed back to the patrol car.

Five minutes of driving, and Adam pulled into the parking lot of the inn. Owen Barclay would be cooperative. Adam didn't doubt that. Barclay was as careful of the inn's reputation as of his own. He wouldn't want a police car at the front door for a minute longer than necessary.

The lobby was relatively empty at this hour on a weekday, and a glance into the restaurant showed that the staff was setting up for lunch. Lifting his hand to the woman at the front desk, Adam went down the corridor to Barclay's office, knocking on frosted glass and opening the door at the same time. "Owen?"

But Owen Barclay wasn't alone. Libby sat across the desk from him, and all the memories Adam had been holding safely at bay flooded back in a surge of longing that nearly pulled him under.

"Sorry. I didn't mean to interrupt." He focused on Barclay, not sure it was safe to meet Libby's gaze at the moment.

"Not a problem." Owen waved him in. "I was just giving Libby some good news."

Libby lifted the camera she held in her hands. "You can call off the search. Owen found my camera."

"Is that right?" Obviously he was the only one made uncomfortable by that kiss. Libby looked and sounded perfectly normal. "Where did it turn up?"

"That's the problem." Owen frowned at the camera, as if it were to blame. "One of the servers found it on the coatroom shelf this morning. But we searched that room thoroughly when Libby reported the camera missing, and I'm sure it wasn't there at the time."

"That is odd." Yet another odd thing happening to Libby, and Adam didn't like it. "Is there any reason to think one of the staff took it and then got cold feet and returned it?"

Owen stiffened, pressing his hands against the polished mahogany of his desk. "I can't believe that of any of my staff."

His staff, just as the office, indeed the entire inn, was Owen's in his view, he'd managed it for so long.

"Sometimes an otherwise reliable person can give in to a sudden impulse." He eyed Owen, wondering if he'd admit it if any of the staff had given him cause to wonder. The staff reflected Owen's taste, just as the elegant lobby did.

"Well, I don't care what happened to it, as long as I have it back in working order." Libby raised the camera, focusing it on Owen, and then lowered it again, frowning.

"Is something wrong?" Owen was quick off the mark. "It's not broken, is it?"

Libby clicked something on the side of the camera. She looked up, not at Owen but at Adam. "The memory card is gone."

He took a step toward her, fixing his gaze on the camera, not on her face. "What was on it? Do you remember?"

"I had just put a new one in partway through the reception. So probably not more than a dozen shots or so. Most of the wedding photos were on another card."

"That's good, isn't it?" Owen said. "At least you didn't lose the important pictures. And we'll be happy to reimburse you for the cost of the card."

She waved the offer away, her gaze still on Adam. "No need for that. Still, it's strange."

He knew what she was thinking. That somehow all these oddities added up to something, if only they could figure out what.

Their gazes clung too long, because all of a sudden he was seeing her face as it had been in the dimly lit parking lot the moment he'd kissed her. The color came up in her cheeks, and he knew she was thinking the same thing.

This time it was Libby who turned away. "I'm sure you didn't come in about my camera." She rose, as if to leave.

"I just had a question for Owen about a couple from Canada who were staying here the night of Esther's accident."

"You've learned something about the driver?" Her gaze sharpened on his face.

"A couple from…" Owen frowned. "You mean the Bradburns?"

"I don't know the name, but they were seen leaving in a damaged black van the next day, and they were apparently staying here."

"Yes, they were. But the damage to their vehicle couldn't have anything to do with the accident. Their van was hit in the parking lot."

That was a blow. "You're sure of that?"

Owen paused. "Well, as sure as I can be. That's how it was reported to me. It was discovered when the valet went to bring the vehicle up when they checked out. Mr. Bradburn was upset, naturally, but we can't guarantee a vehicle's safety in the parking lot, even with valet parking."

"It wasn't damaged when they came in? Or if they took it out again?"

"Certainly not. The valet attendants have strict instructions to check each car for damages each time it comes in."

"Bradburn couldn't have parked it himself?"

"I suppose it might happen, but it's unlikely. We did check up on the possibilities, since it would affect our insurance," Owen said.

"So an insurance claim was filed?" This was beginning to look less and less promising, but it still had to be investigated.

"Well, as it turned out, no." Owen's gaze evaded his. "We're not particularly eager to make a claim against the insurance unless we have to. And since the Bradburns wanted to get on the road to Canada before the weather turned bad again, they agreed to accept a cash settlement."

"You often do that?"

"Trust me, if your insurance premiums were as high as ours, you wouldn't want to push them any higher. If it had been a matter of personal injury..." Owen shrugged. "Since it wasn't, the matter was fairly straightforward, so we settled."

It looked as if his promising lead might be settled, as well. "You'll let me have their contact information."

"Of course, of course. I'll print it out for you." Owen swung to his computer. "It'll just take a few minutes."

Libby moved swiftly toward the door. "I'll be on my

way. Thanks again, Owen." She was out even before Owen could respond.

But it wasn't Owen she was running away from. It was him, and Adam knew it. But there didn't seem to be any way of smoothing things out with Libby that wouldn't dig him in any deeper with her.

LIBBY KNEW WHEN she rushed out of Owen's office that it was a stupid thing to do, but realizing that didn't slow her steps as she scurried through the lobby toward the front door. She'd known when she saw Adam that she wasn't ready to be with him yet. The memory of that kiss was just too fresh in her mind, to say nothing of her heart.

She stepped outside, the cold wind slapping her in the face. Good, that was what she needed—a wake-up call.

The threat to Esther was the crucial thing to deal with now. Next to that, her own problems faded into insignificance. Her job, her future, even Adam, didn't amount to anything next to Esther's safety.

Libby followed the cleared walk to the parking lot. The night of the reception the valets had been rushing back and forth constantly. An accident could easily have happened.

If she hadn't let her emotions get the better of her, she might have found out what Adam thought. Something must have led him to inquire about that particular vehicle. Who had seen the damage?

Libby unlocked the car door and slid inside. Still, there wasn't anything she could do about a tourist who'd returned to Canada. That was obviously a police job. Glancing toward the inn, she saw Adam coming out, saw him look toward her car.

Instinct took over, and she pulled out of the parking lot without looking back. She had an appointment with Tom Sylvester at his office. That was as good a reason as any to evade Adam. He'd just tell her to stop snooping if he knew about it.

A few minutes later she pulled to the curb in front of the construction office. The lights were on, and through the plate glass she spotted Tom at his desk.

She slid out and headed for the door. Too bad she hadn't come up with a plan of attack. She'd just have to wing it.

Tom had suggested they meet at his office, so he could show her the plans for his new motel. Afterward, if she wanted, they could drive out to the site. His tone had made it clear he didn't expect to do that.

Tom must have been watching for her, because he had the door open when she reached it.

"Libby, come in out of the cold. It's raw today. Let me take your jacket."

She hugged it a little closer. "I'll keep it, thanks. I'm not used to Pennsylvania winters, I'm afraid."

"No, I guess you wouldn't be." He returned to his desk, gesturing her to the folding chair. "I bet your mom is glad to have you home for a while. And taking an interest in the community development, too. Your father would be proud of that."

Libby felt her lips tighten, but she managed to produce

a smile. "Dad always cared what became of the land. He never wanted to see careless development."

Did Tom react to that? She thought so, but he bent quickly to spread a detailed drawing on the desk, anchoring the corners with a stapler and a roll of tape.

Interesting. From what she'd seen peering through the window the other day, there'd been nothing at all on the desk. Now it actually looked as if some work was done here.

"Development has to be planned, that's for sure." He waved a hand at the drawing. "I wanted a building that blends in with the surroundings. No sense putting up something that sticks out like a sore thumb." He put one hand down on the plan as she bent over it. "Kind of surprises me, you taking so much interest in it."

And there was the comment she should have prepared an answer to. "Well, coming back after being away, I was struck by how things changed. It seemed to me it would make an interesting article, focusing on the township's growth. Since I'll be here for a while, I'd like to be working on something."

"You sound like me." Tom leaned back, seeming to relax. "That's how I felt about retirement. Two weeks of doing nothing, and I thought I'd go crazy."

"Still, you must have enjoyed the Florida sunshine, didn't you?" She nodded toward the street, where snow had changed to slush, ready to freeze again at the first drop in temperature.

"Tell you the truth, I like the change of seasons, and I just had to get back to work. This little project, now—"

he patted the drawing "—I've had this in the back of my mind for a long time. When the opportunity came up, I just grabbed it."

Libby took the camera from her bag, slipping a new memory card in it. She lifted the camera, taking a step back so she could frame Tom and the plans. She took several shots. He smiled, looking a little forced.

"Just relax. This is your dream project, I gather. You said you'd been planning it for a long time."

"Sure thing. Just daydreaming, you know."

She snapped a few more shots from a different angle. "You like the idea of building something that's yours here in the community where you've lived for so long."

"Well, yeah. I hadn't thought about it like that, exactly, but I've lived in Spring Township all my life. This is sort of giving something back." He gestured expansively. "We all want to have a chance to do that, right?"

"Not many people have the determination and the drive to make that happen," she said. He was relaxing, forgetting her as she seemed to disappear behind the camera. She'd seen that happen often—people sometimes told a photographer all sorts of things they'd never say to a stranger.

"If there's one thing I have, it's determination." Ted didn't seem averse to patting himself on the back.

"It must have taken that to get the variance you needed from the zoning board."

"It's all a matter of knowing—" He stopped abruptly, as if hearing what he was saying.

"The zoning board saw what a benefit this would be to the community." His voice grew stiff.

"Really? I'm surprised they didn't object to prime farmland being rezoned for commercial use."

His face flushed, and she thought he was going to lose his temper. He seemed to force it down. He patted the plans. "I thought this was what you wanted to see."

"I do. But I'll bet people who read the local paper would be more interested in how you got permission to build there."

Tom slapped at the stapler, and the plans rolled shut. "I'm not going to discuss that, so if that's really why you came, you may as well leave."

That was plain speaking. She hadn't expected Sylvester to resist so bluntly. He'd always shown a bit of deference to the Morgan family. But maybe things had changed since Dad was no longer around.

"I'm surprised you don't want to explain. This is your chance to tell your side of the story, so people will stop speculating about it."

"Nobody's speculating but you." His already-ruddy color deepened alarmingly. "Typical. You Morgans always think you've got to put your two cents' worth in."

Her temper rose, but she hung on to it. "Everyone who cares about this area has a right to an opinion."

"Not on my private business." His fist thudded against the desk, and the sound echoed in the nearly empty room. "You're just like your father, always butting into things that didn't concern him."

Libby let the anger go, feeling it surge through her

like a wave of energy. “My father cared about Spring Township and all the people in it. If I am like him, I’m proud of that.”

She stalked out of the office.

CHAPTER TEN

PROPELLED BY A wave of anger, Libby surged onto the sidewalk and stalked toward the car. And stopped. She was blocked in by a double-parked truck.

This was something that happened in the city, not in quiet little Springville. She was surprised Adam wasn't out here already, warning the driver to move on. Mindful of the icy slush, she stepped off the curb and approached the window of the truck on the passenger side.

The driver sat behind the wheel, gazing down the street as if he had nothing better to do. She'd love to give him a piece of her mind, but a tactful request to move would be more likely to get her what she wanted. She rapped sharply on the window.

The driver turned, and her stomach cramped. It was the worker from the construction site. He was just as unkempt as he'd been there, and likely still wearing the same dirt-crusted clothes. Oddly enough, he didn't show any sign of recognizing her.

She pointed toward her car. "You're blocking me in. Pull ahead, please."

The driver smiled then, a narrow grimace that contrasted with the malice in his eyes. He recognized her, all right. Was this some kind of payback for her incursion at the construction site?

Then he nodded, lifted his hand in what seemed to be agreement and started to shift gears. Apparently they weren't going to have another confrontation. Relieved, she headed back to the car.

Climbing in, she started the engine and cranked the heater up. Tom's office had been cold, as if her visit hadn't been worth turning the heat on for.

The truck began moving forward, too slowly for her taste. Restless, she shifted into Drive and edged into the street, her thoughts jumping ahead to what she wanted to do next. She'd drop the camera at home first, checking to be sure it hadn't been damaged.

Then—Libby glanced up to be sure he'd left her enough space to pull out. Barely. Gritting her teeth in annoyance, she began to pull past him.

Halfway out, she realized that the driver had started to back again. She hit the brake and the horn simultaneously. Too late. She jolted backward to the sound of crumpling metal.

For an instant she was too stunned to react.

Then anger flared out of control, and she shoved the shift into Park and flung the door open.

She reached the front of the car just as the driver sauntered back, leaving his truck's motor running so that fumes spewed out at her.

"What is wrong with you? You did that deliberately!"

He smiled, holding up his hands. "Hey, lady, you hit me. Hope you have decent insurance."

She hoped so, too. She had no idea whether Jessica's insurance would cover the damage when Jessica hadn't been behind the wheel. But that was hardly the important thing now.

"I did not hit you. You backed into me while I was pulling out. You knew I was there, and you backed right into me."

"Accidents happen, don't they? Every day. Every night."

Her tension jerked upward. Was that a veiled reference to Esther's accident?

"What do you mean? If you're talking about Esther Zook—"

He lost the phony smile, eyes narrowing. "Don't know what you mean. I'm just saying accidents happen. Especially to people who're too busy minding other folks' business to pay attention."

"If you think you can scare me away with tactics like that, you're mistaken." Her voice rose. "I'm not—"

"What's going on here?" Adam's voice cut through her anger.

She turned, finding him on the sidewalk, almost as if he'd followed her from the inn. He moved quickly between the vehicles, his gaze assessing the damage.

"Well?" He came to a halt, looking from one to the other. "Looks like there's been an accident. Is everyone okay?"

"He hit me deliberately." Libby flung the words at him. "First he double-parked, blocking me in, and then he backed into me." She looked at the crumpled fender, reminded of the crumpled buggy.

Adam's gaze swept over her. "You weren't hurt?" He sounded as neutral as if she were a stranger, but there was concern in his eyes.

She shook her head. "This is the guy who threatened me at the building site," she said quickly, sure he'd remember that conversation.

"Ron Taylor." Adam fixed his gaze on the man. "You actually working these days?"

"You got no call to talk to me that way. I got a good job. I'm the watchman out at that motel Tom Sylvester is building."

Adam didn't react outwardly to that, but she could practically see the wheels turning.

"He threatened me that day, and he just threatened me again," she added for emphasis.

"I don't know what she's talking about." Taylor glared at her. "It's my job to chase trespassers off the job site. They could get hurt. And she drove right into me." He gestured toward the damaged front end. "That's her fault."

"Because I've been too nosy?" she said acidly. She clamped her lips closed. She'd do better to come across as calm and controlled.

He shrugged, hunching his shoulders with a surly glare. "Guess you weren't paying attention. Drove right into me."

"You backed into me!" She couldn't help it—her voice rose.

"Enough." Adam didn't raise his voice, but his steely

tone was enough to subdue Libby. "Get back in your vehicles, both of you, while I conduct my investigation."

"But Adam—" She wanted to tell him that he couldn't possibly doubt her, but his expression said now was not the time. She climbed back into her car, relieved that the heater, at least, was still working.

Not her car, she reminded herself. Jessica's car. Libby wanted to groan at the thought. She'd have to try and have it fixed immediately.

She watched Adam through the windshield as he set up orange cones around the vehicles. Then he began to talk to the few people who had gathered on the sidewalk. Not many people were on Springville's Main Street, given how cold it was.

She'd just have to hope someone had seen what happened, since Adam apparently wouldn't take her word for it. That rankled, even though her rational mind insisted that he couldn't play favorites in a police investigation.

Adam had his notebook flipped open, his head bent as he jotted down whatever people were telling him.

Finally Adam returned, gesturing to both of them to join him. "I have two witnesses who support Ms. Morgan's version of the accident," he said, ripping something off his pad and handing it to Taylor. "I'm citing you for reckless driving. Get that truck off the street, and tell your boss to notify his insurance company."

Taylor clutched the citation in his hand, looking as if he wanted to crumple it up and throw it away. But he seemed to think the better of that.

"You're just doing this because you got a grudge against me. It was an accident."

"You deliberately—" Libby began, but Adam held up his hands.

"Enough. Taylor, get out of here."

Taylor frowned, muttering something to himself. He turned away, but then turned back again, glaring at Libby.

"It was an accident," he repeated. "Accidents happen. They happen all the time, to all kinds of people."

Libby held her tongue and her temper until he climbed into the truck and headed down the street. Then she turned to Adam.

"He hit me deliberately. He's threatening me, don't you see?"

"Let's save this conversation until we're out of the cold," Adam said. "You're not going to be able to drive the car. The fender is rubbing against the tire. I've called for a tow truck."

Libby looked at the damage, wanting to weep. "It's Jessica's car. My brother will never let me hear the end of it."

"You sound like a kid." Adam's voice lowered, and he sounded like himself again. "You know perfectly well Link and Jessica care more about you than a car."

"It's not the sort of impression I wanted to make on a new sister-in-law."

He gave her a sympathetic smile. "Why don't you wait in the township car where it's warm? I'll drive you home as soon as we've dealt with the tow truck."

Nodding, Libby opened the car door. She paused, looking up at him. "That was one of Tom Sylvester's trucks. He's in his office. I was just there, talking to him."

Adam raised an eyebrow. "So that's where you were headed when you rushed away from the inn."

He'd been watching her, then. No wonder he'd turned up so opportunely. "Don't you see? Sylvester is inside. I can see him through the window. He had to know that one of his trucks has just been involved in an accident. So why didn't he come out? Give me a logical explanation for that, if you can. Why didn't he come out?"

ADAM KEPT AN eye on Libby while he dealt with the bystanders and the tow truck driver. She sat in the front seat of his patrol car, holding her hands out to the heater vent.

Libby had a genius for landing right in the middle of things. Maybe that made her a good photojournalist, but he'd prefer she not exercise that gift here. If she ended up getting hurt—

He cut that thought off. No one would harm Libby. An image of Esther's mangled buggy slid into his mind. He'd have said no one would harm Esther, either.

He frowned, apparently looking so forbidding that he discouraged further comments on the part of the few people who lingered on the sidewalk, since they drifted away.

What was Taylor doing involved in this situation? If he'd known Taylor was the watchman who'd warned her off at the construction site, he might have pursued it. The man had been arrested several times on minor theft charges and a drunken brawl or two.

Not the kind of person he'd like to see anywhere near

Libby. For that matter, why would Tom Sylvester hire him? He certainly had to know the man's reputation.

He glanced at the plate glass window of the office. Sylvester was looking out, watching just as Libby had said. When he realized Adam had seen him, he moved quickly away from the window.

What exactly was going on with Sylvester? He'd give a lot right now to know that.

The tow truck pulled up, diverting his attention, and by the time Adam glanced at the office again, the lights had been turned off. Sylvester was gone.

Once the tow truck had moved off, Adam joined Libby in the patrol car. "I'm sorry that took so long. I'll drive you home, and the garage will call you later with an estimate."

"The bad news, you mean." Libby's nose wrinkled.

"Jessica's a nice person. She's not going to come down on you for something you couldn't help. Although if you hadn't been playing Nancy Drew…"

"Don't bother to give me that lecture again," Libby said. "I know it by heart."

"Know it, maybe. Heed it? No."

"Somebody has to find out what Sylvester is up to. And he is up to something." Libby stared out the window at the farms they were passing, but he didn't think she saw the snow-covered fields. "Otherwise he wouldn't have gotten so nervous when I asked him how he'd gotten approval for that building."

Obviously it was useless to point out that she shouldn't have done anything of the kind. "What did he say?"

"He told me I was acting just like my father, butting into things that don't concern me. Not that Dad ever did that. He just stood up for what he believed in."

"Your dad cared, and he did something with that care. That had sometimes made him enemies."

"Yes. He did." Libby's voice softened. "If I am like him, I'm proud of that. But why should my questions make Tom Sylvester so mad, if he's not up to something questionable?"

Maybe, if she knew he was taking this seriously, she'd back off. Adam had a feeling that was a futile thought, but he had to try.

"I've been wondering about Sylvester's business deals myself, although I still don't see how that could possibly connect with Esther. I'll look into it, see if I can come up with anything."

He felt Libby's gaze on his face.

"You're trying to make me feel better, so I'll back off," she said. "You can't investigate a respected member of the community without evidence."

Adam pulled into the lane to the Morgan house. "Not officially, no. But I can do a little quiet poking around." He drew to a stop, leaving the motor running, and turned to her. "Is there any chance you can accept that?"

"Well, I wouldn't if I could think of anything else to do," she admitted ruefully. "I've been away too long. I don't know where to go for gossip anymore."

"Just take care of Esther, okay? Let me worry about the rest of it. I've already talked to the Canadian police about the driver of the van. They'll follow up at that end and get back to me. There's at least a chance the van hasn't been fixed yet, and they'll be able to pick up some evidence from it."

"I'm finding it hard to believe in a hit-and-run driver who escaped back to Canada the next day." She turned in the seat so that she was facing him more fully. "How does that fit in with the things that have happened since?"

"It doesn't," he admitted. "Still, if you…"

She touched his cheek as if to stop his words, and that touch went right through him.

"Don't lecture me anymore, okay?" Her voice was soft. "I can't stay home with my knitting when Esther is in danger."

He closed his hand over hers, drawing it slowly away from his face. "I know you care deeply about her. I know you feel responsible." The truth was that he admired those qualities in her. "I understand."

"Do you?" Her gaze seemed to be entangled with his, and her blue eyes widened.

"Yes." He took a breath, unable to come up with a comfortable lie. "I know how you feel about protecting Esther, because that's how I feel about you."

Her lips curved slightly. "Not exactly the same, I hope."

"Libby, I can't." He tried to evade her gaze, afraid she might really see what was in his heart. "You're Trey's little sister."

She put her hands on his cheeks, tilting his face toward her. "Take a good look, Adam. I'm not a little girl anymore. I'm not made of glass. And I know you're attracted to me."

They'd gone a long way from protecting Esther, but maybe this was what they'd really been talking about all the time.

"It's pretty obvious, I guess."

The dimple at the corner of her mouth showed. "The kiss was kind of a giveaway."

He took her hands in both of his, holding them firmly, resisting the impulse to lift them to his lips. "Look, I admit I'm attracted. But I can't—"

"You couldn't when I was fifteen," she said. "I get that, even though it hurt at the time. But that time in San Francisco..." She paused, as if catching her breath. "Adam, I was afraid you thought I was throwing myself at you. That you looked down on me. And that wasn't it at all, was it?"

"No. Never." He felt as if she'd punched him right in the heart. "Libby, I'm sorry. Don't you see? What happened with Sally showed me that people always hold me to a different standard. They're always ready to think the worst of me. I never meant to hurt you. That's what I was trying to avoid."

She lifted their clasped hands to her lips. "It's a funny way of going about it," she whispered, her breath moving on his skin.

"Don't." He yanked his hands away from her. "I owe your family too much. You think I can forget what I come from? I can't, and neither can anyone else around here."

Libby stared at him, eyes wide. "Adam, that doesn't matter to me. Or to Mom or my brothers."

He had himself under control now, and he wouldn't let go again. Better a small hurt now than a big one later, for both of them.

"It matters to me, Libby." He reached across her to push the door open. "I'm sorry. More than you know."

Her lips parted, and that familiar stubborn look came into her face. But maybe she sensed how determined he was.

She shook her head, slid out of the car and slammed the door.

LIBBY HURRIED INTO the hall, realizing that, as usual, her mother had forgotten to lock the door. Thank goodness no one was home. She didn't know whether to burst into tears or throw something. Preferably something very breakable. At least no one was here to watch.

She did neither. Sam was barking, the sound muffled. Listening, she took a step forward, realizing that the barking came from the powder room. Sam was obviously shut inside. But why? No one would do that, and he was way too big a dog to have been shut in accidentally.

She started toward it and then stopped, her breath catching in her throat as she recognized another noise. The stairs—someone was coming down the stairs.

Heart thudding in her chest, she glanced toward the door. Race out, try to attract Adam's attention before he reached the trees that hid the house from sight? Or run the other way, for the dog?

Another step sounded. Did he know she was here? Maybe not, with the noise Sam was making. Somehow that decided her. She ran toward the powder room, trying to hear any sounds from behind her over the dog's frenzied barking and the pulse pounding in her ears.

She reached the door, grabbed the knob and turned it. Sam bounded past her, showing no signs of his age as he raced toward the intruder.

She pressed back against the door, fumbling in her bag for her cell phone. Before she could find it, a riot of sounds assaulted her—barking, growling, the thumps of someone falling, a high-pitched scream.

Sam…if he hurt Sam—Libby ran toward the noise in time to see a figure break free of the dog with a kick. He reached the door, pulled it open and ran straight into Adam.

It must have been like running into a brick wall. The man reeled back. Adam grabbed him, spun him around and marched him into the hall. Libby blinked, unable to believe the evidence of her eyes. It was Leonard Smalley.

"Are you all right?" Adam's tone was urgent. His gaze swept over her as if searching for injuries, and he held the smaller man like a dog holding a bone.

"I'm fine. He wasn't anywhere near me." She patted her leg, and Sam frisked over to her, tail wagging, obviously proud of himself. "But Leonard…" Words failed her.

Adam hauled the hapless man to the straight chair against the wall and put him in it none too gently. He stood over Smalley, glaring down at him with an expression even Libby found intimidating.

"If you have an explanation for breaking and entering, now would be the time for it."

"I...I didn't. Break in, I mean." Leonard's gaze darted back and forth, as if he looked for a way out of the situation. "The door was unlocked."

"Trespassing with intent to commit a crime, then." Adam leaned over him. "That's not much better."

"But I didn't intend to commit a crime." Smalley was nearly crying. "I just had to find..." He stopped then, maybe afraid to go any further.

"It was you in the house that other time, too, wasn't it?" Hand on the dog's collar, Libby took a step toward Smalley. "You wiped my computer. You took my bag."

"Not...not to keep," he stammered. "I put it back in your room. You look. It's there. All I wanted..." Again he came to a halt.

"This is a waste of time," Adam said, reaching for Smalley. "Let's go. You can call your attorney from the police station. Or your wife, if you prefer."

"Not my wife." Smalley gasped the words. He'd been pale already, and now he turned an almost greenish shade.

Knowing Sandra, Libby could hardly blame him. "Just tell us what's going on," she said, and the dog growled as if to encourage him. "You've been in the house a couple of times, looking for something." Light dawned, and she could only be surprised it had taken her this long. "You're the one who took my camera at the inn. This has something to do with the pictures I was taking, doesn't it?"

Leonard hesitated, looking from one to the other.

Adam gave an impatient shrug. "Let's go."

"You can't arrest me." Smalley's hands shook as he held them out to Libby. "Please, Libby. I didn't mean any harm. Don't let him arrest me."

She hardened her heart. This was the only way to get to the truth. "He'll have to, if you don't tell us everything."

Tears welled in Smalley's eyes. He sniffed, increasing his resemblance to a rabbit. "Friday night. You were at the inn. For the rehearsal dinner, I suppose."

"That's right. I was taking pictures." She began to have a glimmer of where this was going.

"Did Libby catch you with her camera doing something you're ashamed of, Leonard? Something you don't want your wife to know about?" Adam's tone demanded answers.

"I…I…there was nothing wrong." Smalley stumbled over the words. "I was meeting someone. A young lady. Just for a drink, you understand. Nothing wrong with that."

"Just a drink?" Adam's tone dripped disbelief. "I don't think you'd run the risk of breaking into the Morgan's house because Libby photographed you having a drink with another woman."

"It…we were going to a room to have the drink." Smalley forced the words out. "I don't even know for sure if Libby got us. I couldn't find the picture, so I…"

"So you crashed my computer. Unluckily for you, I have everything backed up online." She stared at him, shaking her head. "For pity's sake, Leonard, even if I did get a photo of you with another woman, I wouldn't tell Sandra. What were you thinking?"

He blinked several times in rapid succession. "I was afraid."

"So you wanted to destroy the picture," Adam said. "That doesn't explain why Jason tried to warn me off the accident investigation."

"Jason?" Smalley looked about as blank as Libby felt. "The accident? Why would Jason do that?"

"That's what I'm asking you." Adam leaned over him, planting one hand on the back of Leonard's chair. "What does the hit-and-run have to do with you?"

"Nothing! I don't have any idea what Jason was doing, but..." He paused, and then shook his head. "He wouldn't be acting for me. If he knew about this, he'd think...he'd think it was funny."

There was an odd kind of dignity in his last words that convinced Libby he was telling the truth about that, at least. She eyed Adam's expression. Once she got him alone, they were going to have a talk about Jason Smalley.

"All right. But there's still the matter of stealing a camera, breaking in—"

"But I returned everything." Leonard turned to Libby. "Please, you understand, don't you?"

"No. But I won't press charges against you. Just let him go, Adam. Please." She was suddenly tired, as if all the adrenaline she'd been running on had vanished.

Adam's face turned stony. "The law should take its course."

"We have more important things to deal with right

now, don't we?" She looked at him steadily. Getting involved in Leonard's peccadilloes would just be a distraction neither of them had time for.

For a moment she thought Adam would argue. Then he stepped back and gestured toward the door.

Leonard bolted from the chair, babbling his thanks as he raced toward the door. In a moment he'd run out, letting the door swing shut behind him.

Libby felt herself sag. "Leonard Smalley. So that's it. Not a piece of the puzzle at all. Just a terrified man trying to protect himself."

"You should have let me lock him up. He deserved it." Adam wore his uncompromising look.

"Really? Maybe you want to spend your time dealing with the Smalley family, but I don't." She bent to ruffle Sam's ears, not sure she wanted to ask the obvious question, and the dog pressed against her leg. "Why did you come back?" *Because you regretted something you'd said?*

"I spotted his car, pulled off into the woods." Adam came a little closer. "You sure you're okay?"

"Fine." She looked up at him, managing a smile. "But what was all that business about Jason? Why would he care about the investigation into the hit-and-run?"

"That's what I'd like to find out. He tried to act like the county commissioners thought I was wasting time, but I think he had some other agenda." Adam frowned. "At least we know now that the break-ins here don't have anything to do with Esther."

"There's still the man in Esther's hospital room. And

the attempt to get me out into the parking lot. And that funny business with Sylvester."

"I haven't forgotten," he said, eyes serious. "I'm going to have a little chat with some people who are in the know about the zoning board. See if I can pick up anything about how Tom got that variance."

"Good idea. Maybe my mother knows someone."

"Keep your mother out of it." Adam sounded faintly horrified at the prospect. "If you ask Geneva, the next thing you know she'll be starting an investigation of her own."

She had to smile, because that was exactly like Mom. "You might have a point."

He started for the door and then stopped and looked at her. "Do me a favor. Try to stay out of trouble for a while, will you?"

She choked back a reminder that he didn't have the right to worry about her. "I'll try."

CHAPTER ELEVEN

ADAM HUNG UP the phone and leaned back in his desk chair, staring at nothing in particular as he processed what he'd heard. Since catching Leonard Smalley in the act yesterday, he'd felt as if some of the picture was clearing, at least.

That call from Canadian authorities had muddied the waters again. Charles Bradburn's van had already been repaired, with no way left to prove it had been involved in the hit-and-run. The man had a good reputation as a solid citizen who'd never had so much as a parking ticket. His counterparts north of the border were happy to cooperate, but it seemed there was nothing left for them to do.

That was it, then. Bradburn's van might or might not have been involved in the hit-and-run. But since Charles Bradburn had been well on his way home the next day, confirmed by when he crossed the border, he certainly couldn't have been the intruder in the hospital room or the person who'd tried to decoy Libby out to the parking lot.

His blood ran cold every time he thought of that. Libby just assumed that Esther had been the target, and maybe she was right. But it was equally possible that a person who'd silenced Esther might also want to silence the friend she'd confided in.

Adam moved restlessly, and the swivel chair creaked in protest. If he could put Libby on a flight back to San Francisco right now, he'd feel a lot better, but that wasn't going to happen.

Shoving the chair back, he rose. The office was too small for his mood at the moment. He'd think better when he was moving.

He grabbed his jacket from the hook and strode through the outer office, raising his hand to the dispatcher. "I'm taking a walk around town, Ginger. If anybody wants me, I'll be back in half an hour or so."

"Bring some decent coffee with you," Ginger called as the door swung shut. "And a couple of doughnuts."

He shook his head, smiling a little. Hiring an old friend from high school as his dispatcher guaranteed that he didn't get any respect.

Springville's main street had been slush-covered earlier. Now it was being coated with a fresh coating of snow. Looked nice, but it would most likely bring on a rash of fender benders.

He passed one of the Amish-owned shops, glancing in at handmade rocking chairs. Not much business today, probably. The tea shop and bakery was doing a little better, with folks stopping in for a quick bite and to catch up on the latest gossip.

A car came down the street fast, and then slowed when the driver obviously spotted him. Adam raised his hand, recognizing Judge Judith Waller at the wheel. She looked like a sedate grandmother and drove like a teenage drag racer. He might give her a warning, but professional courtesy dictated that he not ticket her, and she knew it.

She smiled, waved and proceeded down the street at a more decorous pace.

Several buggies were drawn up in the alley next to the hardware store, and he spotted Bishop Amos leaning on the counter, talking to Sam Robertson, the owner. On impulse, he pushed the door open and walked inside. The heat from the wood-burning stove assailed him, and he unzipped his jacket.

"Feels like summer in here, Sam." He approached the counter.

"It's a good advertisement for the wood-burners, don't you think?" Sam, lean and graying, grinned at him, and Bishop Amos nodded gravely.

"Has it sold many of them?" He had his doubts. Most people didn't want the trouble of a wood-burner when they could just push up the thermostat, although sometimes they had cause to regret that decision when the power went off.

"You'd be surprised," Sam said. "What can I do for you today? Does the police department need a fresh supply of locks?"

"No, thanks. Actually, I saw Bishop Amos was here and wanted to have a word."

Nothing seemed to startle the bishop, and his blue eyes were tranquil when he nodded. "I am always glad to see you, Adam. You want to talk about Esther, ain't so?"

With his work-callused hands and slightly stooped shoulders, Bishop Amos looked like what he was, a hardworking farrier. He was also the spiritual leader of the Spring Township Amish community.

Sam faded tactfully into the back with a murmur about stocking shelves. Adam leaned against the counter, not sure how to begin.

"I thought maybe you could tell me if there are any rumors going around among your people about Esther's accident. So far we haven't had much success in tracing the person who hit her."

Bishop Amos shook his head. "That was a sad thing, for sure. Folks are talking about it, but nobody has any guesses as to who the driver was, at least not that I've heard. Whoever he was, we forgive him. It is up to God to deal with him."

"It's also up to the law," Adam said. "But we have to find him first."

Bishop Amos nodded, accepting his words, but Adam knew that didn't mean he'd turn to the law himself. The Amish believed in living separate from the world. *In the world, but not of it.* Strictly law-abiding themselves, they were unlikely to seek redress from the law when they were wronged.

"Libby Morgan received a few letters from Esther recently that indicated Esther was worried about something. Apparently it was something that affected both the Amish and the English. Any idea what that might be?"

Bishop Amos shook his head automatically, but then he paused, frowning. "It might be… But that could have nothing to do with Esther's accident."

Adam tried not to sound too eager. "Anything you can

tell me might help. It might have something to do with why she was out on Dahl Road that night."

The bishop seemed to weigh something. Finally he shook his head. "Some of my people have been a bit concerned about a problem recently, but I did not think Esther was among them."

"If you tell me, it won't go any further."

Bishop Amos's gaze met his. "You have always been a gut friend to the Amish, Adam. I don't forget that. But there are some things I cannot discuss."

Adam shrugged, trying to conceal his disappointment. "I'm always here, if the situation changes."

"Perhaps it may change in a way none of us expected." The bishop's weathered face creased in a smile. "Esther Zook has been improving more than the doctors thought possible. She opens her eyes and seems to understand what people say. There's a rumor she will even go home soon."

That startled him. "Is she talking?"

"Not yet. But once she is home again, perhaps that will happen."

Home. An isolated farm, with no one there to protect her. Esther might improve at home, but she might also be in serious danger, as Libby had pointed out with such emphasis.

He'd have to talk with the Zook family about this as soon as possible. To say nothing of Libby, who'd be involved up to her chin, if he knew her.

THE HOSPITAL WAS beginning to feel way too familiar. Libby walked toward Esther's room, nodding to the nurse who always seemed to be on duty when she arrived. If she felt this way, think how much worse it was for Esther's mother, who'd practically been living here since the accident.

When she opened the door, her heart seemed to stop. Esther's bed was empty.

And then Rebecca came toward her, beaming. "Esther is at physical therapy. Mary Ann has gone with her to learn what to do, so that she can help Esther when she comes home. It is wonderful gut, ja? The doctor says she might be able to leave the hospital this week."

The therapists had been coming to Esther's room every day lately to work with her, mentioning the importance of keeping her from losing muscle tone, but this was the first time she'd gone to them.

Libby collected her scattered thoughts. "Leave? You mean, go to a rehab facility?" They'd have to make new security arrangements at a new place.

"The doctor suggested that." Rebecca took her hand, leading her to a chair. "But we are sure that Esther will get well faster at home."

Esther would go home, and she'd encounter all the dangers that accompanied that. And there would be no guard on duty at the door every night to protect her.

Libby tried to find the argument that would work best on Rebecca. "Surely she would recover faster at a rehab facility. They have all the equipment she would need, and the therapists are trained to help her. You want her to get back to her old self."

"She will do that faster in her own home, with her familiar surroundings." Rebecca sounded stubbornly convinced that she was right. "And the doctor says he will arrange for the physical therapist to come to the house three times every week. The rest of the time, we will help her."

Libby clasped her hand. "What about the danger to Esther? The man you saw in her room? The one who tried to get me to leave her alone the other night?"

"She will be safer at home. Someone will always be there with her." Rebecca seemed to be trying to convince herself. Her fingers tightened on Libby's. "It will be for the best. You'll see."

She didn't agree, but it was obvious that her opinion wasn't going to count for much. Pressing her lips together, she struggled to find another argument, but she couldn't. In fact, she could only think of one possible solution.

"When you do take Esther home, I'd like to come and stay for a while, if that's all right with you." She imagined she felt a slight withdrawal in their clasped hands. "Please, Rebecca. You know I won't be a bother. And I can help with Esther's exercises. Mary Ann has so much responsibility as it is with the children. I'm sure you can use an extra pair of hands."

Rebecca's gaze was troubled. "But what about your job? And your mamm. She probably wants to have you home with her after being away so much."

"I've left my job, so my time is my own for now. And you know that my mother would be the first one to want to help out." She paused. "It would mean so much to me to be able to help Esther."

And to protect her. Even if the only weapon she had was a cell phone, at least she'd be a link with the outside world.

"Ja, I know." Rebecca smiled and patted her cheek. "Esther would like that fine, and so would I."

"Will it be all right with Isaac?" She hadn't forgotten how eager he'd been to have her leave the hospital at first, although he seemed resigned to her presence now.

"Don't you worry about Isaac. He is still my boy, after all. Who I have to stay at the daadi haus is my own business, ain't so? It is settled, so long as your mamm agrees."

Maybe it was best not to point out that she was a grown woman who didn't ask her mother's permission any longer. "I'll talk with her tonight. I know she'll feel just as I do about it."

Of course there was one person who would disagree, and she suspected that he'd do so firmly and at length. But Adam didn't control where she went and what she did.

LIBBY HAD JUST stepped out of Esther's room when she spotted Adam getting off the elevator. Judging by the look on his face, he was on a mission, and probably didn't want to be interrupted.

She'd like to use that as an excuse to avoid another argument, but she certainly didn't want him hearing about her plan to stay at the Zook farm from anyone else. In fact, she didn't even want anyone within earshot when he heard about it.

"Adam, do you have a minute?"

The frowning glance he sent her way wasn't particularly encouraging. "Can it wait? I need to talk to Esther's family."

"I think it's better if you hear what I have to say first." She glanced down the hallway, but the door to the chapel was propped open and the whir of a vacuum cleaner could be heard from within. She turned the other way. "There's a patient lounge down this way."

She walked off quickly, trusting that he'd follow her. And trying to shape in her mind the argument she suspected they were about to have.

The patient lounge was a sunroom, bright even in winter with its array of windows. The furnishings, white wicker and colorful chintzes, were the polar opposite of the usual hospital fare of plastic and vinyl.

"This will do. No one's in here." Unfortunately there wasn't a door she could close, but she walked across to the farthest window, which overlooked the distant ridge. "Nice room, isn't it?"

Adam looked at her with something like surprise in his face. "It should be, since your mother decorated it."

"Mom?" She blinked. How had she not known that?

For an answer, he pointed to a small bronze plaque on the wall. She stepped closer to read it.

"Dedicated to the beloved memory of Blake Winston II, from his family." Her throat seemed to close on the words.

"You didn't know?" Adam moved so that he stood next to her, his body shielding her from anyone glancing in the doorway.

"My mother never mentioned it." She touched the

plaque lightly. "Now I know why the room seems so familiar."

"Yes." Adam was quiet for a moment, but she could feel his controlled impatience. "You wanted to talk to me."

She forced herself to look away from the plaque. "I had some disturbing news from Rebecca when I came in today. It looks as if they'll be taking Esther home, maybe as early as this week."

"That's why I came by. I heard something of that from Bishop Amos." His face looked as if it was carved from stone. "We have to change their minds."

Adam was reacting the same way she had, and she didn't want him upsetting Rebecca.

"I know, but I don't think that's possible. I've already tried. Rebecca is convinced that Esther will do better at home, and she's sure Esther will be safe with all of the family around them."

"A family that embraces nonviolence, that won't turn to the police for help, that couldn't call for help even if they wanted to? How is that safe?" He turned. "I'll talk to her."

Libby put her hand on his arm. It was like grasping a metal railing. "Please, Adam, stop and think before you barge in there. If I couldn't persuade Rebecca, what makes you think she'll listen to you?"

He stood where he was, clenching his jaw so tightly that a tiny muscle twitched. "There has to be a way. If they take her to that farm— You know the danger as well as I do."

"I know. Do you think I didn't try? I suggested moving Esther to a rehab facility, thinking that would be easier to protect. Rebecca won't consider it. I know her. She might seem like a quiet, submissive woman, but she has a will of iron where her family is concerned. But she did agree to one concession."

"What?" He glowered, obviously not liking the feeling that he couldn't control events.

"She'll let me stay at the farm with Esther."

For a long moment he stared at her. Then—"No." And he turned away.

"I'm not asking for your permission, Adam. Rebecca will take Esther home as soon as the hospital will let her go. You know perfectly well they won't allow us to place a guard at the farm. If I'm there, I can call for help at a moment's notice."

"Esther shouldn't be moved from the hospital, and if her family won't listen to reason, then I'll find someone who will." He stalked across the room, frustration in every line of his body.

"What are you going to do?" She was almost afraid of the answer.

"Talk to the doctors, the hospital administrator, maybe the district attorney. There has to be someone who can stop this."

"Adam..." But he was already gone.

CHAPTER TWELVE

BY EVENING, Libby was ready to fall asleep where she stood, but she couldn't. She'd used every excuse she could come up with to avoid telling her mother about her job. Now she also had to tell her about the move to the Zook farmhouse. It was time to clear the air entirely.

She drifted into the family room, her mother's favorite relaxing spot in the house. Looking around the comfortable room, Libby realized why the patient lounge had seemed so familiar.

Mom was curled in a corner of the couch, frowning at the knitting pattern she was following. Never just relaxing, of course. She always had to be doing something.

Libby sat down next to her. "I was in the patient lounge at the hospital today. I didn't realize you had donated it in Daddy's honor."

Mom let the knitting fall to her lap. With her blue jeans and oversize man's sweater, she looked like a child playing dress-up.

"Oh, it wasn't anything. But you should have seen what it looked like before. Institutional green walls and motel modern furniture." She wrinkled up her nose. "I think it's a bit less depressing now."

"It's lovely. Very welcoming," Libby assured her. "It reminds me of this room."

Her mother nodded, glancing around at overstuffed chintz and aged wood. "I hope so. This was your father's favorite room in the house. I think he'd be pleased."

Libby tried to speak around the lump in her throat. "Why didn't you tell us about it?"

Her mother shrugged. "You know how your father felt about charity. Never let the right hand know what the left hand is doing. But in this case, the hospital board insisted on the sign."

"Dad would have loved it, even with the plaque," she said. She cleared her throat. "There's something I've been meaning to tell you since I got home."

"You mean about quitting your job?" Mom said.

"Who blabbed? Did Adam tell you—" She stopped. She was giving too much away, revealing that she'd confided in Adam.

Her mother's eyes brightened, as if she'd heard good news. "Well, what else could it be? You've stayed here much longer than you intended already, and you haven't said anything about asking your boss for more time off. You haven't mentioned the paper once. Just because you always picked your father to confide in doesn't mean that I've lost my mother's intuition where you're concerned."

Libby blinked. "I didn't...I didn't intend to make you feel left out."

Mom patted her hand. "I admit, I felt that sometimes. But Blake was such a good father. How could I wish to change that?"

"He was, wasn't he?" Tears filled her eyes.

"Good husband, good father, good man." Her mother wiped away a tear of her own. "How he'd laugh at us for sitting here crying over that!"

For a moment Libby could almost hear that hearty laugh, and it seemed to pierce her heart.

"I know. We won't stop missing him," her mother said softly.

"Yes, well." Libby mopped her eyes. "About the job… maybe it had been coming on for a long time. Too many pictures of car wrecks and fires and shooting victims."

Her mother clasped her hand. "That must have been especially hard for you. You've always been so sensitive to other people's feelings."

You're like your mother, Rebecca had said. Maybe she was right.

"It all came to a head when the paper published a photo of a grieving mother. I'd asked them not to use that one. It was too intrusive. The editor told me I'd have to toughen up if I wanted to succeed. I decided that price was too steep." She took a breath, realizing that a weight had lifted from her shoulders. "So here I am, ready to start over if I can just figure out what I'm meant to do."

"Darling, you don't have to decide right away, do you? I'd love to have you here forever."

"I'll stay for a good long visit," she said, evading the question of her future. "But first, I have to move over to the Zook farm for a while, to help take care of Esther."

Mom drew back, blue eyes troubled. "They're sending her home already? But isn't that dangerous? If there is someone after her—"

"I know. I tried to change Rebecca's mind, but she wouldn't hear of moving Esther to a rehab facility. She's convinced Esther will do better at home."

"That might be true," her mother admitted. "She's used to being surrounded by her family's love and support. But she has to be kept safe."

"Yes. They wouldn't agree to have someone on guard at the farm. But Rebecca did say that I could stay. You understand, don't you? Adam thought you would try to stop me, but I knew it was what you'd do in my place."

Her mother pressed her lips together, as if holding back her first impulse. "You think you've outsmarted me, don't you?"

Libby couldn't help but smile. Mom always could see right through the three of them. "Did it work?"

Mom sighed. "I have to admit, it's easier to do something yourself than to let someone you love go into danger. But I understand why you have to do this."

"Good." It was a relief not to have to argue about it.

"I'll come over and spell you anytime you want," her mother said. "The crucial thing is that someone be there with Esther all the time, right? And to have a cell phone, of course."

Libby squeezed her mother's hand. "I knew you'd jump right in."

"And that's what you told Adam, I suppose." Mom said the words with such studied casualness that Libby went instantly on the alert.

"More or less," she said cautiously. "He was… Well, naturally he wanted them to keep Esther where he could guard her."

"You've been seeing a lot of Adam, haven't you? He's a good man."

"He is." That quiet comment broke through her reserve. "Everyone knows that. But he's got it in his head that just because of his background, he's not good enough for…well, for…" She let that trail off, because it wasn't going anywhere.

"Oh, honey." Geneva's voice filled with pain. "I had no idea that was still bothering him. He's proved himself a hundred times over. Doesn't he know that?"

"That's not how he sees it." She tried to collect herself. She was giving too much away, and she didn't want Mom thinking she had a broken heart, in addition to everything else.

"He never touches a drop of alcohol, you know." Mom seemed to be looking back through the years. "Determined not to be like his father. That man—" Her lips pursed. "Well, if I had it in me to hate anyone, it would be him. Keeping that child practically in rags and beating him, too. And the mother didn't do a thing to prevent it."

A chill snaked down Libby's spine. "Why didn't child welfare take him away?"

"People weren't as aware of abuse then as they are now. And Adam always denied it, out of some kind of pride, I think. Well, the beatings stopped after your father intervened, though I don't suppose the rest of it was much better."

"What did Dad do?" She'd been younger. That must be why she hadn't been aware of much.

"Adam and Trey were playing in the creek one day, and they'd taken their shirts off. Your father saw the bruises. He came into the house looking…well, I'd never seen him look like that before. He went off without a word, and when he came back, all he'd say was that Adam's father wouldn't lay a hand on him again."

It was a fascinating look at her calm, even-tempered father, but her heart ached for the little boy Adam had been. "I remember that he was around here a lot. I just took him for granted, like another brother."

"We did our best, but he had his pride. We'd have sent him to college, but he wouldn't accept. He insisted on joining the Marines, and he did very well. He could have made a career out of it, but by then he'd decided on law enforcement."

"Why here?" Her heart was sore from the pummeling it was taking. "You'd think he'd want to live anywhere else in the world."

"That pride of his, I suppose," her mother said. "It was as if he had to prove himself to the very people who'd looked down on him as a kid. And we were here, the nearest thing to a family he had." Mom looked at her, a question in her eyes. "Does that help you?"

"I understand a little better, I guess."

"You love him," Mom said softly.

"Yes. I guess I never outgrew that." She tried to say it lightly, but failed.

"Maybe if I talk to him…" her mother began.

"No." Libby caught her hand. "I know you want to fix this." The echo of Rebecca's words resounded. "But you can't. This is between Adam and me. And if we can't overcome it...well, I guess I'll have to live with that."

"YOU CAN'T BE SERIOUS." Judge Judith Waller, black robe open to reveal the sensible suit underneath, shook her head at Adam. "Adam Byler, I thought you had more sense than that."

Adam had caught Judge Waller in the courthouse corridor between hearings. Plump, past middle age, with a no-nonsense manner and shrewd eyes behind her glasses, she looked like a grandmother who'd be more at home baking cookies than in a courtroom, dispensing justice.

"I know it's irregular—" he began.

"It's more than irregular, it's disastrous. In the first place, issuing an injunction to prevent an Amish family from taking their daughter home to care for would bring the ACLU down on us in about sixty seconds. Besides which, it would earn the enmity of half the county. No thanks. Judges are elected, you know."

"I just want to keep Esther Zook safe until we find out the truth about the hit-and-run."

Appealing to the judge had been a desperate act, but Adam felt desperate. He'd spent the better part of two days trying to find a solution, and he'd failed. Esther would be going home today, and Libby was going with her. Once that happened, he wouldn't be able to protect either of them.

"And what if you never do solve it?" Those shrewd

eyes impaled him. "The way I hear it, your case has fizzled out. You can't protect Esther for the rest of her life."

"If I had a little more time..." But he honestly didn't know what he'd do that he hadn't already done, to no avail.

"You've done your duty," she said, her expression softening. "Just get on with things and stop beating your head against a stone wall. That's my advice, but I don't suppose you'll take it."

"I don't drop a case just because it's difficult." He was reminded of Jason Smalley. He still hadn't found out what Smalley's interest in all this was.

Judge Waller began walking again. "The young are always so idealistic. I wouldn't change that." She paused. "And some not so young, like Geneva Morgan." She chuckled. "Well, I wouldn't change Geneva, either, for all the world. But you mind you don't run yourself into trouble, Adam. You've got a career to think of."

She turned into the courtroom, leaving him standing in the hall wondering.

Well, he couldn't just stand here. He glanced at his watch. If he were going to catch Libby before they left the hospital, he'd best get moving.

Libby. He managed to forget her for as long as it took to get his car out of the parking lot and pull into traffic. What could he say to her that he hadn't already said?

She was going to do this thing. When he'd appealed to Geneva, she'd made it clear that she was helping Libby. He should have known that. He had good reason to know what kind of person Geneva was, and it seemed Libby was turning out more like her mother every day.

Funny, how families worked out. Not that he had any basis for comparison. But when they were young, Libby had definitely been her daddy's girl. His little princess. Trey had admired his father and confided in his mother, and Link…well, Link had bounced back and forth between his parents, depending on what mischief he was in at the moment.

The first time he'd gone home with Trey, he'd honestly thought the Morgan family was putting on some kind of an act. But he'd been there often enough to see that it was real. Sensible boundaries, punishment that fit the offense, and an undergirding of unconditional love.

Thanks to them, he knew what family life could be like.

He reached the circular drive at the hospital entrance in time to see a wheelchair-accessible van draw up at the curb where a small group waited—Esther in a wheelchair with an orderly in attendance, Rebecca and Libby. The passenger door opened, and Geneva jumped down. Of course she'd have been the one to arrange this.

Leaving the patrol car behind the van, he got out. By the time he rounded the car to the walk, Libby had come to meet him.

"You're not going to distress Rebecca with any more dire warnings, are you?"

In her bright red anorak, jeans and boots, Libby looked more ready to go sledding than to take up residence at an

Amish farm. Still, when it came to Libby, the Zook family knew what they were getting.

"I won't upset anyone. I tried everything I could think of to stop this, but I failed, just like you said I would."

Blue eyes, so like her mother's, surveyed him. "I don't think I said anything about failing. I said we didn't have any options but this one."

He shrugged. "Same difference. I understand your mother is aiding and abetting you." He glanced toward the van, where the attendant was lowering the platform under Geneva's supervision.

"Did you doubt it?" Libby smiled, the dimple at the corner of her lips showing. "Mom never saw a lame duck she didn't have to help."

"Like me, you mean." It was rubbing salt in the wound, but he couldn't seem to stop himself.

"Don't be ridiculous," Libby snapped. "If you can't talk anything but nonsense, you'd better go away."

He had to smile. Dealing with Libby in a temper was like handling dynamite. He'd better watch his step.

"Okay, no more nonsense," he said. "What are your plans for keeping your cell phone charged? You can't rely on it if your battery is going to go dead just when you need it."

"Two cell phones," she said. "Someone will stop by every day to trade off and recharge the other one. You thought I wouldn't have an answer to that, didn't you? I probably could recharge it from the generator in the barn, but I thought that might annoy Esther's brother."

"Just wanted to be sure." He looked down at her, his

heart twisting at the thought of her in danger. "I want your promise that you'll call at the first sign of something not right. Do not investigate on your own."

"I know, I know." She started to turn away, impatient, and he grabbed her wrist, feeling her pulse pound against his palm.

"I mean it, Libby. No matter how slight it seems, you call me. I'll check it out. Remember that if you're out of commission, Esther is unprotected."

That sobered her, as he'd thought it would.

"All right. I promise."

"Good. And we need a way to check in on a regular basis without alarming the family."

"I don't think that's necessary..." she began.

He swept on as if she hadn't spoken. "I'll wait for you in the stable every evening from eight to nine. Make some excuse to go out in the evening. You need some air, you want to feed the horses a lump of sugar, anything. Just be there."

"You can't do that, Adam. Do you think they're not going to notice a police car pulling into their lane?"

"It won't be a police car, and it won't be in the lane." He'd already thought this out. "I'll use my own car, and I'll leave it out on that old timbering road that runs through the woods. I can walk across from the woods to the stable. It's plenty dark by that hour, and you know how isolated the Zook farm is. The closest neighbor is a half mile down the road. With no outside lights, there's not a chance anyone will see me."

For once Libby didn't plunge into argument. She just looked at him for a long moment. Then she nodded.

"All right. But I might not be able to get out every night, depending on what's going on with Esther."

"I'll wait from eight to nine. Come if you can."

"You're going to freeze out there." Laughter lurked in her eyes despite the seriousness of the situation.

"No more than I deserve for letting you be there. If Trey knew about this, he'd knock my block off."

"Trey couldn't stop me, any more than you can." She glanced to the van, loaded now. "I have to go. I'll try to see you tonight."

"Don't try." His fingers tightened on her wrist. "Do it."

She pulled her hand free. "I'll try," she said, and hurried back to the van.

He jumped in the patrol car and pulled out after the van. They might keep him off the Zook farm, but no one could stop him from seeing them safely there. After that… well, after that it was up to Libby.

He had to admit, despite the hard time he'd been giving her over this, that Libby had been right. This was the only way. And if anyone could do it, Libby could.

CHAPTER THIRTEEN

ARRIVING AT THE Zook farm was like stepping back in time, with the white frame two-story farmhouse sitting well back from its gravel lane, none of the ubiquitous power lines or telephone cables running to it. The fresh coating of snow they'd gotten this morning had dusted the fields with white, and despite the fact that it was only three, the shadows were lengthening.

The van came to a halt at the back door, reminding Libby that country people seldom used the front entrance. She felt as if she were seeing the farm with double vision—the child she'd been, to whom it had been so familiar, and the woman who was nearly a stranger.

Isaac was waiting, and the moment the van door slid open, he began a conversation in Pennsylvania Dutch about how best to transfer Esther.

It took a moment of listening before Libby realized that she actually understood much of what they said. A few weeks ago she'd have said she'd forgotten every word of the Pennsylvania Dutch she'd known as a child. Now, after hearing it spoken nearly every day, the dialect was coming back.

Esther looked exhausted from the trip, and the first thing to do was to get her settled. The daadi haus, a wing of the farmhouse built to house the grandparents when the younger couple took over running the farm, stood at right angles to the main part of the house, conveniently near the lane. Since her father's death, Esther lived there with her mother.

Libby held her breath when the wheelchair was lowered from the van. Esther drooped in the chair, her face white. She blinked against the light of a watery sun reflecting from the snow. Getting her to her bed suddenly seemed an enormous job.

Isaac, at a word from Mary Ann, simply bent and scooped his sister up in his arms, blanket and all. In a few quick strides he was at the daadi haus door. One of his children held it open, and he swept inside.

Rebecca and Mary Ann scurried after him with murmured thanks to Libby's mother and the van driver.

Libby pulled out her suitcase and hugged her mother. "Thanks, Mom. I'll talk to you soon."

Her mother kissed her cheek. "This is a good thing you're doing, dear. Either Marisa or I will be here tomorrow afternoon to swap the phones. Be careful."

"I will." She'd need to be, if they were right about the danger to Esther. She went to the door, held open by a small girl who was a miniature replica of Mary Ann with her soft brown hair and blue eyes.

"Thank you. Denke." She tried the Pennsylvania Dutch word, wondering if the child was old enough to be comfortable speaking English. Amish children spoke Pennsylvania Dutch at home, but began learning English in school when they were six.

The little girl gave her a shy smile, but didn't speak.

The others had gone upstairs, but Libby paused for a moment, orienting herself. The daadi haus had a kitchen and living room downstairs, with a bathroom and pantry between. The staircase was wide enough for easy access, although Esther would have to be carried if and when she came down. As frail as she was now, Isaac had handled her as if she were a feather.

Libby went up the stairs, vaguely uneasy. If she was remembering the layout of the farmhouse correctly, Isaac and Mary Ann's bedroom was on the other side of the house from the daadi haus, meaning they weren't within earshot. Nice for privacy, but not for possible emergencies.

Upstairs the two bedrooms were on opposite sides of another bathroom. Nostalgia swept over Libby as she moved into Esther's room. A hospital bed with a hand crank had replaced one of the twin beds, but otherwise, this looked just like the bedroom Esther had in the farmhouse when they were children…an oval braided rug between the beds, a sturdy oak chest, a handmade rocker, with wooden pegs along one wall to hold clothing. The doll cradle and dolls had been replaced by a businesslike desk and bookcase where Esther had undoubtedly prepared her lessons.

Libby's heart twisted. Teaching had meant so much to Esther. Would she ever be able to do it again?

Isaac retreated, having lowered his sister to the bed, and Libby hurried to help Mary Ann get her settled. She glanced at Rebecca, realizing that the woman looked nearly as exhausted as Esther.

"We must get her to rest," she murmured, and Mary Ann nodded.

"I know."

But at the moment, all of Rebecca's attention was on her daughter, and Mary Ann probably knew as well as Libby did that she wouldn't rest until she knew Esther was.

Libby spread the handmade Log Cabin quilt over Esther, and Rebecca tucked it into place. Esther touched its edge, moving her fingers along it. She smiled.

"Home," she murmured, and drifted into sleep.

If the lump in Libby's throat got any bigger, she wouldn't be able to speak. She blinked away tears.

Mary Ann put her arm around Rebecca's waist. "Komm, Mamm Rebecca," she said softly. "Esther is resting, and you must rest, too."

"Someone must stay with Esther," Rebecca protested. "And you have supper to cook."

"Folks have brought so much food that I won't have to cook for a week." Mary Ann nudged her gently toward the other bedroom.

"I'll stay with Esther," Libby said. "Please, go and rest."

Rebecca smiled faintly. "If you two girls gang up on me, I guess I must." She crossed the hall, and Libby heard her bedroom door close.

Mary Ann smiled, looking relieved. "Denke, Libby. She'll do better, now that Esther is home."

"I'm sure she will." But would Esther?

"We have an upstairs wheelchair here," Mary Ann pointed out. "And a portable toilet seat. When Isaac's daad was ill, everything was made easy for him, so I got those things back out. And I had Isaac put a twin bed downstairs, so Esther can rest there when she's well enough to go down for the day."

"You've thought of everything." Libby firmly dismissed her doubts about Esther's recovery. "You're a good sister-in-law, Mary Ann. I hope I can do as well with my brother's new wife."

Mary Ann smiled, blushing a little, and she touched Libby's arm. "I am glad you are here." She went out of the room and down the stairs, and Libby could hear her hushing the children as she went. Then a door closed, shutting off the daadi haus from the outside, and she was alone with one elderly woman and one helpless one.

Libby touched the quilt. Esther slept, more peacefully, it seemed, than she ever had in the hospital, lips still curved as if she knew where she was, even in her dreams.

Under other circumstances, Libby would agree that this was the best place for Esther to recover, surrounded by her family's love. But these were not normal circumstances.

She moved to the window, orienting herself. The outbuildings were much the same as they'd always been—dairy barn, chicken house, toolshed, twin silos, stable and a few others she couldn't immediately identify. Beyond the stable were the woods lifting to the ridge, much of which was state game land. It was beautiful and peaceful, but it was also very isolated, even though the main road wasn't that far away.

She'd have to come up with some believable reason for going out to the stable to meet Adam every evening. Tonight, at least, she wouldn't have anything to report.

Adjusting the shade, Libby moved to the rocking chair, but she felt too restless to sit. She should have thought to slip some books into her bag.

A pitcher sat on the bedside table, along with a glass and a straw, but the pitcher was empty. Mary Ann had probably intended to fill it with water. Picking it up, Libby headed softly to the stairs.

She'd nearly reached the bottom when a voice spoke. She stopped, startled, and then realized that Mary Ann and Isaac were still in the kitchen. It must have been the children she'd heard going out.

"Was ist letz?" Mary Ann asked. *What's wrong?* The words weren't intended for Libby's ears. She obviously hadn't heard Libby coming down.

Isaac said something she didn't hear. She was about to say something, but his next words came loudly enough for her to hear. To translate and understand.

"...mistake to have her here, that's certain sure. She might find out about it, and then where would we be?"

Libby froze, processing the words and the emotion that had underlaid them. There wasn't a shadow of doubt in her mind that the "she" Isaac didn't want here was herself. But what was it that she might find out about? And why did it upset him so much?

She moved silently back up the stairs. It looked as

if she'd been wrong about one thing. She would have something to tell Adam tonight. She just didn't know what it meant.

ADAM TURNED OFF the narrow blacktop road onto a gravel lane that was even narrower. As he'd told Libby he would, he drove his own dark compact, and in jeans, boots and a navy jacket he looked as far from being a cop as he could manage. He didn't plan to be seen, but if he was, at least it wouldn't look like an official call.

Slowing, Adam moved on, the lane narrowing until it wasn't much more than the logging track it had once been. The car jolted to a stop at the last space wide enough to turn around. He got out, gripping a heavy flashlight. He'd have to use the light to get through the woods, but he'd make do without it as much as possible.

The snow cover lingered in patches here and there in the woods. He skirted what he could, not particularly eager to leave an obvious trail, and brushed his way through the mix of hemlock, pine and maples and around thick clumps of undergrowth where the trees weren't thick enough to shade it out.

When he reached the narrow strip of cleared field behind the stable, he paused. The nearly full moon came out from behind a cloud, glistening on patches of snow. A yellow glow came from the windows of the farmhouse and from the second floor of the daadi haus, but otherwise there was no sign of life. It looked completely serene. He was losing his nerve, imagining danger here.

Finally, sure he couldn't be seen from the house, he

crossed to the stable, slid the door open just enough to slip inside and switched his torch on, covering the beam with his fingers so that the light leaked through.

Reassured by the quiet, he swung the light around. Several of the buggy horses moved, and one whickered softly. The huge pair of Percherons, in the farthest stalls, didn't so much as flicker an eye.

He glanced toward the house. Right on time—the back door opened, and Libby's figure in that red anorak was clearly visible. She turned, and her voice carried in the clear night. "I'll just be a few minutes." She closed the door and started across the lawn toward him, swinging a flashlight in her hand.

He stepped back a little as she entered, making sure that if anyone watched her from the window, he wouldn't be seen.

"You made it."

Libby set her flashlight down on a bale of straw and gave him a quick, preoccupied smile. "I'm here."

"You're sure no one's going to come out after you?" He glanced toward the pale, narrow rectangle that marked the opening.

"I told them I was coming out to call my mother on the cell phone. No one questioned that."

"No, I guess they wouldn't." He frowned, his worries renewed at the sight of her. "Maybe you ought to consider sleeping at home. You could just drive over during the day."

He could see the set of her jaw even in the dim light at the admittedly stupid suggestion.

"What good would that do? Night is when she's most vulnerable. But no one will get to Esther when I'm sleeping in the next bed."

Not without silencing Libby first. Didn't she realize that was what had him jumping at shadows?

"Libby—"

"Don't waste time going over that again," she interrupted. "I'm staying. Is anything new?"

He ought to have sense enough not to beat his head against a wall.

"Not much. I'm still trying to find someone who will talk about how Tom Sylvester got that zoning variance. And why Jason Smalley was so eager to see the investigation stopped."

Libby tilted her head slightly, her hair moving, pale in the dim light. "Have you considered that Jason was just trying to assert himself with you? Lord it over you a bit that he's a big deal township supervisor?" Her tone made it clear what she thought of that honor.

"No. I mean, in theory the township commissioners are responsible for the police, but in actual practice, the police department is autonomous. It wouldn't be ethical to run it any other way."

"I don't mean the police," Libby said. "I mean you personally. He's always been jealous of you."

For a moment he thought he'd heard her wrong. "Why would Jason be jealous of me?" For all his faults, Jason had had what Adam never did…a nice home, a father who put on a clean shirt and went to work every day, a mother who cooked his favorite meals.

"Because Jason was always a bully and a coward, and I don't suppose that's changed any. And because everyone knew you were..." She hesitated, as if searching for a word.

"Trouble?" he suggested. "From the wrong side of the tracks, if Springville had been big enough to have tracks?"

"No." A quick step brought her closer to him. "Honorable. We might not have known the word then, but we knew what it meant."

She'd taken his breath away, and he hadn't thought anyone could do that.

He took his time responding, afraid of what his voice might give away. "Jason still likes to throw his weight around, that's for sure. I still don't see what his interest was in this particular investigation, though."

"Neither do I," she admitted. "But I've found out something."

He raised an eyebrow in doubt, hoping she couldn't see it in the dim light. "What?"

"I overheard Isaac saying something to Mary Ann. I guess they didn't know I was there, and if they had, he probably wouldn't have realized I could understand him. But the dialect has been coming back to me, and I'm sure of this."

"You're starting to sound like your mother, talking in circles," he said. "What did Isaac say?"

And what could Esther's brother know about the situation anyway?

"Mary Ann seemed to be telling him not to worry. And

he said something to the effect of not wanting to have me here, because if I found out about *it,* I would cause trouble. Those aren't the exact words, but close enough."

"What was this 'it' that you might find out about?"

"I don't know." She sounded as if she hated to admit that. "He didn't say, but he certainly sounded worried."

"You can't imagine Isaac would have anything to do with harming his sister." He grappled with it, trying to think of a scenario that fit the words.

"No, of course not. But there's definitely something wrong. Something that's worrying Isaac, and probably Mary Ann, as well."

"Funny," he murmured.

"I don't see anything funny about it."

"Not that way. Funny peculiar. I had a talk with Bishop Amos. He gave me the impression there's some sort of problem in the Amish community. He wouldn't talk about it, but..."

"But it might concern Isaac," she finished, jumping ahead to a conclusion.

"We don't know that." He'd like to damper her enthusiasm, but he doubted that was possible.

"We don't know it yet, but I'm going to find out." She reached for the flashlight.

The determination in her voice filled him with foreboding, and he caught her hand before she could pick the torch up and run off.

"Take it easy," he said. "You can't rush in there and start prying. That would be a quick ticket out of here." Although come to think of it, that might suit him.

They stood facing each other, linked by his fingers clasping her wrist. The air seemed to thicken, pressing him closer to her.

Libby gave a quick shake of her head. "I'll be tactful," she said. She picked up the flashlight. "And careful. You don't need to tell me that."

"You took the words right out of my mouth." He tried to keep it light. He had to, because otherwise… "I'll be here tomorrow night. Meantime I'll see if I can pick up any rumors about Isaac."

"Wait until I get inside before you go." Libby moved to the door. "Isaac might be watching for me, and we don't want him to think I'm meeting a boyfriend out here."

She was gone on the words, and he watched her cross the lawn and disappear into the house.

CHAPTER FOURTEEN

THE FOLLOWING MORNING passed uneventfully for Libby, so uneventfully that she almost began to long for something to happen, no matter what. She found herself thinking of Adam too often for her peace of mind, and when she managed to push him to the back of her thoughts, she'd start worrying about the investigation.

Enough, she scolded herself. She had to learn to immerse herself in the activity of the moment, the way the Amish did. Right now, that activity was brushing Esther's hair gently, avoiding the injured area, and putting in the loose braid she'd worn since the accident.

"The physical therapist will be here soon." Libby realized she'd been quiet too long. They all made an effort to talk to Esther as much as possible. "I'd better get your hair finished."

Esther caught at her hand, frowning a little as she struggled to form a word. "Dress," she said finally. She pointed to the wooden pegs on which her clothing hung. "Dress."

"That's right," Mary Ann said, coming in just in time to hear and exchanging pleased smiles with Libby. Every new word was an occasion to celebrate.

But Esther shook her head impatiently. She tugged at

the nightgown she wore. "Dress," she said firmly, leaving no doubt as to what she meant.

Libby grinned. "Okay, okay, we get it. You want to be properly dressed when the therapist gets here."

It was easier said than done, since Esther still didn't have much control of one side, but with the three of them working, they managed. Until they reached the straight pins that fastened the front of an Amish woman's dress.

Esther's fingers didn't work well enough, Libby had never done it, and Mary Ann, who could do it in seconds on her own dress, was all thumbs trying to do someone else's. All three of them were weak with laughter when they finally accomplished it.

"Ach, I haven't laughed so much since I was home with my sisters," Mary Ann said, still chuckling as she placed Esther's kapp on the back of her head. "What about you, Libby?"

"I only had brothers, and usually they were trying to get me to stop pestering them." Libby held the hand mirror so that Esther could see herself. "There, you look like a proper Amish woman, see?"

Esther smiled at the image. Then she raised her hand and touched the fading bruise on her forehead. "How?"

Libby glanced at Mary Ann. It was the first time Esther had raised the subject of her injuries. They'd agreed not to bring it up until she did. Libby had had to acquiesce, even though she thought Esther might be safer if and when she did remember.

"You had an accident," Mary Ann said, her tone soothing. "You're getting better now."

Esther's frown lingered, and Libby held her breath. If she remembered—

"Hello." The therapist's cheerful voice sounded up the stairwell. "Ready for me? I'm coming up."

Esther's frown vanished, and with it probably any faint memory of what happened to her. Libby's clenched her hands in frustration. But there'd be another time. There had to be.

The physical therapist from home health services was young, cheerful and relentless. So tall his curly red hair nearly brushed the door frame of the upstairs rooms, Keith Longman combined a gentle touch with an optimistic determination to get the best from every session.

The next half hour was strenuous enough to tire all of them. At the end of it, Esther was clearly ready for a nap, but she was smiling. She had actually stood and taken a couple of steps with help.

"Excellent job." Keith handed Libby the soft balls he'd had Esther squeezing. "Add this to the routine every day. It will help with that left hand."

She nodded. "Will do. Anything else?"

"Just keep it up." His glance took in all three of them. "You're doing a great job. At this rate, Esther will be outside planting a garden come spring."

"Ach, that's gut to hear." Mary Ann spread a quilt over Esther. "Ain't so, Esther?"

But Esther's eyes were already drifting shut. Libby resigned herself to waiting for another opportunity to lead the conversation toward the accident.

"I'll walk down with you." She followed the therapist

toward the stairs, waiting until she thought they were out of earshot to continue. "Esther really is doing well, isn't she? None of us know quite what to expect from her recovery."

"Nobody knows that with head injuries," he said bluntly. "But she's doing very well physically. Much better than her physician initially thought she would. She was very fit before the accident, and that helps. And she has a great attitude and lots of support. You can't ask for much more than that."

Libby nodded. She was beginning to think Keith had more maturity than his boyish grin would indicate. "What about her mental recovery? How much might she remember?"

"About the accident, you mean?"

She nodded. She was probably being too obvious, but this was important for reasons Keith couldn't know.

"That's hard to say. Some head injury patients never recall the trauma, and maybe that's a blessing. But it could return at any time. You just have to keep reassuring her and answering any questions she asks."

She nodded, knowing she couldn't expect more than his honest opinion. "She brought it up this morning, asking how she got the bruise on her head."

"Natural enough." He reached for the door and paused, hand on the knob. "Well, she's sure got a lot of people pulling for her. Even people who aren't Amish. There was a guy at the coffee shop this morning asking how she was doing and if she remembered the accident. He seemed to know where I was coming."

Libby's heart seemed to skip a beat. "What coffee shop?"

"The one right in Springville. I was running a bit early, so I stopped for a cup of coffee." He grinned. "And a sticky bun, I confess." He patted his flat stomach.

"I don't think you need to worry." She gave the expected answer. "But this man—what did he look like?" That sounded too blunt, and she tried to qualify it. "I mean, he's probably someone we know, so I'll mention his concern to Esther."

"Youngish," Keith said. "Maybe thirty. Well dressed. Looked like a businessman, I'd say."

Jason Smalley fit that description. Of course, a few other people in Springville did, including her brothers. "What did you tell him?"

"Just something vague and polite. I don't discuss my patients. Is something going on I should know about?" His glance was suddenly shrewd.

Now it was her turn to be vague. "The accident was a hit-and-run, and the police still haven't identified the driver. It's just as well to be careful."

"Gotcha. Nobody will get anything from me." He pulled the door open. "Keep up the good work. Your friend's relying on you."

That was more serious than he realized, Libby thought, her mind busy with the ramifications of what the therapist had told her. Natural enough, she supposed, that someone in the coffee shop would assume, seeing the logo on Keith's jacket, that he was coming here. Natural enough to ask how Esther was or to express good wishes. But to ask specifically if she remembered? That wasn't quite so natural.

She went through the enclosed porch between the main house and the daadi haus, intending to let Rebecca know they were finished with the therapy. Rebecca had been happy to turn the exercises over to Libby and Mary Ann, since the prospect of pushing Esther to do more than was comfortable brought Rebecca to tears.

The door opened into a hallway off the kitchen of the farmhouse. As she closed it behind her, she heard Isaac's voice in the kitchen.

"…need the money now, not sometime in the future." He sounded…what? Not angry, exactly, but worried and somehow fretful.

"Maybe you should have listened to Esther," Rebecca said. "Maybe your sister was right about it."

Libby had reached the doorway by that time, and Isaac saw her.

He seemed to make an effort to banish the worry from his face. "So, how did the therapy go today?"

"Very well. Esther actually took a few steps with help."

"Gut, gut." Tears glistened in his eyes for a second. "That is wonderful gut, ja, Mammi?"

Rebecca had turned from the stove, wiping her hands on a towel. "Thank the gut Lord. Does she need me?" She looked ready to fly up the stairs.

"She's sleeping," Libby said quickly. She didn't want Rebecca to escape before she'd made an attempt to find out what she and Isaac had been talking about. "She was tired, so we thought it best to let her sleep. Mary Ann is with her. Maybe we can keep some lunch warm until Esther wakes. Can I help you?"

Isaac murmured something about the barn and went out. Rebecca gave her a doubtful look.

"Do you know how to make the dumplings for the chicken stew?"

"It's been a while since I've done it, but my mother insisted I learn. You'll need to remind me of the ingredient amounts."

Libby pushed her sweater sleeves to her elbows and washed her hands. Another thing her mother had taught her was that women shared confidences while they cooked together. If she wanted to get Rebecca talking, there probably wasn't a better opportunity.

With Rebecca's sometimes anxious glances over her shoulder, Libby mixed up the light dough in the earthenware bowl, the technique coming back to her as she worked. She kept talking as she did, giving Rebecca a detailed description of the therapy session.

When the stew was bubbling, she began spooning the dumplings carefully on top.

"You know, I couldn't help but hear that Isaac was worried about something when I came in," she said casually, her gaze on the dumplings.

"You understand the Pennsylvania Dutch?" Rebecca said. "Ja, I remember you did when you were a child."

"It's coming back to me." She put the lid on over the dumplings. "What did you mean, when you said that maybe Esther was right?"

"Ach, it was nothing." But Rebecca's anxious eyes and twisting hands denied her words.

Libby turned from the stove and took the older woman's hands in hers to soothe away their twisting. "It might be important. Don't you see? If something was wrong, something that troubled her, that might have something to do with the accident."

"Ach, no." Rebecca seemed startled at the thought. "No, no, it couldn't be. He wouldn't do anything like that. And he couldn't be driving a car anyway."

"Who?" Her tone was urgent. "Who, Rebecca? Please tell me what's going on. I promise I won't repeat it to anyone unless it has to do with the accident."

Rebecca seemed torn between her natural reticence and the urge to share the burden she obviously carried. Her hands twisted in Libby's grip.

"You know you can trust me," Libby said.

"Ja." Rebecca sighed. "It's a worry, but it couldn't have anything to do with the accident. You'll see."

"Just tell me." She glanced out the window, praying Isaac wouldn't come back before she'd gotten the story out of Rebecca.

"You wouldn't know Eli Bredbenner," Rebecca said. "He lives over toward Paradise. Amish, but from a different congregation. He does construction and carpentry, and he's a gut man with money, so people say."

She nodded, not sure what an Amishman from Paradise could have to do with a hit-and-run on Dahl Road, but wanting to hear it anyway.

"People wonder what's best to do with their money

these days, ain't so? Whether it's gut to expand businesses or put it in the bank or what. Anyway, Eli, he has an investment that he said he's making a lot of money from, and so some of the brothers from the church decided to invest with him."

Difficult economic times hit the Amish just as they did everyone else. To invest in something with a fellow Amishman must have seemed a logical place to put extra cash.

"So Isaac was one who invested with this man," she said.

"Ja." Rebecca seemed relieved just to have gotten her worries out. "He was supposed to start getting money back already. But Eli, he said he was having trouble with all the government rules and such, and it would be a little longer." Her forehead wrinkled. "He's Amish. We trust our brothers."

"It sounds as if Esther didn't think it was such a good idea, though."

Rebecca shook her head. "Esther tried to tell Isaac not to put his money into something he couldn't see for himself. And she asked a lot of questions when the returns didn't start coming on time. But Isaac couldn't admit that his little sister maybe knew more about it than he did." She shook her head. "I don't like to see my children fussing. And you know Esther. She's as stubborn and determined as Isaac is."

Yes, Esther was. And if she thought someone was cheating her brother, she wasn't one to sit back and let it happen.

"What exactly did they invest in?"

"Eli said it was a very nice resort place up in the mountains in Maryland. He showed us pictures of it. There's a lodge and a lot of cabins for folks to rent. A nice family place, and he said it would make a lot of money. Wait, I'll show you."

With a quick glance around, probably to be sure Isaac didn't see, Rebecca crossed to the jelly cupboard and opened one of its shallow drawers. She came back with a colorful brochure. She shoved it into Libby's hand as the outside door rattled.

"Take it," she whispered. "Don't let Isaac see. He wouldn't like me telling you."

Libby just had time to slip the folder into the waistband of her jeans and pull her sweater down over it before Isaac and the two youngest children came into the kitchen, knocking snow from their boots, cheeks ruddy with cold.

Libby edged toward the connecting door to the daadi haus as Rebecca began dishing up the chicken stew. "I'll tell Mary Ann to come down for her lunch. I can get mine later, when Esther has hers."

Isaac lifted his youngest, two-year-old Jacob, onto a chair. "You could leave Esther while she's sleeping, ja? Then you can both sit and eat."

"That's all right." She exchanged glances with Rebecca. It was useless to repeat her concern that Esther was in danger to Isaac. Convinced that was nonsense, he wouldn't listen.

"Ja, that's best," Rebecca said. "I'd be worried we

wouldn't hear Esther call if all of us were over here. Denke, Libby."

Seizing the opportunity to escape, Libby slipped out quickly. She had to make an effort not to pull out the brochure the minute she reached the daadi haus. Better not let Mary Ann see that she had it.

She hurried up the stairs, the stiff brochure sticking into her skin, and tiptoed into the room. "You go down and eat," she whispered to Mary Ann. "Isaac and the children are already at the table."

Nodding, Mary Ann went softly out, and Libby listened while her footsteps faded.

Finally she felt safe enough to pull out the brochure. Glossy, colorful and professionally printed, the first thing that struck her was how sophisticated it was. The usual advertisement for an Amish business was a fairly simple affair, not a full-color brochure.

The cover featured a photograph of a timber lodge surrounded by wooded mountains and a description of the amenities of Hidden Valley Resort that would do credit to a Madison Avenue adman. Folded open, the brochure showed cabins, a children's playground, a lake, tennis courts and swimming pool.

She had to admit, Hidden Valley looked the sort of place that should be a gold mine for its owners. So why weren't the investors seeing any return? She flipped to the back, where the owner was listed as Mountain Treasures, Inc., with an address in Frederick, Maryland. A sketch map seemed to put the resort not far from Frostburg.

Libby turned it over in her hands, wondering. If this

outfit was incorporated, there had to be records somewhere. Unfortunately, she hadn't the slightest idea how to find out.

If Trey were here, with his position as head of the family businesses, he'd know exactly how to proceed. Link? She considered her twin, but dismissed him with a shake of her head. Link ran the construction business, but his strength was engineering, not business. She'd have to hope Adam would know how to go about this.

She studied Esther's face, relaxed in sleep, every tiny line wiped away. *How would you react if I showed you this brochure, Esther? Would you remember? Tell me about it?*

Well, she couldn't risk it; that was all. Any upset might throw back Esther's progress. Until Esther started to remember on her own, she didn't feel she dared ask too many questions.

CHAPTER FIFTEEN

ADAM HEADED INTO the Springville Inn a little before noon, blinking a little as his eyes adjusted to the interior after the brightness of sunshine against the snow. With any luck, today's warm-up would melt what remained before the storm that was forecast for the weekend.

He was meeting an old high school buddy, Danny Whitman, for lunch, something he did every month or so. Danny, like Trey, was one of the handful of people who had never jumped to negative conclusions about him. Usually Trey joined them, since the three of them had been classmates. As Trey said, they could relive their glory days on the high school football field together, since no one else was interested in hearing about long-ago games.

Trey, of course, was still on his honeymoon, and whether he'd want to continue these get-togethers after marriage was up in the air. Marriage tended to change friendships, he'd noticed.

Adam headed for the coatroom to get rid of his heavy jacket. Danny was probably already here. He'd developed an alarming promptness since joining his father's real estate firm as a very junior partner. The old man, according to Danny, didn't cut his son and heir any slack in the office.

This lunch meant more than catching up with an old friend. The senior Whitman knew all there was to know about pricey real estate in Lancaster County, having handled most of it at one time or another. Maybe, through Danny as an intermediary, Whitman senior would be willing to shed some light on how Tom Sylvester had finagled his way past the zoning board. To say nothing of why he would hire Taylor as a watchman.

Adam stepped back from the coatroom door as Sandra Smalley sailed out, with Leonard a step behind her as usual. She gave Adam that arch smile she always seemed to wear when she saw him, as if to remind him she knew what he came from.

"Well, Chief Byler. Imagine running into you here."

He nodded, doing his best impassive expression. "Mrs. Smalley. Leonard. Nice day to go out to lunch."

Leonard looked like a horse about to shy. "We...we're going to the civic club luncheon."

Adam nodded, edging past them as he shrugged off his jacket.

"Nice to see we pay the police enough to lunch at the inn," Sandra said, loudly enough for him to hear as she walked off toward the private room the inn reserved for club luncheon meetings.

Adam hung up his jacket and turned, realizing that Leonard was still there.

"I'm sorry about that. Sandra doesn't know...she doesn't understand...."

Well, obviously not. Smalley could hardly tell his wife what Adam knew about him.

"No problem." He waited, wondering if that was the only thing on the man's mind.

"I just wanted to thank you again for…well, you know." Leonard sent an apprehensive glance after his wife. "I owe you for not talking. Anyway, you asked me about Jason—about why he'd want to see the investigation into that hit-and-run dropped."

"Yes?" He came to alert. Was he actually going to learn something?

"I tried to bring it up casually, you know, just to see what he'd say." Leonard seemed to fumble for the words. "Jason just laughed. He said it never did any harm to do favors for influential people. He wouldn't say anything else, so I don't know who. Or if it's important. I just wanted…"

Adam was beginning to understand why Libby felt sorry for the man. "Thanks."

Leonard nodded. He darted off after his wife.

Danny waved his arm like a semaphore the minute Adam reached the restaurant archway. A born extrovert, he was probably a natural at real estate sales, even in the current market. With his open, boyish face and broad smile, he didn't look all that different than he had in high school.

"Hey, good to see you." Danny pumped his hand when he reached the table and then waved for the server. "Don't know why you have to come armed, though. It could make the clientele nervous."

"The weapon goes with the uniform," he said easily, never bothered by Danny's comments. Insulting each other was part of the ritual.

"Uniform, is that what it is? Doesn't the township budget extend to anything better-looking than that?"

"Better than that junior executive look you're going for," Adam said, studying the menu and settling, as usual, for a steak sandwich. "Did your father pick out that tie for you?"

"The old man has one just like it," Danny said complacently. "He likes to see me wear it. Makes him stop moaning about how I'm going to ruin the business. For a day or two, at least."

The server came to take their orders. When she'd left, Adam figured he'd better get to the subject on his mind before Danny got off on one of his frequent tangents.

"You being such a big shot in the real estate world, I thought you might be able to help me with something."

"Sure thing. You finally going to settle down? Looking for a vine-covered cottage with a white picket fence? Or a Spanish-style rancher?"

"Neither," he said. "And I'm not settling down. I need to get some behind-the-scenes info in regard to real estate."

"Well, it's the old man who knows where all the bodies are buried, but he doesn't talk easily. That's probably the secret to his success. He says I shoot my mouth off too much ever to make it, and he just might be right. What do you want to know?"

"Tom Sylvester," he said promptly. "And that parcel of land where he's building a new hotel."

Danny brightened. "Actually, you've hit upon one deal where I know something. See, I had my eye on that piece of property for a client who wants to build a house near Springville. So when the owner passed away, I went snooping around."

"You reduced to studying the obituary pages for business?" Adam couldn't help the crack.

"Shut up," Danny said. "So, anyway, it turns out the old guy who died was the maternal uncle of Tom Sylvester's wife. And everyone knew they were retiring to Florida, so I figured she'd be putting it on the market. Turned out I was wrong. Tom said his wife wasn't interested in selling, and they were thinking of putting up a little hotel there. A retirement hobby, he said."

"And what did you say?" Adam asked, sure a disappointed Danny would have had some colorful remarks.

"Told him he was nuts," Danny said promptly. "That it was zoned farming/residential, and he'd never in this world get a variance granted. So anyway, it turns out the laugh was on me, because next thing I knew, that hotel was going up. But it's no mom-and-pop operation, for sure. I couldn't believe the zoning board let that go through. Quick and quiet, that's for sure."

"So why did they? Influence?"

"Influence, definitely," Danny said. "But not from Sylvester. He's a nice guy, but he doesn't have that kind of clout. Somebody must have gone to bat for him."

"Any ideas floating around as to who that someone might be?"

Danny looked faintly embarrassed. "To tell the truth, some people think it was the Morgan family. After all, Sylvester ran their construction firm for a lifetime or so."

"It wasn't." It had never occurred to him that people were saying that.

"I'll take your word for it, but if that's the case, I don't have a clue as to who the person doing the pushing was. But I might know who the pushee on the zoning board was." He dropped the bombshell casually.

"Who? And how do you know?" He shot the questions, leaning across the table.

"Frank Albright." Danny came out with the name as if he was sure.

"Coach Albright?"

Adam frowned. Frank Albright had been their football coach, and Adam had always considered him one of the most ethical people he'd ever met. His boys would have done anything for him, and he never accepted less than their best. He was principal of the high school now, still a public-spirited guy, volunteering for various drives and charity events as well as serving on the zoning board.

"Right. Coach." Danny's expression was that of someone who didn't like what he was saying.

"What makes you think it was Albright?" He couldn't help the skepticism in his voice.

Danny shrugged. "I can't prove it. But a few of us were in here one night after a basketball game, just shooting the breeze, and somebody started ragging on the zoning board for passing that variance. You know Albright. Usually he never turns a hair—probably comes from all those years of dealing with high school kids. But this time he lost it. Very defensive. Too defensive."

"Maybe he thought you guys were out of line."

Danny flushed at Adam's doubtful look. "Listen, Owen will back me up." He reached out and waved at Owen Barclay, the inn's manager, who was making his usual round of the lunch crowd. "Hey, Owen, come here a minute."

"Don't..." Adam began, but it was too late.

Owen had already reached their table.

"I hope your lunch was to your liking," Owen said, as gracious as if he'd cooked it just for them.

"Fine, fine." Danny brushed aside the pleasantries. "Listen, Owen, remember that night we were talking about the zoning board decision on that hotel of Tom Sylvester's?"

"Lower your voice," Adam muttered. "You don't need to tell the whole dining room." Why had he thought he could talk about something discreetly with Danny?

Owen, with a glance of sympathy, sat down. "Adam's right," he said. "Let's not advertise it when we're talking about someone."

"Yeah, right." Danny didn't look impressed. "I was just telling Adam that Frank Albright got really defensive about that decision, and it made all of us wonder what he had to do with it."

Owen glanced at Adam, a question in his eyes. "Is this a police matter?" His voice had lowered even more.

"Not exactly," Adam admitted. "It came up in connection with something else, and I'd like to clear it out of the way."

Owen nodded as if he understood, which was more than Adam did himself. "I don't know anything definite, but one does hear rumors." He smiled suddenly. "At least ninety percent of which are nonsense, of course. But I'd have to agree with Danny on this. Frank did seem a bit overheated on the subject." He shrugged, spreading his hands. "I'm not suggesting anything crooked, you understand. But sometimes people will let their decisions be influenced by others."

"Any idea who those others might be?" Adam asked.

Owen shook his head, rising. "Not at all." His tone suggested that if he did, he wouldn't say so. "I have to get back to work. By the way, I suppose you know Libby is staying over at the Zooks' place, helping with Esther. She's certainly a good friend."

Adam tried not to let any expression show in his voice. Owen was implying he was in on Libby's plans, no doubt trying to needle him. He'd probably given away too much that day they'd both been in Owen's office.

"Yes, she is a good friend." He'd like to be able to say that Libby was someplace far, far away.

No, he wouldn't. He wanted her right here. Safe. With him.

He wasn't starting to think that was possible, was he?

A SMALL DISPUTE among the Zook family developed after lunch. Mary Ann wanted to take advantage of the sunny day to go to Springville for groceries, taking five-year-old Elizabeth, and she wanted her mother-in-law to go, as well.

"Komm, please, Mamm Rebecca," she coaxed, helping her small daughter tie her black bonnet. "It will do you gut to have an outing. Libby and Isaac will both be here to see to things."

"We'll be fine," Libby said. "If I leave the doors open, I can easily hear it if Baby Jacob wakes from his nap before you get back."

"Ja, and I'll chust be out in the stable while Bishop Amos shoes the other horses." Isaac added his voice to the rest. "You need to get out a bit, Mamm."

"If you're sure you don't mind..." Rebecca looked at Libby. It was obvious that she'd enjoy the outing and probably the return to a normal routine.

"Go, or you'll make me think you don't trust me," Libby said.

Mary Ann didn't waste any time at that sign of weakening. She had her mother-in-law hustled into her coat and bonnet and out to the buggy before Rebecca could change her mind.

"Denke, Libby." Isaac hesitated at the kitchen door, almost as if he wanted to say something more.

Libby studied his face, the blue eyes so like his sister's, the beard that hid his chin. *What are you holding back, Isaac? Tell me.*

He pulled on gloves. "Chust shout if you need me. Or ring the bell outside the door." Not waiting for a response, he went out.

Strange, to be so alone in a house that was normally bustling with activity. It gave her the chance to do one thing she wouldn't want anyone to see.

Libby went straight to the drawer from which Rebecca had taken the investment brochure. There must be more paperwork about the project somewhere, if Isaac had invested money in it. She slid the drawer open.

Apparently this was the storage space for such papers as the Zook family might need. It held several manila folders, all neatly labeled in what she recognized as Esther's hand. Dairy company agreement, tax records, children's medical records, bank receipts. And one labeled Investments.

Libby slipped the file out and flipped it open with only a passing pang of guilt. If this contained a clue to what had happened to Esther, she wouldn't let anything stop her from investigating.

The folder contained only two things: a prospectus on the investment and Isaac's investment agreement. She whistled under her breath at the amount. The dairy farm must be doing better than she'd expected, and it was probably an amount Isaac could now ill-afford to lose, with Esther's hospital bills looming. No wonder he seemed worried.

She started to look through the prospectus and realized another paper had been stuck inside. It was a letter dated December 3, addressed to "Dear Shareholder." In it, Eli Bredbenner apologized for the delay in delivering the returns he'd promised, blaming endless delays with the government paperwork necessary for setting up the corporation. He asked for patience, insisting that shareholders would begin to see a return on their money by spring, at the latest.

Libby turned the paper over in her hands. The letter was obviously computer-generated, and again she had the sense of some sophistication at work that she wouldn't have expected.

A sound from outside drew her attention to the window. A buggy was coming down the lane. Quickly she jotted down the particulars from the prospectus on a notepad from the counter, ripped it off, and shoved it into her jeans pocket. She could hear the creak of harness now and the clop of hooves. Shoving papers back into the file, she slid it into the drawer and closed it just as someone knocked at the door.

Breath coming quickly, Libby smoothed her sweater down over the pocket and opened the door. An Amish couple stood there, the woman with a basket over her arm.

She managed a smile. "Are you here to see Isaac and Mary Ann? Mary Ann is out, I'm afraid, but Isaac is in the stable."

The man nodded. "Ja, I see Bishop Amos's buggy parked there. We have komm to ask about Esther. You are Libby Morgan, her Englisch friend, ja?"

"I am." She held on to the door, not certain whether she should invite them in or not. "I'm sure Mary Ann will be sorry she missed you."

"My wife has brought pies for the family." The man put his hand on the door. "Mary, chust put them on the counter."

Before Libby quite knew how it happened, they were both inside the kitchen. The woman set her basket on the table and lifted out two pies, moving them to the counter.

"That's lovely," Libby said. The pies were works of art, perfectly browned and crisp-looking, with an intricate flower design forming the top crust vent. "Who shall I say brought them?"

The wife didn't speak, but the man took off his hat, putting it on the table as if he expected to stay. "I am Eli Bredbenner, and this is my wife, Mary."

That was almost too coincidental, to have them show up so promptly after most of the family had left. Or maybe it wasn't coincidence at all. Maybe Bredbenner had planned it that way.

"It's nice to meet you." *Interesting* might be a better word, Libby realized.

So this was the Amish investment broker. He looked like any other Amish man she might see in town, wearing traditional black clothing. His beard was almost chestnut in color, full and bushy in contrast to his bald head. He was probably in his fifties, at a guess. His wife, pale and thin-faced, seemed intent on fading into the woodwork.

"We were pleased to hear that Esther was well enough to be out of the hospital already. When we heard, my wife insisted that we must visit and bring some of her pies. Esther especially enjoys them, and we wanted to celebrate her homecoming. How is she feeling?"

It was a good thing she recognized a snow job when she saw it, Libby decided. Bredbenner obviously wanted something, but what was it?

"Esther is doing better physically, the doctor says. The family is so pleased to have her at home."

"And she is herself again?" His gaze seemed to probe Libby's face. "Back to talking with the family, remembering things?"

Remembering...the question everyone seemed to be asking.

What would he do if she asked him directly about the investment scheme? Or if she implied that Esther remembered everything about her accident?

She couldn't. It wouldn't be safe. A cold knot formed in Libby's stomach. She was alone in the house with a sleeping toddler and a helpless woman. Isaac and presumably Bishop Amos were only as far away as the stable, but Eli Bredbenner stood between her and the back door, with the bell rope that hung right beside it.

"I'm afraid Esther doesn't remember or communicate."

She almost said "yet" and deleted it. Eli Bredbenner might be nothing more than an inept businessman who'd bitten off more than he could chew, but she wasn't taking any chances.

"Too bad," he said. "We would like to see her now, ja?"

Libby's gaze flickered to the daadi haus door before she could stop it.

"I'm afraid not," she said quickly. "She's not seeing anyone but family."

"But you are not family," he pointed out.

"I'm only here to help with Esther." She moved, positioning herself between them and the daadi haus door.

"But we are such old friends." He took a step toward her. "She will want to see us."

Libby stood her ground, but her heart was thudding uncomfortably. "I'm afraid not. It wouldn't be appropriate for me to let you see her when the family's not here."

"My wife can slip up for a moment." Bredbenner caught his wife's arm, pushing her forward. She certainly didn't look as if she had any need to see Esther.

"Esther is sleeping. She can't be disturbed." An icy trickle fluttered down her spine. What would she do if he tried to walk right past her?

Bredbenner took a step closer, his smile seemingly forgotten on his face. Libby froze, fists clenched. It was one thing to practice self-defense moves in a gym and another to anticipate using them on someone in a quiet Amish kitchen.

The back door opened, and Bishop Amos walked in, wiping his boots carefully on the rag rug, and the tension in the room dissipated into nothingness.

"Ah, Libby, there you are. Isaac said there might be some coffee on the stove for me." He nodded gravely to the other two. "Eli. Mary. Have you come to call?"

"Ja, but this Englischer won't let us see our sister Esther." Bredbenner spoke in the dialect, but Libby had no trouble understanding.

"Ach, Libby is the nurse, and we must mind what she says," Bishop Amos said in English, his tone cheerful. "We will tell Rebecca that you came to call."

Bredbenner stood for a moment, his face stiff. Bishop

Amos never lost his smile, but something inflexible appeared in his face.

Bredbenner shrugged, taking a step back. “Ja, denke. Tell her that we wish her well in her recovery. Komm, Mary. We must go.”

Shepherding his wife ahead of him, Bredbenner went out the back door. Libby let out a breath she hadn’t realized she’d been holding and met Bishop Amos’s gaze.

“I’m glad you came in when you did. He didn’t want to take my word for it that Esther was sleeping.”

Bishop Amos’s expression was unreadable. “Esther is fortunate to have such a loyal watchdog on duty, ja? I am glad that you are here, Libby Morgan.”

CHAPTER SIXTEEN

LIBBY COUNTED THE minutes until eight o'clock. If Adam didn't turn up tonight…

He would. She didn't really doubt that. However much he might disapprove of her actions, he wouldn't let her down.

She stepped into the enclosed porch, zipping her jacket. She patted her pocket, making sure the brochure and her notes were there. As she reached for the flashlight that hung from a nail, the door into the farmhouse opened. Isaac stood there, and she stiffened.

But he didn't seem to be wearing his usual disapproving frown when he looked at her. "You are going out to call your mamm, ain't so?"

Libby nodded. She held up her cell phone. Thank heaven she'd thought to slip it in her pocket. "I promised I'd be in touch every evening."

"That's gut. I…I think that you are going outside to call because I would not like the use of the phone in the house." He seemed to struggle with what he wanted to say. "You are Esther's friend. If you want to use your phone in the house, I do not object."

For a moment Libby didn't know what to say. From Isaac, this was a huge concession.

And all the while, she was lying to him by her actions. Saying she was doing it for Esther's sake didn't make her feel any better about it.

"Thank you, Isaac. That's very kind of you. But I—" She glanced at the phone, still in her hand. "For some reason, I get better reception outside, anyway. But thank you."

Managing a smile, she hurried out before she had to tell any more lies. She had no choice. But that didn't make her feel any better.

Clouds had thickened, and a chill wind snapped at her cheeks. She'd really need the flashlight tonight. She headed across the yard.

Be there, Adam. I don't want to carry this information alone any longer.

The stable door stood open a few inches. Isaac wouldn't have left it that way, so Adam must be here.

Libby slid through the gap, swinging the beam of the flashlight around. "Adam? Are you here?"

A step sounded behind her, too close. She whirled, raising the flashlight as a weapon.

"Easy." Adam caught her hand. "It's me."

Libby took a shaky breath. "Sorry. I guess I'm a bit jittery."

"A bit?" He took the flashlight and set it on a straw bale. "What's going on?"

Where to start? "Do you happen to know if Jason Smalley makes a habit of stopping at the coffee shop in Springville?"

"Maybe. I don't follow him around. Why?"

"Because a thirtyish guy who looked like a businessman asked Esther's physical therapist a lot of questions about her at the coffee shop this morning."

Even in the dim light, she could see Adam's eyes narrow. "Jason. That's suggestive, especially after—" He stopped.

"After what?" He was trying to hold something back from her. She knew it. "Listen, if you're going to start keeping secrets from me..."

"All right, all right." He lifted both hands palms toward her in a gesture of surrender. "I had a little chat with Jason's father today. Leonard actually tried to find out why Jason wanted the investigation stopped—maybe he feels he owes us something. Anyway, Jason's answer was that he liked doing favors for influential people. What did the therapist tell this person?"

"Just something vague. He wouldn't talk about a patient." She shook her head, trying to shake off the nagging worry. "But Esther *is* doing better. She's starting to talk. People are bound to hear about it, and that could increase the danger to her." She shivered, rubbing her arms.

"Sit down here. You're cold."

Adam drew her down onto a straw bale. Reaching up to the row of hooks above her head, he pulled down a buggy robe and tucked it around her, then sat down beside her.

The warmth she felt was from him, not the blanket. She gave in to the temptation to slide a little closer.

"If Jason Smalley is involved somehow—" She

stopped. “I just can’t imagine that. He doesn’t strike me as brave enough to do anything worth killing for.”

“No, but obviously he’s not too scrupulous about using his influence. Maybe trading favors with people.” Adam made a sound of exasperation. “Ever since that business your brothers got involved in, I’ve been looking at people differently. Who’s trading favors with each other, bending the rules in someone’s favor? It doesn’t matter to me whether they fancy it up by calling it a secret society, it’s still wrong.”

“The old boys’ network is just another version of it.” She considered. “I suppose, human nature being what it is, people are always more ready to do something for someone they think can return the favor.”

“So who is Jason Smalley doing favors for? I wonder what he’d say if I asked him that.” Adam’s voice always had that edge when he spoke of Jason.

“I don’t think you’d better,” she said. “He does have some political clout.”

Adam seemed to draw away from her, even though he didn’t actually move. “That won’t keep me from doing my job.”

“Look, I’m not arguing with you.” Adam’s unbending allegiance to the law was admirable, but she didn’t want to see him sacrifice his career to it. “I’m just saying you don’t have any evidence that he’s done something wrong. Better wait until you do.”

“Maybe you’re right.” Some of the tension seemed to ease out of him. “Guess I’m feeling a little touchy on the subject. It’s beginning to look as if Frank Albright might be the person who swayed the zoning board in Tom Sylvester's favor."

"Albright? Wasn't he your football coach in high school?" She could hardly forget that when Trey had spent four years quoting "Coach's" advice on anything and everything.

"Yeah." A muscle in Adam's jaw twitched. "If there's one person I figured was a straight arrow, it was Frank Albright. And your dad, of course."

"I'm sorry." What else could she say? "It's tough to find that your idol has feet of clay. Are you sure?"

"No." He snapped off the word. "I'm going to see him tomorrow."

He obviously wasn't looking forward to it, and she couldn't blame him. Adam would follow the trail wherever it led, even when it hurt him, because that's the kind of man he was.

"Something else happened today." She pulled the brochure and prospectus notes from her pocket. "I found out what's been troubling Isaac. He's invested a considerable sum in a building project, mainly because it's run by another Amishman, Eli Bredbenner."

"There's been a problem with it?" His interest was sharp.

"It hasn't been paying off the way Bredbenner promised. Apparently, from what Rebecca told me, a number of others from the church invested, as well as Isaac. And Esther didn't want her brother to get into it. Apparently she questioned this Bredbenner pretty intensely."

Adam adjusted the flashlight to scan the papers, not speaking.

"And if you're going to tell me that an Amish person wouldn't run an elaborate scam like this—" she began.

"Quit putting words in my mouth," he said, still focused on her notes. "I wasn't going to say anything like that. Seems to me the Amish would be particularly vulnerable to being cheated by someone they trust, especially another Amish person. Did Isaac talk to you about this?"

"No, Rebecca did. Apparently he's very sensitive about it. He certainly wouldn't be happy if he knew she'd told me. Is there any way you can investigate it?"

He nodded, stuffing the papers in his pocket. "I know a guy with the state police who's handled cases like this. I'll start with him."

"Good." She shivered again. "The way Bredbenner looked at me—"

Adam jerked around, grabbing her shoulder. "What do you mean, looked at you? You didn't go after him on your own?"

"Of course not. But he came here, he and his wife. They acted as if it was a friendly call, and they wanted to see Esther. I didn't let them." Cold snaked down her spine. "Maybe I'm overreacting, seeing menace from everyone who asks about Esther's health. But I didn't like it—"

The stable door scraped, and a light flashed on. Libby's breath caught. Isaac Zook stood there, staring at them.

"So this is what you do when you say you are talking to your mother."

It was over. Isaac would make her leave, and then Esther would have no protection.

"Isaac, I—"

Adam stood, his arm around her bringing her up, as well. He actually chuckled.

"Come on, Isaac. Don't tell me you and Mary Ann never slipped off to the barn to steal a few kisses during your rumspringa, because I wouldn't believe it." His hand tightened on her shoulder, as if compelling her to agree. "Libby and I aren't doing anything worse than that."

Isaac took a step closer, his gaze going from one to the other. "This is true, Libby?"

She slid her arm around Adam's waist. "Guilty, I'm afraid."

Isaac's face relaxed in a half grin. "Why? You two don't need to hide, do you? Now, Mary Ann's father—he figured she could do better than me."

"Mary Ann knew her own mind," Adam said easily. "As for Libby—well, she's just not ready to tell everyone about us yet."

"Ach, Adam, you could still find a better place for your sweet-hearting than a cold barn." Isaac chuckled. "I won't tell on you, but komm in soon, before you're frozen." He walked away, and she could hear his chuckle for another moment or two.

"That was close," Adam said, his lips so close to her cheek that she could feel his breath. "Looks like he believes us."

"Don't laugh. I feel like a jerk, telling lies left and

right, acting as if I…" She let that trail off, because it was coming too close to the truth.

She started to pull away, but his arm tightened, drawing her closer. "What are you doing?" She was suddenly breathless, and her heart had begun thudding.

"I wouldn't want you to feel like a liar," he murmured, and his lips found hers, catching them on a startled gasp and deepening the kiss.

For an instant she was stiff with surprise. Then she seemed to melt against him, feeling nothing but the strength of his arms around her and the warm, teasing pressure of his lips on hers.

Heat began to build between them, until she wondered how she could have thought she was cold. She wanted to yank off her jacket, press herself closer to him….

His lips moved across her cheek, leaving a trail of heat in their wake. He drew back at last, and she realized that his breath was as ragged as her own.

"Good night, Libby." His voice was husky. "Sleep well." He dropped a light kiss on her lips, turned her around and pushed her gently to the door.

THE HIGH SCHOOL parking lot was almost completely filled with cars. Teenagers were obviously better-equipped than he and Trey had been, back when Trey had driven them to school in the beat-up old sedan he'd earned the summer between their junior and senior years.

Leaving the police car at the curb, Adam headed inside, trying not to get sucked back into nostalgic memories. Classes were in progress, and he could glance into the rooms as he passed. Here was the chemistry lab, where Danny had started a fire one fine May day; there the room where Mrs. Fredericks taught Principles of Democracy to reluctant seniors.

She was still there, still wearing her gray hair pulled back in a bun. They'd thought her ancient then, but she probably wasn't more than sixty now. Even as he watched she slammed a textbook down on the desk of a kid who must be twice her size, jerking him to scared attention.

And then he was standing at the office door, feeling pretty much the way he had whenever he'd been hauled to the principal's office. A different secretary sat behind the desk now. She glanced at his uniform and waved him into the inner office.

Frank Albright looked up, grinning when he saw who his unexpected visitor was. "Adam Byler." He came around the desk, hand outstretched. "It's good to see you, son. It's been a while. Have a seat."

"Thanks, Coach." Adam didn't suppose any of Coach Albright's boys would ever call him anything else. He sat down in the chair usually reserved for parents in front of the gray metal desk.

"So what can I do for you today?" Coach sat in the swivel chair, leaning back. Light from the side window highlighted the gray in his hair and the lines in his face. "Some project you need volunteers for?"

"No, nothing like that." He couldn't sit here in front of the man he'd idolized, surrounded by plaques and photographs memorializing Coach Albright's service to the community, and seriously suspect that this man had done anything wrong. Danny and Owen must have misinterpreted his reaction.

"Not one of our kids in trouble, I hope." Albright's eyes narrowed with concern.

Adam shook his head. There was nothing to do but push on with it. "I wanted to speak to you about the zoning board. There have been some questions raised about how Tom Sylvester got that land of his rezoned."

"I see." Coach looked down at his desk, but not before Adam had recognized the uneasiness in his face.

His heart sank. "It's true, then. You had something to do with it." He thought of what Jason Smalley had said about doing favors for influential people. "Doing someone a favor, were you?"

Albright planted his elbows on the desk, studying Adam's face. "I suppose, in a way. That shocks you, doesn't it?"

He stiffened. "I never thought you were a man to make decisions out of pressure. What happened to all those ideals you used to hold up to us, like honor and dignity and self-respect?"

I modeled my life on those. That was what he wanted to say.

Albright shook his head slowly, looking tired and old without his usual smile. "You're not going to understand this, Adam. You only see things as right or wrong."

Disappointment was an acrid taste in his mouth. "I'm a cop. In the law, there is only right and wrong. I thought that was what you believed, too. That was what you taught us. Or was it just talk?"

Something that might have been pain flickered in Albright's eyes. "I taught you what I believed, but life is more than winning football games. Sometimes there are shades of gray." He shook his head impatiently. "Look, if I approve a zoning variance, nobody gets hurt. I didn't break any laws, and maybe the next time I need support for an after-school program or an extra teacher, I'll find someone willing to go to bat for it."

"Trading favors," Adam said. What had happened to the man he thought he knew?

"That's how the game is played." Coach's smile was a sad shadow of his usual confident grin. "It's not as if I'm getting anything for myself. I'm trying to do my best for the kids."

Adam wanted to turn the clock back, to return to what he'd thought he knew about Frank Albright. But he couldn't. Albright wasn't a hero, but he wasn't a villain, either. He was just a man, trying to do his best for the most people.

He tried not to let his disappointment show in his face. "What would Tom Sylvester's goodwill do for you?"

"Not Tom," he said quickly. "I wouldn't let someone who was petitioning the board influence my decision. But if an elected official calls and says the variance is a good thing that will benefit the community, I listen."

Adam wasn't even sure he wanted to know the answer, but he had to ask. "Who was it?"

Albright met his gaze for a moment, and then his eyes slid away. "Judge Judith Waller."

Adam could only stare at him. Judith Waller, that fixture of the county judicial system. Why on earth would she take such a step for Tom Sylvester?

Influence. Trading favors. The more he learned, the more confusing the situation looked. And maybe none of it had anything to do with the attack on Esther at all.

CHAPTER SEVENTEEN

ESTHER HAD COME downstairs that afternoon for the first time, and despite her worries, Libby joined in the general rejoicing. Esther's little nieces and nephews were so excited that they couldn't be still for more than an instant. At first Libby thought the children might be shy of the changes in Esther, but she soon realized they simply accepted her as she was.

Supper had been a happy meal, with the children vying to be allowed to help their aunt. Mary Ann finally stopped the wrangling by appointing the two oldest girls, Leah and Esther Jane, to sit on either side and help her.

Libby, glancing around the table at the happy faces reflected in the lamplight, couldn't help but wonder at how normal it all seemed. Anyone looking at them from outside couldn't know about the fears and worries they hid.

Once the meal was over, Isaac carried his sister into the living room, where the older children proposed to read to her from one of the *Little House on the Prairie* books, a perennial favorite with Amish children. It must be a hilarious project, judging by the laughter that echoed from the room.

Libby took a dishcloth from Rebecca's hand. "Go and

join them. I'm sure the children want you to hear them read. I'll help Mary Ann finish up the dishes."

"Ja, Mamm Rebecca, do." Mary Ann plunged a stack of plates into soapy water. "Libby and I will visit, and the dishes will soon be done."

"If you're sure..." Rebecca began.

Libby gave her a little nudge toward the living room. "Go, please."

She and Mary Ann exchanged smiles once Rebecca had hurried into the other room.

"Denke, Libby. Mamm Rebecca needs to take a little break now and then." Mary Ann set a rinsed plate on the rack.

Libby began drying, the towel making soft squeaking sounds. "She's been pushing very hard since the accident. But she looked so happy to have Esther back at the supper table."

"Ja. That was gut." Tears glistened in Mary Ann's eyes. "When we went to town yesterday, everyone we met asked how Esther was doing. I started to worry that Mamm Rebecca was too optimistic in her answers, but maybe she was right."

"She needs that optimism to help her through this, I suppose."

But all the same, Libby couldn't help a sense of apprehension at learning that Rebecca had been talking in public about how well Esther was doing. If the person who had driven the van that hit her believed Esther was well enough to remember, he might feel the need to stop her from talking.

Each time they'd attempted to convince Esther's family that she might need protection, they hadn't been willing to accept it. The refusal to allow a guard at the farm was typical. She was tempted to press the subject again, but if she pushed too hard, she might become unwelcome here.

Still, Libby had been here since Esther came home from the hospital, and nothing had happened. Two apparent attempts at the hospital, and nothing since—had the attacker been scared off? Convinced himself that she could never identify him?

What would Adam say if she asked him that? Probably he'd remind her that they didn't have hard evidence that anyone had ever been after Esther. Just lots of fears and suppositions.

She glanced at Mary Ann, realizing that she had been quiet for a long time, but Mary Ann was humming softly as she worked. Then she met Libby's gaze and smiled.

"You are thinking of your sweetheart, ain't so?"

"Isaac told you," she said, trying to buy time. She didn't want to lie to Mary Ann, who had turned into a friend.

"Ja, he told me." A smile played around Mary Ann's lips. "I wasn't surprised. I saw how Adam looked at you, those times at the hospital. And how you looked at him."

"I guess I wasn't hiding my feelings as well as I thought," she said, resting a heavy cast-iron skillet on its edge to dry it.

"It is ser hard to hide love." Mary Ann's smile was

reminiscent. "I remember. But you and Adam could tell folks. You don't want to keep things from your mamm."

"My mother knows how I feel." That was true, anyway. "But Adam is my older brother's best friend, and Trey is still away on his honeymoon."

That sounded like a feeble excuse to her, but Mary Ann nodded, seeming to accept it readily.

"You'd want to tell him before you let everyone else know," Mary Ann said. "I understand. We try not to tell folks until the wedding is published in church, but people always seem to guess, anyway."

"As you said, it's hard to hide love," Libby said, relieved to move the conversation onto Amish wedding customs.

What would Adam say if he could hear this conversation? Well, this fictitious relationship had been his brainstorm, hadn't it?

And it hadn't exactly felt fictitious when they'd kissed.

"Ach, look at the time," Mary Ann exclaimed as the last dish was put away. "I must start getting the young ones to bed."

Libby glanced at her watch. It was not quite time for Adam to show up. Would he drive openly up the lane? He might as well, given that Isaac and Mary Ann both knew of his visits. Doing so would save him a trek through the woods.

Or would he even show up, given last night's fiasco? She was suddenly restless, needing to see him yet half-afraid of how he might react. Or how she might react.

"I think I'll step outside for some air," she said, moving toward the door.

"Ja, some air would be gut," Mary Ann agreed, eyes twinkling.

Sure she was flushing, Libby reached for the hook in the hallway where she normally hung her jacket, only to discover that it wasn't there. She'd worn it upstairs when she'd come in earlier, she realized.

"What's wrong?" Mary Ann paused in the doorway.

"Nothing. I left my jacket upstairs. I'll run up—"

"Don't bother," Mary Ann said. "Chust take mine. It's hanging next to the door."

Libby grabbed the black wool coat from its hook. "Thanks. I won't be long."

"Take your time," Mary Ann said, laughter in her voice.

Well, at least she was providing Mary Ann and Isaac with some much-needed humor in a worrisome time. She shrugged into the heavy coat, buttoning it against the cold, and stepped outside.

Light snow flurries dusted the shoulders of the coat almost at once, and she flipped the hood up. What was she doing out here? It was too early. Adam wouldn't be here for another ten minutes, probably. Still, he'd been there before her each night.

She started across the lawn, the flashlight swinging in her hand. The snow wasn't heavy enough to coat the ground, frozen hard from the January cold.

Would Adam mention what had happened last night? At least he hadn't backed off and apologized after that embrace. That was a first. Maybe he was getting over this ridiculous idea of his that he wasn't good enough for her.

She slid the stable door open, leaving it ajar. One of the buggy horses whickered a welcome. They must be getting used to her nightly visits by now.

But Bess, the big Percheron, moved restlessly in her stall, hooves the size of dinner plates thudding against the boards. Libby moved toward the stall with some vague idea of quieting the animal.

"Was ist letz, Bess?" she asked, using the dialect the animal was used to, her voice soothing. She leaned against the stall door. "Hush."

Bess threw her head up, eyes white in the dim light. A board creaked. Gripping the flashlight, Libby turned.

Something struck her arm, knocking the flashlight from her grasp. Before she could react, hands closed around her throat.

For an instant panic overrode every other impulse. She clawed at the hands, frantic, trying to find enough breath to scream, but she couldn't—couldn't scream, couldn't breathe, could see only blackness shot through with red—

The horse whinnied, huge hooves shaking the floor. Her flailing hand struck the stall door—the latch—if she could pull it over—

Please, please, help me. Please...

Her fingers hooked through the latch. She slid it, pulled with her last bit of strength, feeling herself sinking, falling—

The stall door swung open, carrying her to the side with it, the attacker stumbling, the grip of her throat easing, she could breathe—she had to run before he caught her again—

The mare charged through the open stall door. A high-pitched cry shattered the night.

She scrambled to her feet, forced her shaky legs to carry her toward the pale rectangle of the door; he could be after her—

She staggered out into the night, finally finding the breath to scream, over and over.

ADAM DROVE UP the narrow lane to the Zook farmhouse. Not much sense, as far as he could see, in trudging through the woods when the whole Zook family probably knew he was coming.

Yellow light glowed from the windows of the farmhouse, but beyond it, all was dark. He stopped by the back door. Would Libby expect him to come to the stable or the house? No use wondering. He may as well go to the door.

Almost before he could get out of the car, Isaac appeared in the doorway, gesturing urgently. "Adam, komm schnell!"

Heart thudding, adrenaline soaring, he ran toward the house. Who? Esther? Libby?

He bolted into the kitchen. A figure in black slumped in a chair, fair hair spilling over the coat. For an instant he thought it was Esther, but it wasn't. Libby—

He reached her, touched her, felt warm skin, heard shaky breathing and knew she was alive. "Libby. How bad is it?"

She raised her head, tried to smile. A red lump swelled

on her forehead. Without a word, Rebecca lifted the compress she held to Libby's neck and he saw the bruises, darkening quickly—the marks of a man's hands.

"I'm all right," she murmured, voice rasping. "Don't..."

"Paramedics," he said, yanking the cell phone from his pocket.

"We have already called," Isaac said. "Our Leah knew how to use Libby's phone." He cast a glance at his oldest girl for confirmation.

"Where did it happen? Who?"

"In the stable," Isaac said. "Libby, she came running out screaming, Mary Ann and I ran out. We got her into the house."

His voice shook a little, and Adam realized that Isaac's ruddy face was pale. The women were shocked and silent, save for soothing murmurs as they tended to Libby.

Adam knelt beside Libby, taking her hand gently. "Don't try to talk, just nod. You were attacked when you went to the stable?" She'd gone to meet him, and he hadn't been there.

She nodded. "He was waiting," she murmured.

"Don't talk," he said again, wanting nothing so much as to put his arms around her and hold her close. "Do you know who it was?"

She shook her head slightly, hand going to her neck.

"Nothing that would give us an idea who it was?" He hated to persist, but time was slipping away. He ought to be securing the scene and looking for the assailant.

"No," she whispered. "Bess saved me."

He frowned. Was she out of her head?

"Bess is the Percheron mare," Isaac said. "She was clean out of the stable when we got there. I tied her outside, thinking you'd want to see things first."

Adam nodded, rising and flipping his cell phone open. Call for some help first. He couldn't do this alone. Much as he wanted to stay right here holding Libby's hand, he'd have to leave her to the women until the paramedics got here.

He called for the patrolman on duty, giving terse instructions, and then clicked off. "I need to have a look at the scene," he said.

"I will go with you." Isaac was already shrugging on his jacket.

"Good." Adam allowed himself to touch Libby's hand lightly, and then he went quickly outside, detouring to the car to turn on the headlights and grab a torch.

He and Isaac walked toward the stable, their flashlights moving, probing the darkness. He studied the ground for any signs, but now that he would welcome the snow cover, it was gone, and the iron-hard ground didn't give up any clue.

A massive white form appeared ahead of them, resolving itself into the draft horse. The animal moved restlessly, as if resenting these unprecedented interruptions in her quiet night.

"I take it this is Bess."

"Ja, we have the pair of Percherons." Isaac wouldn't want to display pride, but there was pleasure in his voice. "Libby said something about letting the mare out. She maybe did it when the man attacked her. Bess is big enough to scare anybody off."

"Maybe so." Adam shone his light over the animal, checking for signs of injury or blood, but there was nothing. "Was the door standing open like that?"

"Ja. Libby would maybe have left it open."

"Good thing." That might have meant the difference in getting away.

He stepped cautiously into the stable, stopping to swing his light around. The assailant wouldn't still be here. He'd had plenty of time to get away. In fact, he'd probably come and gone the same way Adam had the past few nights.

Nothing. Aside from the stall door hanging open, the stable appeared undisturbed. He turned back. "I don't want anything touched until my people get here with their equipment."

"But the mare—" Isaac began.

"I'm afraid she'll have to stay out until we've checked the scene thoroughly. Sorry."

Isaac nodded. "We will do as you say. I think…I fear I am at fault. I did not believe that Esther was in danger, and now see what has happened."

"I'm not sure it would have made a difference. Why did he attack Libby?" The question pounded at him. If anything, he'd have expected the assailant to try and get into the house.

"We…Mary Ann and Mamm and I…we were wondering. Talk is going around about how much better Esther is doing. She even came down for supper tonight. Anyone looking in the window could have seen."

"And thought Esther well enough to start remembering." He finished the thought.

"Ja. When Libby came out, at night, in the black coat and with her hair the same color as Esther's, maybe he thought he was attacking Esther." Isaac's voice shook on the words.

"Maybe." It made more sense than thinking the man had targeted Libby. "I didn't realize Esther was doing so well. Has she said anything about the hit-and-run?"

They had started back to the house, and he saw the rescue truck pull in, closely followed by the township's two police cars.

"She is not talking much yet," Isaac said. "She has asked about what happened to her, but she does not seem to remember it herself."

It would be too much to expect it would be that easy. And as long as the secret was locked in Esther's mind, the danger existed.

He nodded toward the paramedics, who were heading toward the house. "If you'll take care of them, I'll get my people started."

Without a word, Isaac hurried toward the paramedics. Adam resisted the desire to follow him. He had to get the stable area secured until the crime scene investigation team from the state police arrived. Had to behave as if this were just any investigation, no matter how much his instincts cried for action.

Only after Adam had seen the stable secured and

started a search of the other outbuildings did he allow himself to head back to the farmhouse. Another vehicle had joined the police cars and rescue truck in the driveway. He recognized Geneva's car. Good. It looked as if little Leah had been busy with the phone again.

He entered the kitchen to find it crowded with people. The paramedics were checking out Libby, while Geneva hovered and the Zook women busied themselves setting out coffee and shoofly pie.

Link detached himself from the group around his sister. "Did you find anything?" he asked. "Do you know who it was? What are you doing about this?"

Adam couldn't resent the rapid-fire questions. That was how he felt himself. "No sign of him. He probably ran the minute Libby started screaming."

"Thanks to Bess," Isaac said, smiling a little. Adam figured that story would get a lot of mileage in the Amish community.

"Bess?" Link said, diverted.

"Your twin apparently turned a draft horse loose on her attacker," Adam said. "Look, we're doing everything that can be done. If he left any traces at all, we'll get him."

Link's jaw tightened. "If I'd had any idea Libby's staying here would really put her in danger—"

"You wouldn't have been able to stop her," Adam pointed out.

The paramedic turned from Libby just then, and Adam caught his eye.

"Are you transporting her to the hospital?" That would be the safest place for her.

"She refuses to go." The paramedic shrugged. "And I can't really say she needs to. She's going to be mighty sore for a few days, but she'd probably be more comfortable at home than in a hospital bed."

"That's right," Geneva said. "We'll take her home and get her into her own bed."

Well, that wasn't a bad choice, as far as safety went. Link would probably sit up all night making sure no one got to his sister.

"No." The word was hardly more than a whisper, but it held a note of finality, and Libby's face wore its stubborn look. "I won't leave Esther."

"Libby, he's not going to try anything else tonight."

She glared at him. "You don't know that," she murmured.

True, he didn't. "Then let someone else stay."

"I'll stay," Geneva said. "If that's what it takes to get you home. Marisa can come and look after you."

It was obvious to everyone in the room that Geneva wanted to be doing that herself. And he didn't particularly want Geneva on guard duty, either.

"Seems to me the best answer is for me to leave an officer on guard." He turned to look at Isaac.

Reluctance mixed with the guilt in Isaac's face. The guilt was what Adam was banking on.

"Ja," Isaac said finally. "A policeman may stay."

CHAPTER EIGHTEEN

ADAM STOPPED AT Judith Waller's house the next morning, his eyes gritty from lack of sleep. He'd been up half the night, making sure every inch of the Zook property was thoroughly searched and that the officer he'd left on duty was prepared for anything.

He could have waited, caught Judge Waller at the courthouse later, but he'd decided that an informal approach was better. What he had to say to her was difficult enough without a formal setting.

The Waller house was a fine old brick Victorian on Main Street, one of a row of similar houses. Some had been turned into insurance offices and apartments, but Judge Waller still lived alone in the house that had been in her husband's family for generations.

He rang the bell and heard the sound of footsteps coming toward the door. This wasn't going to be pleasant, no matter how he put it, and he didn't have any illusions. Judge Waller would be a bad enemy to make.

She swung the door open, clearly dressed for the office in a wool skirt and jacket. "Adam, you're out and about early. Come in out of the cold."

Closing the door quickly behind him, she raised her eyebrows, obviously wondering what had brought him here at this hour. "There's still coffee left in the pot. Would you like a cup?"

"No. Thank you." He hesitated, but there was no good way to bring this up. He may as well plunge in. "I'd like to talk with you."

Judge Waller's face seemed to tighten, very slightly. She glanced at the grandfather clock that stood against the wall of the center hallway. "I can give you fifteen minutes before I have to leave for the office. Come into the study."

Following her, he tried to assess her reaction. Had she been expecting this visit? Certainly Coach Albright might have called her, might have warned her as to what had passed between them.

The study was to the left of the hall, behind a formal dining room. Bookshelves lined the walls, and a huge old-fashioned globe stood on an oak pedestal in front of a side window whose heavy drapes were drawn back. Judge Waller sat down at the desk, waving him to a chair in front of it. The arrangement was obviously meant to put her in charge.

"What can I do for you?" Her tone gave nothing away.

He balanced his uniform hat on his knee, letting the question hang for a moment. Then he met her gaze.

"I understand from Frank Albright that you called him on behalf of Tom Sylvester's application to the zoning board."

She didn't move a muscle. "Is that a matter for police investigation?"

"It may be."

"I fail to see how. Unless you give me an explanation, I don't see any point in discussing the matter."

"You don't have to, of course." Admitting that was only the truth. "But the subject is not going to go away. You must have realized that as soon as Albright spoke, there would be questions."

"And if I say that I made no such call?"

Her years on the bench had given Judith Waller a commanding presence. She sat here in a room that was a symbol of prestige, wealth and influence. In spite of all that, he sensed something in her that didn't quite match her outward persona. Fear? Shame? He wasn't sure what it was.

She was someone he liked; someone he respected. But he had to have the truth.

"If you say that, I'll believe you are lying. And somehow, I don't think you want to do that."

She stared at him, expressionless, for a long moment. Then she let out a long breath. "Frank Albright told me about your conversation. He also told me that he discovered he couldn't lie to you. It seems I can't, either. Yes, I made the call. I didn't offer anything to Frank, and he didn't ask for anything."

"What about Tom Sylvester? What did he offer?"

Pushing the desk chair back, she rose. If she was going to refuse to answer, there was nothing he could do about it. He could talk to the district attorney, of course. The matter would wind its way slowly and painfully to some sort of conclusion.

She stood, hands on the desk. Funny," she said slowly.

"I've always said I wanted to travel. Retire. See the world. But I could never bring myself to let go." She shook her head slightly. "Or maybe I didn't believe anyone else could do the job as well as I do."

"Maybe not. You have a reputation for common sense and fairness. I'd have said it was well-earned."

"Until now, you mean. All right. Tom Sylvester came to see me a couple of months ago. He said that he had a project in the works for a hotel near Springville, but that he needed a variance from the township zoning board to make it happen. He wanted me to use my influence with the board."

Influence. The word was beginning to leave a bad taste in his mouth.

"What did you tell him?"

She turned toward him then. "I told him no, of course. And then he reminded me of something I'd prefer to forget."

She paused for a long moment. He could feel her reluctance. He waited.

"Twenty-five years ago I was an ambitious young attorney bumping her head against the glass ceiling." Her lips twitched. "Or maybe it would be better to say I couldn't crack the old boys' network, for obvious reasons. Then someone gave me an opportunity to join with a group of like-minded individuals who agreed to use whatever influence they had to further each other's interests."

His mind spun. "You're talking about the Brotherhood. Allen Morgan's version of a secret society." Allen, Libby's uncle, whose little group had led, inadvertently, to the death of Marisa's mother. He'd thought they'd laid that to rest when he'd made a belated arrest in that case. It seemed not.

"Allen was a hobbyist. A history buff who'd let himself get carried away by what he read." She sounded contemptuous. "I had no interest in secret symbols or handshakes or any of the rest of the trappings Allen was so fond of. But I did see an advantage to being involved with people who had a certain amount of power and were willing to use it."

Judith Waller's name had never come up in all the publicity that had surrounded the group when the story behind Marisa Angelo's mother's murder broke. The murderer had died before he could reveal anything further about it.

"So Tom Sylvester knew you were a part of that group, and he used the threat of exposing that as leverage."

"A favor, he said. From one friend to another. I would help him get what he wanted, and he'd forget all about seeing me going into Allen Morgan's house for a meeting the week the Angelo woman was killed." She sat down, back still straight but a resigned look on her face. "I didn't know anything at all about the murder, but after all the publicity that surrounded it...well, being connected no matter how peripherally would have meant the end of my career."

"If the killer hadn't died himself—" he began.

"He would undoubtedly have named names," she said. "I had no illusions about that. But it didn't happen, and

I began to believe that I was safe. Until Sylvester came calling."

He tried to untangle it all. Tried to make the attack on Esther Zook fit into it. He couldn't. Tom Sylvester had broken the law, attempting to blackmail a judge, but how could Esther have possibly known anything about that?

"Did Sylvester ever mention Esther Zook to you?" he asked abruptly.

"Esther Zook? Is that what this is all about?"

"That's what started it." He'd pulled a string, and it seemed the whole fabric of the community had started to unravel.

"No. No, I'm sure he wasn't involved in the hit-and-run. He's been too busy with his own little crimes." She paused. "I could resign. Maybe do that traveling I've always talked about."

"And let Tom Sylvester get away with blackmailing a public official?"

She sighed. "No, I guess not. Your ethics wouldn't allow that, and oddly enough, mine wouldn't, either. I'll prepare a full statement for the district attorney."

There wasn't anything else to say. He rose. Nodded. Walked out of the study and out of the house. Everything didn't seem quite so black-and-white just now.

SAFE IN HER own bed, Libby had slept for fourteen hours, only rousing when someone changed the ice packs on her neck. But by midafternoon, she couldn't hide under the covers any longer.

A hot shower eased away some stiffness. She frowned

in the mirror at the black bruises on her neck. Those she could, and did, cover with a turtleneck sweater. The black eye that had started to blossom wasn't so easy—makeup just seemed to make it look worse.

Well, she'd have to tell people she ran into a door. Come to think of it, that might be true...Bess's stall door. Bess deserved a handful of carrots and a sugar lump. She'd have to see to that.

She went downstairs, hand on the banister, and followed the sound of voices to the kitchen. Link sat at the table, a mug of coffee in front of him, while Mom cut into what looked like an apple walnut cake.

He broke off whatever he was saying at the sight of her. "Look who's rejoined the land of the conscious. How do you feel?"

"Fine." Her voice was husky, and her neck hurt when she talked. She waved that consideration away. "What's been happening? Is Esther all right?"

"She's perfectly safe." Her mother shooed her into a chair. "What do you feel like eating? Soup? I have chicken soup on the stove, and Mary Esch brought over a potpie this morning, if you'd rather have that."

Neighbors brought food in time of trouble. Everyone knew that.

"Soup sounds great, Mom." Obviously her mother would only be happy if she could feed her little chick. "But what about Esther? Is the guard still there?"

"Only at night," Link said. "Don't worry. Marisa is there now. I made her promise the cell phone wouldn't be out of her hand."

"Are the Zooks okay with that?" After all, Link's fiancée must be a stranger to them.

"They've made her very welcome," Link said. "After all, Marisa's mother was Amish. As far as they're concerned, she's almost kin."

Of course. She'd forgotten, for a moment, the discovery of Marisa's long-missing Amish mother, buried on Morgan land.

"I could go back to the farm—" she began.

"You'll do no such thing," her mother snapped. She shook her head, looking a little tearful. "Sorry. But you need to get feeling better first. Marisa and I will take turns until then."

Given that she had about as much strength as a six-week-old kitten, that was probably for the best, much as she hated to admit it. She took a spoonful of the soup, easing it down her still-swollen throat. "Has Adam found out anything?"

"Not much." Link frowned. "This character is either very lucky or very careful. There weren't any identifiable fingerprints."

"Even an amateur would know enough to wear gloves, with all those forensics shows on television," Mom said. She set a mug of tea in front of Libby and a wedge of cake in front of Link.

"No fair," Libby protested. "Don't I get cake?"

Her mother smiled at the feeble joke. "After you eat all your soup," she said.

"I've been causing you a lot of worry. I'm sorry."

The words came out impulsively, but she was glad she'd voiced them.

"I guess I should get used to my children finding trouble." Mom divided a smile between the two of them. "But I can't not worry, even when I know you're doing what's right."

"You and Dad didn't raise a bunch of wimps." Link's tone was teasing, but he clasped Mom's hand for a moment.

Libby's thoughts had skipped in another direction. Rebecca's children had been raised to do what was right, as well, but for them, that right included a firm injunction against violence.

"Is Isaac in trouble with the church for allowing the guard there at night?" He'd looked so young and frightened when she'd stumbled screaming from the stable.

"There's some criticism," her mother said. "But Bishop Amos says it's not wrong to let the Englisch police deal with an Englisch criminal, so I hope that will set the matter to rest."

Libby fidgeted in the chair. She must be a glutton for punishment, because she wanted to be right back in the thick of things.

"I wonder if Adam has—"

"Adam is doing a thorough job," Link said firmly. "He knows more about police work than you do. Just sit still and let him do his job."

"Right. Like you did when Marisa was in trouble," she retorted.

"That was different." Finishing his cake, Link shoved

his chair back. “Well, maybe it wasn’t, but what do you think you could do that Adam isn’t?”

“I don’t know.... Wait a minute, yes, I do.” The idea took root in her mind. “Someone ought to take an actual look at that resort Eli Bredbenner has been getting the Amish to invest in. It’s not that far to Maryland. I could drive there in a couple of hours.”

“Elizabeth Morgan, you’re doing no such thing.” Mom sounded scandalized at the thought.

Link reached for his jacket, grinning. “You’d better hide all the car keys, Mom. Relax, Libby. I’m sure Adam has thought of that, and he told me he’s been in touch with someone at the state level to look into that scheme. You’ll just mess things up if you jump into it.”

She subsided, glaring at him. “Maybe. But I don’t see what harm it would do to take a look.”

“Stay home and let Mom pamper you for a while.” Link dropped a kiss on top of her head. “And put some ice on that shiner. The way it looks, you’d scare small children and dogs.”

Libby threw her napkin at him. “Not dogs, anyway.” She patted her knee, and Sam ambled over and rested his big head on her lap.

Link laughed, going out.

“It’s not that bad,” Mom said, tilting Libby’s head to look at the bruise. “And you will take it easy, won’t you, dear?”

“I will.” She couldn’t very well do anything else at the moment.

But tomorrow…tomorrow she'd feel better, and everyone would stop fussing over her.

And if no one else had done it, she could take a drive down to Maryland and see for herself.

LIBBY COUNTED THE hours until she was finally alone in the house the next day. Link had gone to work, and Mom had left for the Zook farm early, obviously eager to take Libby's place.

She ought to feel guilty, making her mother think she was going to stay quietly in the house today. Still, what good would it do to have Mom worrying about her? With any luck, the rental car she'd ordered would arrive shortly. She could drive to Maryland and be back before Mom got home.

Not bad rationalization. The trouble was that it didn't alleviate her guilt.

She hurried downstairs, laying out her jacket, handbag and camera bag in readiness for the car's arrival.

One good thing had come of her enforced idleness yesterday. She'd uploaded all the photos she'd taken recently and started editing them. Happy pictures from the reception, serene photos from the Zook farm.

Somehow the images had brought her more pleasure than any she'd taken in a long time. No one had been looking over her shoulder, rushing the photos from camera to page. She could take her time, editing them until they satisfied her artist's eye.

A vehicle appeared, coming down the driveway, winter sunshine reflecting from the windshield. Libby pulled on her jacket, grabbed the bags and hurried out, locking the door behind her.

The vehicle pulled to a stop at the base of the porch steps. Not the rental car at all—it was Adam's car, with Adam at the wheel.

At any other time she'd be delighted to see him so she could pump him about the investigation, but not now. Not with the rental car due to drive up at any moment. That would precipitate questions she didn't want to answer.

Adam got out and came around the car. Instead of approaching her, he opened the passenger-side door. "Your ride to Maryland is ready," he said.

CHAPTER NINETEEN

LIBBY COULD ONLY stare at Adam for a moment. "How did you know?"

"Link stormed into the diner last night and interrupted the only hot meal I've had in days," Adam said. "Oddly enough, he was convinced you were going to take off to check out Hidden Valley Resort all by yourself. I told him you wouldn't be foolish enough to do that. But here you are."

"There's nothing foolish about it," she snapped. "I'm perfectly capable of driving myself to Maryland."

"Maybe so, but you're not going to." His tone was implacable. "Get in the car, Libby. Trust me, this is the only way you're getting down there today."

She'd ask how he expected to prevent her, but something about the way he was looking at her made her decide against that. Not speaking, she walked to the car and got in.

She didn't say anything until they were out on the road. Then she pulled her phone from her bag. "I'll have to cancel the car I had ordered. They'll probably make me pay for the day anyway."

"That's okay," he said. "I won't charge you anything for the trip."

She snapped the phone open and called the car rental company.

Once she'd returned the phone to her bag, she glanced at him. "What were you going to do if I refused? Lock me up?"

"That's what your brother suggested," Adam said.

"I'll get even with him," she said darkly. "I guess I should be glad you're willing to investigate the place."

"Believe it or not, I intended to do that. I'm not ignoring this business of the investments. Just because Eli Bredbenner is Amish, that doesn't guarantee he's not a crook. In fact—"

He cut that off, instantly arousing her curiosity.

"Well? What have you found out about it? You're not going to hold out on me, are you?"

He removed his gaze from the road ahead to glance at her. "This is in confidence," he said.

"I won't say anything. Did you find out that it's a scam?"

"Not that," Adam said, his forehead furrowing. "A friend in the state police put me in touch with a guy in the justice department in Harrisburg."

"And?"

"According to him, they had one person call in reference to this particular investment, asking how to file a complaint. But it never reached the formal complaint stage."

"Does he know the person's name?"

"No. But it was a woman." Adam's tone was expressionless.

"It must have been Esther." Surely he saw that. "She's probably the only woman in the community who would make such a call. She was worried about Isaac's money, don't you see? It all fits."

"It fits, yes. But we don't know that for sure. If we had a list of Eli's investors, we'd be further along."

"This man from the justice department—is he going to follow through?"

"After he heard what I had to say, he agreed that an investigation was warranted." Adam glanced at her. "That doesn't mean it will move fast. You think I'm cautious, but he's a lawyer and a CPA. Caution squared."

"Surely it can't be that complicated. If Eli Bredbenner is cheating his investors...well, this resort either exists or it doesn't."

"That's why I agreed to this little road trip," Adam said. "Remember?"

She had to admit, Adam was doing all he could on that front, but she burned with impatience to move faster. She touched her neck. Someone was getting desperate.

"We have Esther protected." His deep voice comforted her. "We'll get to the truth."

"I know." She glanced at him, but his face was impassive behind the sunglasses that shielded his eyes. "What about Judge Waller? Have you found out why she helped Tom Sylvester with the zoning board?"

"I have." His voice was short.

She watched his face, curious at what put that tone in his voice. "Are you going to tell me?"

He didn't speak for a moment. "There's one thing you

should know about being close to a cop. Sometimes they can't talk about what they know."

"If she used her influence to get him a variance..." She let that die off at the forbidding look on his face.

There was that word again. Influence. Did everything have to come down to that? Maybe she'd had too rosy a picture of her hometown.

"Will you be satisfied if I tell you that it had nothing at all to do with the attack on Esther?"

She'd like to demand answers, but unfortunately she knew he was right. He couldn't talk about everything he discovered as a police officer. And maybe she really didn't want to know other people's dirty laundry.

"I'm satisfied. I trust your judgment."

He shot her a look. "You really mean it this time?"

"Yes, I mean it." Small wonder he doubted, after all the times she'd said she'd stay out of things and hadn't. Including today, obviously.

Finally he looked at her again, as if studying her face. "You're looking pretty beat-up." His voice was gruff. "Try to sleep a little."

In other words, he was signaling her that he didn't want to talk any further. She leaned her head back against the headrest, watching him through half-closed lids, thinking about the boy he'd been and the man he'd grown into.

She couldn't imagine what it must have been like, growing up the way he had. She'd probably said a hundred insensitive things to him over the years.

The other night, when he'd kissed her and hadn't pulled away, she'd actually thought they were making progress toward being something more than friends. But since the attack on her he'd withdrawn behind that stoic facade of his. Was it just a matter of not mixing their personal relationship with police business? Or was it more than that? She wanted to demand answers, but maybe she was afraid to risk it—afraid of what he might say.

Ironic, really. She'd begun to think she knew what she wanted from her life. A relationship with Adam. A chance to use her photography to share the joy of life instead of its pain, right here where she belonged.

But if Adam couldn't get past the barriers he imagined existed between them, could she stay here? See him often, accept being nothing but friends?

She didn't know. She closed her eyes, unable to keep looking at him.

She must have fallen asleep for a while, because the next thing she knew, Adam was nudging her awake.

"It looks like this is it."

She sat up. The sign for the resort could use another coat of paint, and the lane that shot up the mountain a fresh layer of gravel.

"Are you sure?"

"The sign's right, and according to my GPS, this is the place." Adam pulled onto the gravel road and the car started to climb.

The lane wound through dense patches of woods and then into the open again. Around them, the smooth, rounded peaks of the Catoctin Mountains raised their heads. The ground was covered with snow here, unmarked and glistening.

The lane swung around the curve of the hillside and petered out to nothing more than a track at a gatepost she recognized from the brochure picture. Beyond it stood a crumbling log cabin and a few ramshackle outbuildings.

"So." There was a note of satisfaction in Adam's voice. "I guess we know now, don't we?"

Libby nodded. "No lake, no lodge, no cabins. The resort doesn't exist."

ADAM SLID OUT of the car, surveying the quiet mountainside. It was a beautiful spot, but as Libby said, it had none of the amenities the brochure had promised.

"You see?" Libby rounded the car to join him, her face tense with excitement. "This has to be what Esther was trying to tell me. Somehow she'd realized the investment was a scam. She must have wanted my advice on how to proceed."

He gave her a skeptical look. "Because you know so much about investment fraud?"

"No, because she couldn't bring herself to go to the police," Libby snapped back. "She'd have expected that I'd consult with Trey probably, or even have gone to Leo Frost for her. And somehow Bredbenner found out and decided to silence her."

That was Libby, jumping ahead to conclusions. She was a lot more like Geneva than either of them could see.

"An Amish man, driving a black van," he said.

His commonsense tone didn't seem to deter her any. She waved his comment away. "It's not any more unlikely than an Amish person creating a scheme like this to begin with. And we know he's done that."

His instincts told him she was probably right on target, but the law didn't operate on instinct. "We still don't know exactly what Bredbenner promised his investors. It's possible the photos on the brochure are meant to represent what the resort will look like when it's finished. If so, and if he can show he's making a good-faith effort to build what he's promised, I'm not sure we'd have a case of fraud."

"I should have tried to get more information from Isaac." Her forehead wrinkled. "But I didn't want to cause trouble with Rebecca for having told me. I do know Bredbenner told them the place would be open this spring. That's not likely, is it?" She gestured toward the ramshackle buildings.

"No, not likely. At least this should get the justice department moving. I don't suppose you have a camera, do you?"

Her smile flashed. "Of course I have a camera." She darted back to the car, reappearing a moment later with a camera bag. "What do you want shots of?"

"Anything and everything," he said. "Enough to show that no improvements have been made." He nodded toward the log cabin. "I'm going to check inside."

He watched Libby move off, her expression intent as she adjusted camera settings. Then he strode to the cabin. He was prepared to do a little housebreaking if he had to, but the door wasn't locked. That argued he wouldn't find anything of value, but he had to look.

The furnishings were sparse—a few broken chairs, a scarred kitchen table, a bureau against one wall. Clearly no one had lived here in a long time, if ever.

The bureau was the only place where anything could be stored. He pulled open a drawer, disclosing some faded newspapers and a few mouse droppings. Through the dirty front windows he glimpsed Libby's red anorak, bright against the snow. He shouldn't have brought her along, but short of locking her in a cell, he didn't know how he'd have stopped her.

He knelt, pulling out the bottom drawer. Nothing. He'd have to—

The shot was obscenely loud, shattering the mountain stillness into a thousand echoes. He was at the door in seconds, weapon in his hand, heart beating so loudly it thundered in his ears. Libby—

He bolted outside. Saw her—facedown on the ground, red anorak like blood against the snow. His heart stopped entirely.

He ran to her, gaze searching for the shooter's location even as every fiber of his being focused on Libby.

Another shot, wide of him, a flash of movement giving away the shooter's location some hundred yards off in the woods. Adam squeezed off a couple of shots and dropped to the ground, grabbing Libby. Had to get her to safety, see where she was hit—

Then he realized she was struggling in his grip, fighting him, and thankfulness swept over him in a tidal wave of relief.

"You're alive. Can you walk?" He crouched over her,

shielding her with his body, alert for any movement from the woods.

"I can if you get off me," she muttered, sounding reassuringly normal.

"When I roll free, you run for the car. Get inside and on the floor, you hear? Don't stop."

"But you—"

"I'll be right behind you," he lied. "Just go. Ready?"

He felt her body tense as she gathered herself to move. "Yes."

"Go." He rolled off her, weapon steadied in both hands as he pulled off a volley of shots toward a flash of movement in the trees. He spared a quick glance at Libby. Good, she'd reached the car.

Jumping to his feet he bolted after her, his back muscles tense as he prepared for a shot. None came. Maybe he'd scared the guy off. Maybe.

He dived into the car, shoving Libby to the floor. He turned the ignition. Libby popped back up, and he shoved her down again.

"Stay down," he barked. He threw the gearshift into Reverse, backing until he reached the lane. Grabbed the door as it swung wide, slammed it and shot off down the narrow road.

The shooter had been using a rifle. Adam sent the car bucketing down the lane. He didn't dare stop. They reached the main road and he swung out on it, narrowly missing a truck headed the other way. Around several bends—the shooter couldn't possibly spot them here. He pulled into a farm lane and hit the brakes.

"Where are you hit?" He reached for Libby, helping her up into the seat, running his hands down her arms.

"I'm not." She pushed his hands away and brushed snow off the front of her jacket. "I'm fine."

"Then why were you lying in the snow?" Relief made his voice harsh.

"That first shot barely missed me. Playing possum seemed like a good idea." Libby managed to smile, but her face was pale and the fear hadn't entirely vanished from her eyes.

"I thought—" He stopped. He couldn't betray his feelings.

Not now, not ever. This was how he repaid the Morgan family for all their kindness, nearly getting Libby killed not once, but twice.

"Put your seat belt on," he said, pulling out his cell phone.

She grabbed the belt to pull it over and frowned at his phone. "What are you doing?"

He raised his eyebrows at her. "We just got shot at, remember? I have to report it."

"But it had to be Bredbenner. Who else would care if we were snooping around up there? Although—" A thought gave her pause. "How would he have known we were coming here?"

"Given that your brother blurted it out in the diner last night, almost anyone might have heard it by now."

"So Bredbenner found out and tried to stop us. You surely don't want to bring the Maryland police into this."

"I don't have a choice. I'm out of my jurisdiction. I

fired my weapon. I can't just drive away and pretend it didn't happen."

"But—" A hundred objections seemed to bubble in Libby's voice.

"Listen," he said sharply before she could get going. "This is what we're going to say. I'm collecting information for a complaint to the justice department about a possible scam centered in my jurisdiction. You're the complainant, and I brought you to have a look at the site. I shouldn't have done any such thing, but if we stick to that, maybe we can brush by without getting too involved. Understand?"

Libby looked a bit mutinous, but she nodded. "Okay."

"Good."

Adam returned to the phone. All he wanted to do now was get through this as quickly as possible and get Libby safely back to her family.

LIBBY COULDN'T RELAX, even once their business with the local police was finished and they were on their way back to Lancaster County.

"Are you sure Esther is well-protected? Someone reckless enough to shoot at us might be in such a panic that he'd attempt to get to her in broad daylight."

Adam didn't take his gaze from the road. "I've sent someone to stand guard around the clock from now on. No one is going to get near her."

Adam sounded as if he were trying to control his impatience. He was completely focused on the job at hand, so focused that he seemed to forget she was there.

It probably didn't help that she had a tendency to babble when she was upset. At least she'd managed to contain that quality during their interview with the county sheriff.

The man had probably suspected that there was more to the story than they were saying, but he'd let them leave at last, with a few caustic comments on proper police protocol. Adam's stoic face had seldom been more in evidence.

She glanced at him. Hands tight on the wheel, lips clamped together, he looked as remote and distant as the blue ridge of mountains receding behind them. He was eager to get on with the job. That was natural enough, but she wasn't imagining the size of the wall he'd built between them. It had been bad enough after the attack on her in the stable. Now it seemed completely impenetrable. The moments when they'd kissed might never have been.

They'd nearly reached Springville before Adam roused himself from his abstraction and looked at her. "I'll take you home. Then I have to meet with the district attorney."

"You may as well drop me at the Zook farm. It isn't any farther, and my mother will still be there."

To her surprise, he didn't argue. Maybe he figured she'd be safer at the Zooks', with plenty of people around, than at home alone.

She stared out the window at the passing farms, most with smoke curling from their chimneys. Somehow, she had to find the words that would break through the barrier between them. If she didn't succeed now, with that memory of their narrow escape so fresh, she probably never would.

Adam stopped behind the patrol car in the Zook driveway, keeping the motor running, obviously impatient for her to get out. She turned to him, longing to reach him and not knowing how.

"Adam…how do I thank you? You saved my life today."

His gaze met hers, his eyes darkening. His hand lifted toward her face, and the air seemed to thicken until she could barely take a breath.

Abruptly his hand dropped. His expression closed. "I was the one who risked your life. Remember?"

She could feel him slipping away. This wasn't the perfect time, but if not now, when?

"Please, Adam, listen to me. I know I'm not imagining things. We have feelings for each other."

He was shaking his head, but she rushed on, afraid to let him speak.

"Look, I'm not that fifteen-year-old girl any longer. I'm a grown woman, and I know what I want."

"Not me." The words were as sharp as a slap. "I owe your family everything. I can't do this. You're out of my reach, and even if you weren't, I've nearly let you get killed twice." His lips twisted with what she thought was pain. "That's enough to convince me to stay away from you."

Grief formed a hard, cold ball inside her.

"This isn't about my family. Whatever you think they did for you—don't you know how much they love and respect you?"

"Libby…" He turned away, shaking his head.

Over. That's all she could think. It was over.

"The problem isn't what anyone else thinks of you, Adam. It never has been, even back in high school. It's what you think of yourself." Her voice choked on the edge of tears. "If you can't get past that, there's nothing anyone else can do."

She groped for the door handle, found it and stumbled out of the car.

CHAPTER TWENTY

THE LINEUP of official vehicles in the driveway of an Amish home had a disconcerting appearance. Eli Bredbenner's house proved to be a modest ranch-style house on the outskirts of Paradise. Adam hadn't even reached the front porch yet, but already cars were slowing on the road, drivers peering at them, and a woman stared from the picture window of the house next door.

"You should make the initial approach, Chief Byler." Quinton Foster, the new district attorney, glanced at the state investigator for confirmation. "You have a better rapport with the Amish than anyone else here."

The *anyone else,* in addition to Foster and James Donato, the state investigator, included two state police officers. At a signal from Donato, they hung back by their vehicle. This was a balancing act between jurisdictions and departments, and fortunately everyone was treading lightly at the moment. He'd seen this sort of thing go badly in the past, as people jockeyed for position.

With a brief nod, he stepped up to the front door and knocked, his muscles tense. He wouldn't normally expect trouble from an Amish household, but if half what they believed was true, Eli Bredbenner was not the average Amish person.

A shade twitched on the front window. A few seconds later, the door opened a careful two inches, and a woman's face appeared.

Scared, that was his first thought. Her faded blue eyes were round with shock.

"Mrs. Bredbenner?"

"Ja, I am Mary Bredbenner. Was ist letz?"

"Nothing's wrong," he said. No point in escalating the situation any sooner than he had to. "I'm Adam Byler, from over in Springville. I'd like to speak to your husband."

"Eli's not here." She looked as if she'd like to close the door on him but didn't quite dare.

"It's important that we speak to him. Do you know where he is?" To say nothing of where he'd been earlier in the day.

She shook her head, and the hand on the door trembled. "He did not say."

"When did he leave?" Adam could sense the restlessness of the men behind him, but he wasn't about to rush this.

"Early," she said. Worry furrowed her forehead. "He went early. I do not know when he will be back."

Donato moved a step closer. "We're wasting time. Explain about the search warrant."

The woman's gaze swiveled to Donato and back to Adam, and he wasn't sure how much of that she'd understood.

"This paper is a search warrant." Adam showed it to

her. "It gives us the right to look through your husband's papers. We have to come in."

She clung to the door a moment longer, and then she stepped back, holding it wide so that they could enter. Donato beckoned to the state troopers.

Five big men made a crowd in the small, neat living room of the house. "I'm sorry for the disturbance, Mrs. Bredbenner." Adam nodded to the sofa. "Suppose you just sit there while we have a look around."

She nodded, eyes downcast. Then she darted a quick glance at his face. "Is Eli in trouble, then?"

"What makes you say that, Mrs. Bredbenner?" Quinton Foster seemed to find his voice. "Has Eli been doing something wrong?"

She shook her head slowly. "I do not know anything about Eli's business."

Adam gave Foster a warning glance. The woman's words might or might not be true, but antagonizing the Amish community by pressing the woman wouldn't do either of them any good.

"Looks as if Bredbenner does most of his work in here," Donato said. He'd walked into the adjoining room—probably intended for a dining room, it contained a gray metal desk and filing cabinets, along with a folding table littered with papers. "We'll start here."

The troopers carried cardboard file boxes into the room and set them on the floor. One of them reached for the papers on the card table.

"Don't touch anything," Donato snapped. "Not until I tell you to."

Face expressionless, the trooper stepped back.

Donato obviously knew what he was looking for. Adam had no objection to leaving him to it. He moved to a rocking chair near the couch.

"May I sit down, Mrs. Bredbenner?"

At her nod, he drew the rocker a little closer and sat.

"Eli will be upset." Her hands twisted together. "He never lets me touch his papers."

"He'll understand that you couldn't stop us," Adam said. "You have to obey the law."

She nodded, her tension easing a little.

"You said that Eli has been gone all day. Is that usual for him, to go away and not tell you where he's going?"

"Sometimes," she said, her voice soft. "When he has business to tend to." She glanced at the clock. "But he's usually home by now. I have supper almost ready."

"Does Eli use a car when he's off on business?" If Eli had been today's shooter, he must have had transportation to Maryland.

She frowned, considering. "Sometimes he hires an Englisch driver."

He'd hardly have hired a driver for the trip to Maryland with a loaded rifle. "Does Eli know how to drive?"

"No." She looked shocked. "We follow the church rules. No cars."

"He might have learned to drive when he was a teenager," Adam suggested. "Plenty of kids do."

"Well, ja, I suppose. But he wouldn't drive now, not after joining the church."

He wouldn't cheat his neighbors, either, but he was obviously doing that.

The two troopers were moving through the rest of the house now, searching. Mrs. Bredbenner clenched her hands together. The thought of strange men looking through her belongings was obviously painful. Whether or not she knew anything about her husband's activities, there were more painful times ahead of her.

"Will you come here for a moment, Chief?" Donato's voice held a note of satisfaction.

Adam hurried into the other room, to find Foster peering over Donato's shoulder at the sheaf of papers.

"He didn't cover his tracks very well," Donato said. "I'd say everything we'll need to make a case is right here. And look at the sums of money involved. This was no nickel-and-dime operation."

"Any indication of where the money is?" Somehow Adam didn't think Eli would have put it in a bank.

Donato shook his head. "We'll have to go through the property inch by inch."

"He probably has it with him," Foster said. He ran a hand over thinning fair hair and rubbed the back of his neck. "Too bad we didn't get onto him a couple of days earlier." He glanced at Adam, as if considering where to fix the blame. "After assaulting an officer of the law, he'll be on the run. Better get the machinery in motion to apprehend him."

Adam nodded, mind ticking over the possibilities. The sooner they caught up with Eli Bredbenner, the better. At least, with him on the run, Esther was safe.

So why did he have this niggling feeling at the back of his mind that it wasn't going to be as easy as that?

LIBBY TURNED FROM the window overlooking the Zook farmyard, forcing a smile for Esther.

"The children have found an icy spot perfect for sliding," she said. "Would you like to see?"

Esther nodded. Then she frowned, as if impatient with herself. "Ja." She articulated carefully. "I would."

"Great." Libby's pleasure in the improvement of Esther's speech momentarily eclipsed her grief over Adam. "Let's have a look." She wheeled Esther's chair to the window, pulling a straight chair next to it for herself.

Esther leaned forward, smiling at the sight of the children in the yard below. The younger ones had discovered a spot where a strip of ice had formed, and they were taking turns getting a running start and seeing how far they could slide.

Esther actually laughed out loud as one of her nephews ended up facedown in the snow. She turned to Libby, eyes alert, looking like the old Esther. "Remember?" she said.

Libby nodded, her thoughts slipping back to a snowstorm so heavy that school had been closed for several days. The boys had created a snow fort—no girls allowed. So she and Esther had found a patch of black ice on the driveway and were busily enlarging it by pouring kettles of water on it when Dad found them, nearly falling in the process.

"I still say that would have made a perfect skating

rink," she said. "But I understand why the grown-ups didn't agree."

Esther pointed to her and then down to the children. "Try it," she said.

"No, thanks." Libby's answering smile was a bit forced. Adam had been at the Morgan house that cold day, too. He'd helped to spread ice melt on the driveway.

Esther leaned forward, taking her hand. "What?"

"Nothing." Libby tried to smile, but how convincing could she be when her heart felt as if someone had been using it for a punching bag?

Esther's fingers gripped harder. "What?" she demanded.

"I'm being stupid about Adam." She blinked, determined not to shed any more tears over the situation. "This…the accident, the investigation…it brought us close together. A second chance, I thought." Her lips twisted despite her efforts to control them. "But Adam can't get past this ridiculous idea that he's not good enough for me. Stupid."

"Ja, stupid," Esther echoed. Her sympathy was so strong Libby could feel it—as if arms wrapped around her, holding her tight. "I am sorry. My fault."

"Not your fault." How could she think that? "The wedding would have thrown us together, even if not for the accident."

"Accident." Esther's forehead puckered, as if she struggled to remember. "Not accident?" She made it a question, her look questioning.

"No, I don't think so. It looks as if someone hit your

buggy on purpose." They still didn't have proof that Eli Bredbenner was behind the attacks on Esther, but… "Did you find out something about Bredbenner's investment scheme?" She held her breath, hoping she wasn't doing the wrong thing by asking the question.

Esther's frown deepened. "Eli…" She hesitated, and Libby had the sense that Esther was pressing her way through the clouds that surrounded the crash. "Not gut," she managed. "Isaac wouldn't listen."

"He wasn't the only one. A lot of people apparently invested their money with Eli." Surely it couldn't do any harm to push a little. "Did you find out? Were you coming to tell me that night?" She clasped Esther's hands in hers, blocking out the peaceful room and the children's squeals, intent on her friend.

"Cold," Esther murmured, and Libby knew she wasn't talking about the present. "Couldn't… Buggy couldn't outrun them." She leaned back in the chair, eyes closed, looking drained.

"Them?" Libby seized on the word. "Esther, who was after you that night? Was someone with Eli?"

Esther opened her eyes. Shook her head. "I…I don't know. Why can't I remember?" Her voice rose on the question.

Libby patted her. She shouldn't have pressed. "It's all right, Esther. You'll remember when it's time. Don't be upset, or your mamm will scold me."

The anxiety faded slowly from Esther's face. "I'll remember," she repeated.

So close. Esther had definitely used the word *them*

when she thought of that night. Did she really know who had been in the vehicle that hit her?

A tap sounded on the door frame. Libby turned to find Leah hovering there, as if afraid she was interrupting something.

"Hi, Leah. We were watching the little ones sliding." She gestured toward the window. It probably wasn't a good idea to let Leah or anyone else know that Esther had started to remember the night of the accident.

Leah's mind was clearly on something else. "Bishop Amos is here, and Chief Byler. Daadi says will you komm, please, Libby?"

Libby nodded, rising. Adam. She wasn't ready to see him again, but obviously she didn't have a choice.

Leaving Leah with Esther, Libby went downstairs. As she passed through the enclosed porch between the daadi haus and the main house, she could hear the rumble of voices. The visitors were obviously in the kitchen.

She paused at the door, taking a deep breath. No more crumbling in front of Adam. He didn't need to see any further evidence of her feelings.

At least no one would expect smiles and good cheer, as serious as the situation was. Steeling herself, she walked into the kitchen.

Bishop Amos, Isaac and Adam sat at the table, while Mary Ann filled mugs from the ever-present coffeepot. At the sight of her, Isaac gestured to an empty chair.

"Komm, sit. We must hear what is happening."

Isaac's face showed the strain he was under. What

would it mean to the family if the money he'd invested was gone for good?

She sat down, nodding to Bishop Amos and letting her eyes skim past Adam. She wasn't quite ready to meet his gaze full on yet. Bishop Amos looked fully as distressed as Isaac, the lines deep around his eyes.

"Denke, Mary Ann." Bishop Amos nodded his thanks as Mary Ann put the mug of coffee in front of him and then focused on Adam. "We are ready to hear whatever you can tell us about this sad situation."

Adam nodded, his gaze distracted as he seemed to gather his thoughts. "Well, first of all, there seems no doubt that Eli Bredbenner was deliberately cheating the people he'd talked into investing."

Bishop Amos shook his head gravely. "It is ser hard to believe that of a brother. Are you sure he didn't chust make mistakes, as anyone might?"

Mistakes that included trying to kill Esther? Libby kept the question to herself.

Adam met the bishop's gaze. "I'm sorry. I wish I could say otherwise, but I can't. He had never filed the necessary paperwork to form the corporation he talked about. He didn't even have a clear title to that parcel of land in Maryland."

She tried not to think of those moments when she'd lain in the snow, not knowing where Adam was or if the shooter was aiming at him.

"I don't see how he thought he'd get away with it." Isaac's voice was rough, as if it hurt him to speak. "Sooner or later he would have to account to us for the money."

"Maybe he didn't plan to be around that long," Adam said. "He may have thought to take off with the money before anyone grew suspicious, but it didn't work out that way. Your sister began asking questions."

"I should have listened to Esther from the beginning. Then maybe she would not have been hurt." Tears filled Isaac's eyes. Mary Ann put a gentle hand on his shoulder.

"You can't know that." Libby had to reach out to him. Behind the beard, Isaac was still the boy she'd known. "Once Esther decided something was wrong, nothing would stop her from trying to make it right."

"Ja, that's true," Bishop Amos said. "But what has happened to Eli? What does he say about his actions?"

"Nothing," Adam said. "He hasn't been back to his house since he left yesterday morning. He must be on the run."

The bishop shook his head gravely. "What does his wife say?"

"She claims not to know anything about his business. And she seems genuinely worried about him. Apparently it's not unusual for him to travel on business, but he's always come back the same day."

"Poor woman," Mary Ann murmured. "This must be so hard for her. Is anyone with her?"

Of course that was the first thing Mary Ann would think of, even in the face of their trouble.

"Her congregation is supporting her," Bishop Amos said. "There does not seem to be any other family, but she is staying with a neighbor."

"Where would Eli go?" Isaac moved restlessly in his

chair, as if needing to take some positive action. "Is his buggy accounted for?"

"The horse and buggy were found at the general store in Paradise," Adam said. "No one seems to have any idea where he went from there. If he was the person who fired the shots at us yesterday, he had to have traveled by car, but none of his usual drivers admit to seeing him."

Bishop Amos frowned. "How could he leave Paradise? There are no buses through there. Where would he go?"

They seemed to have come full circle. Where was Bredbenner?

"That's the question," Adam said. "You understand that there's a warrant out for his arrest. If he's seen, he will be arrested, and if anyone shelters him, that person would be guilty of a crime, also."

"A crime in the Englisch courts," Bishop Amos murmured.

"A crime," Adam said firmly. "You wouldn't encourage anyone to shield him after what he's done, would you?"

"No, no. I am chust concerned for the state of Eli's soul. I know he must pay the penalty for his crime to the courts, but we forgive him."

Bishop Amos glanced at Isaac. Isaac's lips clamped together, but he nodded. Forgiveness was the Amish way, no matter how difficult it might be.

"About someone hiding him…" Libby hesitated, wanting to reflect what Esther had said accurately. "Esther spoke to me about the accident just a short time ago. She said something about knowing she couldn't outrun them."

"Them?" Adam caught the word at once, of course. "She's sure there was more than one?"

"When I asked if more than one person had been after her, if she knew who hurt her, the memory seemed to slip away." Libby tried to avoid looking into Adam's eyes as she spoke, but that was impossible. And impossible not to be hurt.

"I'd like to talk to her." He half rose.

"No, don't." She put out her hand to stop him, careful not to touch him. "The little she did say tired her out, and she didn't remember anything else. You can't push her on it."

"Ja, that's so," Mary Ann murmured. Isaac glanced at her, clearly surprised that she would offer an opinion in the presence of the bishop and the police chief.

Adam frowned, and Libby sensed the impatience that rode him. "All right. But tell me immediately if she remembers anything else."

He was looking at her, so Libby nodded. She would, but if Esther confided in a family member, she wasn't so sure that person would talk. That was yet another reason why she needed to be here.

Bishop Amos frowned. "Even if Eli has done what you say, surely he would not have been driving a vehicle. And to harm a sister in the Lord…"

"People do things that are out of character when they're desperate," Adam said. "And plenty of Amish have driven at one time or another. Why not Bredbenner?"

The bishop sighed, palms up, indicating that he didn't have an answer for that. "I suppose. But if the driver was

Amish, a teenager seems more likely. I can't deny that some of them have cars hidden from their parents."

"The only way we're going to get the answers we need is to find Eli Bredbenner." Adam stood, reaching for his jacket. "We're doing all we can, and if you hear anything at all, I hope you'll get in touch with me. Eli will be a lot better off if he comes forward and tells the truth."

"Ja, he will," Bishop Amos said soberly, and Libby felt sure he was thinking of Eli confessing before the congregation, not in a court of law. "But there is something I must ask you before you leave."

Adam paused, looking at the bishop with his eyebrows slightly raised.

"We are having a meeting this evening at the fire hall at seven for all of those who might be affected by the investment business. Too many rumors are flying around, and that is not gut." Bishop Amos's face drew tight. "We must talk together about it. If you could be there, I think it would be helpful."

Adam nodded. "I'll do my best. I'll try to get at least one of the other investigators to come, as well."

"Gut." Bishop Amos stood. "I must go and spread the word about tonight."

There was a little flurry of activity as Mary Ann brought the bishop's coat and Isaac helped him put it on. Libby, standing, found herself too close to Adam.

"Excuse me." She stepped past, trying not to look at him but unable to prevent herself. "I must get back to Esther."

He nodded, looking as if he wanted to say something to her. Then his lips clamped shut, and he turned away.

Libby went quickly to the door into the enclosed porch, unable to breathe until she'd closed it behind her. This was more than difficult—it was impossible. Whatever her long-term plans might be, they certainly couldn't include staying where she might run into Adam at any time. Even for her family she couldn't do that.

CHAPTER TWENTY-ONE

THE TOWNSHIP FIRE hall might have seen odder meetings than this one, but Adam couldn't think when. The Amish had begun filing in just before seven, as solemn as if they were walking into Sunday worship. Instead of separating into a men's side and a women's side, though, families sat together on the rows of metal folding chairs someone had set out. The chairs faced an empty table.

Adam stood at the back. He'd brought Donato along, but the state investigator was clearly out of his depth in a room full of Amish people. He kept stealing cautious glances at them, as if afraid to offend by staring.

"Bishop Amos will conduct the meeting." Adam spoke under cover of low-voiced conversations in Pennsylvania Dutch. "Just don't forget that we're here at his invitation."

Donato shifted from one foot to the other. "I can't say I've ever been in on anything quite like this in my career."

"Neither have most of these folks, I'd guess. It's unusual, but these are odd circumstances."

"If they've been swindled by Bredbenner, I'd rather interview them separately, someplace where I could take notes." Donato shifted again, restless. "This isn't how we do things."

"Maybe not, but if you want cooperation from the

Amish, you'll have to let Bishop Amos run the show. Otherwise, you can ask for all the interviews you want, but no one will talk to you."

"But they've been swindled." Donato clearly didn't understand. "Don't they want to help put the perpetrator away? Don't they want to retrieve their investments?"

He shook his head. "It's not that simple." He should have explained the Amish viewpoint to Donato, but the man hadn't shown up until the last possible moment. "You'll have to take my word for it."

Donato nodded, but Adam didn't miss the skepticism in his eyes. If he'd heard Bishop Amos talking about forgiveness this afternoon, he probably wouldn't have understood that, either.

The Amish viewpoint was simple. If you wanted God to forgive you, you had to forgive others. Period. No waffling, no extenuating circumstances.

Libby had understood that without question, but she'd grown up close enough to Amish people to take that forgiveness of theirs for granted—or at least, to accept it.

He didn't want to think about Libby, because that set his gut churning with all the things he'd gotten wrong. Better to concentrate on the job. That was the only side of his life he hadn't managed to mess up.

Bishop Amos, along with the bishop from the Paradise church district, drew chairs up close to the waiting group.

The bishop closed his eyes for a moment, perhaps asking for guidance. Then he began to speak.

"We will talk tonight in Englisch, as we have guests who must be able to understand what we say."

No one looked around, but Adam knew that every person in the room was aware of them.

"You are here because you have invested money with Eli Bredbenner. So many rumors have been flying around the community about Eli that it seemed right to bring us together to hear the facts. You will not wish to believe it, as I do not, but it seems clear that our brother Eli has acted wrongfully, falsely presenting his investment and taking your money."

A low murmur swept through the group. Maybe they'd been hoping against hope that what they'd heard wasn't true.

"Eli is not here to speak for himself," Bishop Amos went on. "It appears that he has run away. I will ask Mr. Donato, an investigator from Harrisburg, to tell us what he can of this investment scheme."

Donato walked to the front of the room, looking stiff and uncomfortable. He set a box on the table, sliding out some of the glossy folders and the prospectus they'd taken from Bredbenner's files.

He turned, clearing his throat. "Thank you, Bishop Amos. We appreciate your cooperation." He picked up one of the brochures, tapping it against his palm. "I wish I had better news for you, but after going through Mr. Bredbenner's files, it seems clear that his entire investment scheme was just a scam."

Donato paused, glancing around the room as if waiting for a response. There was none.

"That is, he was trying to take money from people without giving anything in return." He held up the brochure. "These photographs, for instance, are not really of the site of the supposed resort. No development has taken place there, and there's no sign any was ever planned."

Joseph Miller, a local farmer who ran a lucrative greenhouse operation, cleared his throat. "But we saw the plans. All of us." He looked around, and others nodded in agreement.

"Fakes," Donato said. "Very clever fakes. Bredbenner apparently had the plans drawn up, but he never attempted to follow them. In fact, he never filed any of the paperwork with the state that would be required for such a development."

"He told us that it was the state that was holding things up." Miller seemed more willing to speak, maybe because of his own business experience.

"That's not true." Donato produced a thin smile. "I agree, the state often takes too long to process requests, but in this case, Bredbenner hadn't even attempted to get the necessary permissions. It's not clear that he owns the land in question."

That was a blow. Adam could sense the truth sinking in as well as the despair that accompanied it.

"What about our money?" Isaac raised the question. "Will we get our money back?"

Donato spread his hands wide. "So far, we haven't been able to find the money Bredbenner took from his investors. Either he has a hidden bank account under another name, or he took it with him when he went. If he's found and any of the money recovered, some repayment will be made, but it may take a long time for that to happen."

He hesitated again, maybe expecting a reaction. There was none, at least not out loud.

"Well, now, I'm sure you want to know what efforts we're making in that direction." Donato spoke quickly, gesturing to Adam. "I'll let Chief Byler discuss that aspect of it. If that's all right." He glanced toward the bishop, apparently remembering Adam's words.

Bishop Amos nodded gravely.

Adam took his place at the front of the group, frowning at the brochures that still lay on the table. "As you may know, the police are actively looking for Eli Bredbenner. At the least, he has committed fraud. It is also possible that he has been involved in attacks on two people."

A low murmur went through the crowd at that. Isaac and Mary Ann stared straight ahead, while Rebecca pressed her lips together, eyes downcast.

"If any of you have suggestions as to where Bredbenner could have gone, the police would appreciate your help. If you don't care to speak to me, perhaps..." He glanced at Bishop Amos, who nodded.

"Ja. Tell me if you know anything." The bishop's face was grave. "You may feel that you don't wish to be involved with the police, but remember that until our brother comes back and confesses his sin, he will not be right with God."

Adam read reserve on some faces, but there were those in the crowd who nodded. He could only hope they were the ones who knew something.

"Are there any questions you'd like to ask?" He didn't expect there to be, and there weren't. He nodded and went back to join Donato.

"That's it?" Donato's eyebrows rose. "The last time I had to attend a meeting of victims, I was nearly deafened from the yelling and screaming and blaming that went on. Won't these people miss the money Bredbenner took?"

"They'll miss it, all right. But they'll help each other. That's the Amish way."

"What I don't get is how Bredbenner has managed to disappear so completely." Donato sounded fretful. "I figured somebody as unsophisticated as an Amish man would trip up in a matter of hours."

Adam found he was staring at the brochure Donato held in his hand. *Unsophisticated,* Donato had said, and the word triggered a train of thought. There was something…a vague thought teased at the back of his mind.

He took the brochure from Donato, turning it over in his hands. "Tell me something," he said abruptly. "In all the files you went through, did you see any hint that someone else might have been involved in this scam?"

Donato blinked. "A partner? No, not at all. What makes you say that?"

Adam held up the brochure. "You said it. Unsophisticated. And yet the glossy brochures, the prospectus, everything we've seen has been exactly the opposite."

"That's true," Donato said slowly. "Some of the paperwork I went through was computer-generated, but there was no computer at the Bredbenner house."

"No. There wasn't." Adam's mind raced, fitting pieces

together. "If Bredbenner had a non-Amish partner, it would answer a lot of questions—the production of the paperwork, the fact that vehicles were used in the attack on Esther Zook and the shooting in Maryland, the use of a cell phone in an attempt to decoy Libby Morgan out of the hospital room. All those things would be difficult for an Amish person."

The reluctance faded from Donato's face, and he rocked back and forth, toes to heels, as if he wanted to dart into movement. "That makes more sense than anything else we've run into in the case. But who? I've been through those files with the proverbial fine-tooth comb and I assure you, there's no clue to another conspirator."

"There has to be. We're looking for someone familiar with the area and the people. Someone who came into contact with Bredbenner in some way. Someone who has the business savvy to mastermind a scheme like this."

Donato listened, head on one side like a robin eyeing a worm. "That makes sense, but I don't see how you're going to find out who it was unless we get Bredbenner and he's willing to give up his partner."

Adam glanced at Bishop Amos. A small group had surrounded him, talking quietly, with Isaac and his wife and mother among them.

"There's someone else who might be able to tell us. Esther Zook."

Esther, who was back at the farm right now, with Libby and the children. And one of his officers, he reminded himself. Joe Carmody was there tonight, and he was a bright kid. He wouldn't let anyone get near them.

Somehow that didn't reassure him as much as it should. He yanked his cell phone from his pocket.

"Who are you calling?" Donato watched him, dark eyes curious.

"The officer on guard at the farm." Adam punched in the numbers, not sure himself what was driving him, just knowing he had to be assured that everything was all right there.

The cell phone rang. And rang. And rang. No one answered. Something had happened to Carmody.

ESTHER SEEMED A little more tired than usual, so Libby had her tucked up in bed before eight. Once there, though, she wanted a pillow behind her back.

Libby settled her and sat down in the rocker next to the bed. "Okay now?"

Esther nodded. "The children?"

"Leah is getting the little ones to bed. Your mamm and Mary Ann went with Isaac to the meeting."

There had been no point in trying to keep what was happening from Esther. And maybe knowing about it would help her remember.

A frown formed between Esther's brows. "Wish I could be there. Could help."

"You've already helped." Libby clasped her hand. "Without you, they might never have known that Eli Bredbenner was cheating people."

The frown deepened. "How could he cheat—" her hand moved restlessly as she searched for the word "—the

Leit." She'd resorted to the Pennsylvania Dutch word, but Libby knew it. The Leit. The People, the Amish.

"That's what so hard on everyone," Libby said. "Bishop Amos is grieved, and I'm sure it's even harder for Eli's own ministers and bishop over in Paradise."

"How…how did I know?" Esther's voice was fretful. "Why can't I remember?"

"It'll come. Don't push it. The whole situation is in police hands now, anyway. We can leave it to Adam."

"Ja." The frown vanished, and Esther studied her face. "You and Adam—"

Libby tried to manage a smile, but it wasn't easy. "There's not going to be any Adam and me. For a while I thought…" She let that trail off.

"I am sorry." Esther's voice was soft. "That is ser hatt."

So hard. Yes, it was. "I'm all right." She forced a confidence she didn't feel into her voice.

"It will be as God wills." Esther's eyelids started to droop. "We are in His hands."

"Yes." She found comfort in the thought. "Ready to sleep now?"

Esther nodded, eyes closing. "You can outen the light."

She did so, thinking how appropriate the phrase was. Standing for a moment at the window, Libby stared out at the dark. There was no moon visible, and ice had formed on the outside of the pane.

A circle of light moved across the yard, reflecting from the snow cover. The police officer had probably been checking the outbuildings.

Carmody was on duty tonight—just as he had been

the night of Esther's injury. He was young, but Adam had faith in him. He'd keep Esther safe.

There was probably no need to worry now, anyway. She glanced at Esther and then tiptoed quietly to the door. No need to worry. After all, Bredbenner was on the run, his crimes out in the open now. If he had any sense, he'd be far from here.

And his partner, if he had one? She paused at the bottom of the stairs, hand on the newel post. Surely the same applied to him. If he had any sense, he would run before the investigators found him.

She shivered a little and zipped up her sweatshirt. They'd been keeping Esther's room toasty with a kerosene heater, but the downstairs of the daadi haus was chilly.

Chilly and quiet. Leah and her brothers and sisters were shut away with two closed doors between them. She and Esther were virtually alone.

Giving herself a shake, Libby hurried into the daadi haus kitchen. There was light there, and warmth from the stove. She'd make some hot chocolate…Mom's remedy when anyone needed comforting.

She put the milk on to heat, adding extra. Joe Carmody would probably appreciate a mug of something to warm him up about now. It had to be cold work, prowling around out there in the snow.

Once the milk was warming and she'd found the chocolate and the mugs, she peered out the window, trying to spot the patrolman. There was no sign of his flashlight. He must have gone around the house. She'd have to catch him on his next pass.

A sound at the door startled her into spilling a few drops of hot milk on the counter. Not a knock exactly—a sort of scratching sound, grating on nerves that were already stretched.

It had to be Carmody, probably trying to avoid disturbing Esther by knocking. She went quickly to the door and twisted the dead bolt. She eased the door open a few inches.

Nothing. No one was there. Maybe one of the barn cats, looking for shelter? Libby swung the door wider, so that the light from the kitchen flowed out.

And saw him—a huddled figure, sprawled in the snow.

"Joe!" Grabbing a flashlight from the hook beside the door, she ran to him, knelt next to him.

"Joe, what's wrong? Are you hurt?" She touched his face, the warm skin reassuring her. Her fingers fumbled for his throat, finding a pulse, relief flooding through her when she felt it beating.

"It's all right, don't worry." No idea if he could hear her, but she had to say it. "I'll call for help." She started to pull the cell phone from her pocket, only to hear a groan, sense movement.

She swung the light around, catching another figure in the snow, this one groaning, trying to move. She took a step toward him and froze, recognizing the dark brown beard. Eli Bredbenner. He and Carmody must have fought—

She had to get help. Pull the phone free, run for the house, call 911, lock the door, keep Esther safe—

She sensed, rather than saw, a movement behind her.

Dodging, she flung up her arm to protect herself. Something struck her head a glancing blow, landing on her forearm, sending indescribable pain radiating through her arm. The phone went flying, and she stumbled forward. Eli must have been playing possum; he'd be on her in a second. If she could make the door—

She couldn't. Hands grabbed her shoulders, sending pain surging through her arm. She cried out, trying to get away. She had to stop him, had to, couldn't let him get to the house, Esther, the children—

Hands searched for her throat, still painful from the last encounter. She grabbed at them with her left hand, struggling, had to get away from him, feet slipping on the ice beneath. If she fell she'd be helpless, he'd finish her off and go after Esther.

Somehow she managed to keep her balance, keep the hands off her throat. His breathing was harsh in her ears, he was so close, the scent of him sharp in her nose, and then she realized where they were, why it was so slippery. They were on the icy slide the children had made. If she could knock him off balance she might have a chance.

She struggled, trying to kick him, unable to connect, feeling her own feet slip. If she fell, it was all over. Frantic, she threw herself backward against him. They fell together, and there was a sharp crack as he hit the ice.

His hands lost their grip. She rolled free, scrabbling away from him, right arm useless…

And she realized he wasn't moving. She tried to get to her feet, but she couldn't, not with her arm dangling helplessly. She couldn't see where he was, if he came after her again—

The roar of an engine shattered the silence, and headlight beams pierced the dark. Doors swung open, men's voices, people rushing toward her. She turned, forcing herself to look at the man.

He lay flat, apparently knocked out when his head hit the ice. But it wasn't Eli Bredbenner—he still lay in the snow. It was Owen Barclay.

CHAPTER TWENTY-TWO

"LIBBY, IF YOU DON'T hold still, the doctor isn't going to be able to fix your arm." Mom sounded as if she were scolding an eight-year-old, but the strain in her eyes was acute.

"I will." She forced herself to lie still, biting her lip a bit.

"Not to worry." The emergency room doctor smiled reassuringly. "It's a simple break, and it should heal fine. Just don't do any more fighting on the ice."

Heaven only knew what the doctor had heard. It had probably been impossible to keep things quiet when paramedics had come in with four victims.

"Just tell me," she muttered, glaring at her twin, figuring he'd be more forthcoming than Mom, who still seemed to think she could protect her little girl. "Is the police officer okay? What about the others?"

"As long as you hold still, I'll talk," Link said, reaching around Mom to pat Libby's free hand. "Carmody has a mild concussion. One or the other of them must have hit him from behind as he was coming around the house."

"What about Eli?" Her brief glimpse of him hadn't been reassuring.

"Ironic, in a way. He has a head injury, too. Looks like a case of crooks falling out, as far as anyone can tell. He's in the hospital under guard, and the doctors expect him to be able to answer questions tomorrow."

She closed her eyes for a moment. Knowing the Amish, they'd be surrounding Eli's wife with comfort and praying for him.

"And Owen?" If he hadn't attacked her, she wouldn't have believed it. Owen Barclay, of all people.

"His injury wasn't serious. He's lawyered up, of course, and so far he isn't saying anything. Probably hoping to cut the best deal he can."

"Why did he do it? That's what I don't get." At a frown from her mother, she managed to keep from moving. "He surely didn't need the money."

Link shrugged. "The police are digging into that now. One thing that's surfaced already is a rumor that the owners of the inn are preparing to sell. It may be that his position wasn't quite as secure as people thought it was."

She still couldn't quite grasp it. "Esther's all right?"

Mom patted her hand. "She's fine. She slept right through it. And the children are all right, too. The older ones didn't know anything was going on until the police car drove in."

"I should go back there—"

"No, indeed you won't," Mom said firmly. "Esther is perfectly safe now that those two have been caught, and plenty of people are there to help. Marisa insisted on staying the night, just in case, and she has her phone."

Libby let herself sink back against the pillow. Good thing she wasn't needed, because she felt as if she'd been hit by a steamroller.

"I hope you realize what a great person Marisa is," she said, giving her twin a mock frown.

Link's expression softened. "One in a million."

Her heart seemed to twist. If only...but there was no point in indulging in wishful thinking. Adam had made his attitude clear. The fact that he hadn't even checked in on her since she reached the hospital just added a punctuation mark to that.

ONCE AGAIN SHE'D slept half the day away. Libby got up, groaning a little as she moved. She had to get going, find out what had been happening, and she couldn't even think how she was going to get into her clothes with this cast on her arm.

Someone tapped on the door, and Marisa peeked in. "Good, you're awake. Adam is downstairs, and he's about to fill us in, but he insists that you'll want to hear it, as well."

Adam. Libby wasn't sure she was in any condition to face him. She caught a glimpse of herself in the mirror and recoiled.

"I can't go down looking like this."

"You take all the time you need," Marisa soothed. "I'm here to help you, and they can just wait for us."

With Marisa's help, getting dressed wasn't so hard after all, although she'd clearly need to learn the tricks of managing the cast. Marisa talked soothingly while she brushed Libby's hair and touched up her face. Clearly she'd been told not to answer any questions.

"There," she said finally. "You look great."

"I look as if I've been pulled through a knothole backward, and you know it, but thanks for the help." She discovered that her legs would indeed support her. "Okay, let's go down."

And face Adam. She only wished she could do the poker face as well as he could.

Adam, Link and her mother were waiting in the family room. She managed to avoid taking a good look at him while Mom fussed over her, making sure she had a pillow to support her arm.

"I told the boys that you'd need something to eat first, but they're both too impatient to wait." She gave Adam and Link a look that relegated them to about the third grade.

"Geneva, if you want to give Libby something to eat—" Adam began.

"Never mind," Libby said. "I want information more than I want food. What is going on?"

Adam took a chair a careful distance away from her. "I suppose Link told you that Owen's attorney isn't letting him say a thing so far."

She nodded. It was probably the only thing he could do.

Her mother made a sound of disapproval. "I should think he'd want to get all of it off his chest. Owen Barclay, of all people, involved in such things. It's hard to believe."

"His attorney will probably count on people thinking that," Adam said, his expression disapproving.

"He's not going to get away with it," Libby said. "After all, I'll testify that he attacked me."

Adam nodded. "Carmody caught a glimpse of him, as well. And Bredbenner is talking."

"He's recovering then?"

"He was stunned, but he seems to think Barclay intended to finish him off and leave him to take the blame for everything." Adam shrugged. "That could well be, but we'll never be able to prove it. Still, we have enough to put Barclay away without it."

"I just don't understand why." Mom sounded genuinely distressed. "Owen had everything, you'd think…he was respected, well-off, with a secure future. Why would he risk it all on such a scheme?"

"I doubt that his future was as secure as all that," Adam said. "The owners of the inn are fairly elderly, and there's talk they plan to sell. He must have known that was coming. Investigators are looking into his finances now. With a little luck, they'll come up with a motive."

"I don't get how Barclay and Eli Bredbenner ever came together," Link said. "That seems so unlikely."

Adam planted his hands on his knees. "That we do know. According to Bredbenner, he'd done some carpentry work at the inn, and he'd padded the bill. He'd done it before, and none of his Amish customers had ever questioned it. But Owen caught him. Instead of reporting him, Owen proposed a deal. With Eli's Amish background, other Amish would trust him automatically. Owen would provide the know-how, and Eli would handle the sales. A perfect combination, they must have thought and apparently it was, until questions were raised."

"Esther," she murmured.

"It seems pretty clear that they considered Esther a threat." Adam leaned back in the overstuffed chair that had been her father's, but there was nothing relaxed in the pose.

"There must have been more to it than that. They wouldn't attack Esther just because she was asking questions." Link sat down on the arm of Libby's chair, putting a protective hand on her shoulder.

"We know Bredbenner's version of it. If and when he talks, Barclay will tell it differently, I suppose." Adam's expression suggested distaste for both men. "Bredbenner says Esther had been asking a lot of questions, wanting to see documents. He got nervous, contacted Barclay, wanting to get out of the whole deal. Barclay wanted to talk, and they set a place to meet—that pull-off where the township shed is, just down from the Amish school. Bredbenner thinks Esther must have been leaving the school. She saw him, followed him, maybe overheard enough of their conversation to know what was going on."

Libby shivered, and her brother's hand tightened on her shoulder. "They must have seen her. They chased her down that road."

Adam nodded. "Bredbenner blames it all on Barclay, of course. Says he just wanted to talk to her, but Barclay said they had to silence her."

"Barclay didn't use his own vehicle, I take it," Link said.

"He apparently took a vehicle from valet parking and returned it later. That way, if anyone happened upon their meeting, he wouldn't have been easily identified." Adam's jaw tightened. "Eli claims it was Barclay who tried to get at Esther afterward, and Barclay who shot at us at the site in Maryland. Naturally he would say that."

"They're not going to get away with blaming each other, are they?" Mom looked like a hen ruffling its feathers at the thought.

"Their lawyers will fight it out, but neither one is going to get off, not with the evidence we have." Adam glanced at his watch and stood. "Look, I'm sorry to rush off, but I have a meeting with the D.A. in less than an hour."

"That's fine." Libby could only hope her expression looked more like a smile than a grimace. "Thanks for bringing us up-to-date."

He stopped, looking down at her, his face set in that mask he did so well. "I didn't want you to be worrying. Now you can relax and let your family take care of you."

"We're doing that," Mom said. "Believe me, I'm not letting her out of my sight until I'm satisfied that she's well."

"I'm fine," Libby said, knowing nobody believed that. But that was okay, as long as they couldn't look into her heart and see what was really wrong with her.

LIBBY SAT WITH Esther and her family in the farmhouse kitchen the next afternoon. She'd just finished sharing all she knew about the arrests.

It was Esther who finally broke the silence. "I have little pieces of memory." She shook her head slowly. "Ja, I saw Eli with Mr. Barclay, but if I heard anything…I just don't know."

"Maybe you should stop trying." She'd certainly be happy if she could forget some of the events of the past few days. "Adam is trying to convince the district attorney not to make you testify, according to what he told my brother. He knows how hard it would be."

"Adam is a gut man," Isaac said. "He understands us better than many."

He was a good man. Just not her good man. Libby made an effort to dismiss that thought from her mind.

"Esther can work on getting well now," Rebecca said. The relief in her face wiped away the look of strain she'd worn for so long. "Her pupils are missing her, I hear."

Esther smiled, but didn't speak. Was she thinking that she would not return to the classroom? Libby wasn't sure.

At least Esther would be able to move forward without worry now. The shadow that had hung over the Amish community had been banished.

At the sound of a car, everyone glanced toward the window. Libby didn't have to move from her chair to see that it was the township police car. Or that it was Adam who got out.

Isaac opened the door. "Adam, wilkom. Komm in."

"Thanks." Adam stamped snow from his boots and stepped inside. At the sight of Libby his movement seemed to check. "Libby. I didn't realize you were here. You're not driving with that broken arm, are you?"

She shook her head. "Link dropped me off, and Mom will stop by later to pick me up."

"Good." His attention went to the others.

While he was greeting them, Libby had a small battle

with herself. She would treat him as she always had—a sort of adjunct big brother. And sooner or later, it would stop hurting.

"I can't stay," Adam was saying, in answer to Mary Ann's offer of coffee and shoofly pie. "But something has come up I thought you'd want to hear about right away. The investigators who are checking into the financial end of things have found several bank accounts Barclay opened since the resort scheme started—a couple in Lancaster and at least one in Harrisburg. It looks as if much of the money the two of them took is safe, and the district attorney is taking action to seal the accounts, so that Barclay can't get access."

"So that means we will get our money back?" Isaac couldn't disguise the hope in his face.

"It looks promising that eventually that will happen. But you have to understand that it may take time."

"That's wonderful gut. We have plenty of patience." Isaac's grin split his face, making him look like the boy he used to be.

"Good." Adam shifted his weight, almost as if he was uneasy. He glanced at Libby. "I hate to break up your visit, but I need you to come into town with me. We have to take a formal statement from you." He gestured toward the door.

Every protective instinct she possessed rebelled at the thought of being alone with him. "Can't that wait until later? I can have Link or my mother bring me to your office."

"Now, please." He sounded his most official. "The

district attorney is very insistent." He turned toward the door, not waiting for her agreement.

A few minutes later she was buckled into the seat next to him, shifting to get comfortable with the seat-belt strap over the cast. Adam didn't speak as he drove out the lane, but he seemed to be making an effort to ease the vehicle over the rough spots.

Once they were out on the county road, he cleared his throat. "I had a little chat with Jason Smalley this morning."

"You did?" Her thoughts scrambled after the memory of Jason's apparent efforts to interfere in the investigation. "Did he admit to being involved with Owen Barclay?"

"Not exactly." Adam's smile was sardonic. "He danced all around the subject, but eventually he admitted that Owen had said he'd like to see the investigation into the accident ended. Jason claimed Owen didn't tell him anything, but Jason supposed that he was trying to protect the inn from any bad publicity. Naturally Jason went along with it. Doing favors for important people is his method of operation."

She studied his face. So upright himself, he couldn't understand the shortcuts other people took to what they considered success.

"Things haven't changed that much, have they?" she said. "I gather that was the reasoning behind that little group my uncle tried to start—influential people using their clout for other people like them."

Adam's jaw hardened. "It's wrong, no matter who does it."

"Of course it is. I guess I'm just not surprised when the old boys' network rears its ugly head. They might not have secret meetings or hidden passwords anymore, but they're still trying to bend the rules for themselves, without regard for other people's interests."

She studied his face, wondering what was going through his mind. "I trust you put the fear of God into Jason, even if you couldn't charge him with anything?"

He grunted an assent. "We'll see how long it lasts." He seemed on the verge of saying more, but instead he pulled into a turnaround near a farm lane.

"What are you doing? I thought I had to rush into town to give you my statement."

He swiveled in the seat so that he was facing her. "That was the only excuse I could think of to get you alone. If you haven't been surrounded by your own family, you've been surrounded by Esther's."

She stared down at her hands, not sure how to react to that. "If you needed a statement…" she began.

Adam put his hand over hers, linked in her lap. "Forget the statement. I mean, I do need it, but that's not what I want to talk to you about."

"Oh?" She couldn't resist looking at him, and she found his face was very close.

"Yes." He seemed to be struggling to find the words he wanted. "You said something to me the other night. Something I haven't been able to get out of my head, about my family."

"I shouldn't have," she said quickly. "I didn't have the right to—" She had to stop, because he'd put his palm over her mouth. His hand was warm against her lips, and that warmth seemed to move through her.

"Don't apologize. You were right." He was frowning, as if what he had to say was too difficult. "All my life, no matter how I worked or what I tried to make of myself, I knew at bottom I was…trash. Just like my parents."

"Don't say that." She snatched his hand away so that she could speak. "I wouldn't try to judge your parents. I don't know what drove them. But I know you. I know what kind of person you are, all the way through." Grief had a stranglehold on her throat, and her eyes prickled with tears, but she was determined to get this said. "You're honorable, and brave, and—"

He cut her short again, this time with his lips. The kiss was long and lingering and possessive, and she had a sense that he only drew back so that he could find the breath to speak.

"Nobody's as good as all that," he murmured, his lips against her cheek so that she felt his breath with each word. "But you were right about one thing."

He drew back a few inches, maybe so that he could see her face, but his arm was secure around her, and with his free hand he stroked her face.

"What was that?" Her heart seemed to be beating somewhere up in her throat.

"It's not who your parents were that count. It's who you are." He shook his head, frowning a little. "This investigation led me places I didn't want to go. It showed me things I didn't want to know about people I'd looked up to, people I thought had the status I'd never had."

She touched the lines between his eyebrows, wanting to ease the hurt away. "As you said. It's who you are that counts."

"Yeah." He captured her hand in his and kissed her fingers. "I guess it doesn't matter what other people think, as long as I know who I am."

She let herself believe, let herself smile. "I'm glad you finally came around to my way of thinking. So who are you, Adam Byler?"

He smiled, his face relaxed and open to her, so that she could see his heart. "I'm the man who loves you, Libby Morgan. And don't you forget it."

There was no chance of that, she thought, as he kissed her again. She'd come home after all this time and found what she'd been looking for, and she wasn't going to let him go.

EPILOGUE

June, with roses spilling over the hedges and the last of the lilacs blooming. June was also the month of Esther's birthday, and the Zook family had decided that a picnic was the way to celebrate both her birthday and the fact that she was doing so much better.

Libby helped Mary Ann and the girls carry trays of desserts and plates out to the picnic table under the trees in the Zook yard.

"Ach, Libby, do you think there is enough here?" Mary Ann frowned at the pies she was carrying. "Maybe I should have made another dried apple pie, ain't so?"

"If we had any more desserts, we will probably burst." Libby set her tray on the picnic table and placed the birthday cake in front of Esther. "There. You have to have the biggest piece, Esther."

Esther's answering smile warmed her heart. "I will, since my sweet sister-in-law made my favorite."

Her speech had improved enormously over the past few months, and if she hesitated in finding a word now and then, no one thought anything about it. Esther even talked about returning to her classroom in the fall, and Libby didn't doubt that she'd manage it.

Mary Ann blushed at her words, her rosy face a little

rounder these days with the expectation of her next baby. In true Amish fashion, no announcement had been made, but of course all the women knew.

"It made me very happy to bake," Mary Ann said. "And the kinder like chocolate cake with buttercream icing, too."

Libby glanced at Trey and Jessica, deep in conversation with Bishop Amos. Jessica was expecting, as well, even though she wasn't showing yet, but Mom had already told the immediate world about the new little Morgan who'd be arriving.

That news, combined with Link and Marisa's plan to marry next month, would keep Mom busy and out of mischief for quite some time, Trey had declared.

Libby stepped away from the table to give Rebecca space to put the candles on the birthday cake. As Esther healed, her mother had, as well. Her face was serene now, and the worry was gone from her eyes.

Adam put his hand on her shoulder, and she leaned back against him. "Happy?" he asked.

"Who wouldn't be? Esther is herself again, and the community has finally settled down. I think Mom would be pleased if no member of the Morgan family appeared in the newspaper for some time to come, though."

The revelations of the investment scheme and the attacks on her and Esther had provided the newspapers with fodder for the front page issue after issue, it seemed. In contrast, the revelation of Sylvester's attempt to improperly influence the planning commission had barely made a dent in the news.

Judge Waller had resigned with a letter of censure, Tom Sylvester had been heavily fined, and word had it the property would be going up for auction sometime soon. More importantly, Owen Barclay and Eli Bredbenner were both going on trial in the fall court term.

"Well, I think maybe your mother would like to see one more news item," Adam said. His hand found hers and squeezed. "Maybe the announcement of her only daughter's engagement. What do you think?"

She looked up at him, knowing love for him shone in her eyes. "I think that would be absolutely perfect," she said.

* * * * *

AVAILABLE MAY 2012

HANNAH'S JOY

Pleasant Valley, Book Six

Unexpected tragedy has left Hannah without her soldier husband or a home for her baby son, Jamie. Seeking refuge, she comes to live with her aunt in the Amish community of Pleasant Valley and finds an unexpected sympathetic listener in furniture maker William Brand. Hannah is irresistibly drawn to the shy, caring William—but how can she encourage his attention when she might someday leave Pleasant Valley and when her father-in-law, a military officer, is scheming to take Jamie away from her?

FROM BERKLEY

A Member of Penguin Group (USA)

Available wherever books are sold

penguin.com

martaperry.com

PHMPBERK

New York Times **bestselling author**

SUSAN MALLERY

is back with a charming new trilogy!

Three California cowboys are about to find love in the most unlikely of places…

Available now!

July 2012

August 2012

Read them all this summer!

PHSSMT2012R

REQUEST YOUR FREE BOOKS!

2 FREE NOVELS FROM THE SUSPENSE COLLECTION PLUS 2 FREE GIFTS!

YES! Please send me 2 FREE novels from the Suspense Collection and my 2 FREE gifts (gifts are worth about $10). After receiving them, if I don't wish to receive any more books, I can return the shipping statement marked "cancel." If I don't cancel, I will receive 4 brand-new novels every month and be billed just $5.99 per book in the U.S. or $6.49 per book in Canada. That's a saving of at least 25% off the cover price. It's quite a bargain! Shipping and handling is just 50¢ per book in the U.S. and 75¢ per book in Canada.* I understand that accepting the 2 free books and gifts places me under no obligation to buy anything. I can always return a shipment and cancel at any time. Even if I never buy another book, the two free books and gifts are mine to keep forever.

191/391 MDN FEME

Name (PLEASE PRINT)

Address Apt. #

City State/Prov. Zip/Postal Code

Signature (if under 18, a parent or guardian must sign)

Mail to the **Reader Service:**

IN U.S.A.: P.O. Box 1867, Buffalo, NY 14240-1867

IN CANADA: P.O. Box 609, Fort Erie, Ontario L2A 5X3

Not valid for current subscribers to the Suspense Collection or the Romance/Suspense Collection.

Want to try two free books from another line? Call 1-800-873-8635 or visit www.ReaderService.com.

* Terms and prices subject to change without notice. Prices do not include applicable taxes. Sales tax applicable in N.Y. Canadian residents will be charged applicable taxes. Offer not valid in Quebec. This offer is limited to one order per household. All orders subject to credit approval. Credit or debit balances in a customer's account(s) may be offset by any other outstanding balance owed by or to the customer. Please allow 4 to 6 weeks for delivery. Offer available while quantities last.

Your Privacy—The Reader Service is committed to protecting your privacy. Our Privacy Policy is available online at www.ReaderService.com or upon request from the Reader Service.

We make a portion of our mailing list available to reputable third parties that offer products we believe may interest you. If you prefer that we not exchange your name with third parties, or if you wish to clarify or modify your communication preferences, please visit us at www.ReaderService.com/consumerschoice or write to us at Reader Service Preference Service, P.O. Box 9062, Buffalo, NY 14269. Include your complete name and address.

SUS11